THOSE TYRANNISING LANDLORDS

Seán Damer

Ringwood Publishing
Glasgow

Issued in 2022
by
Ringwood Publishing

Flat 0/1 314 Meadowside Quay Walk, Glasgow
G11 6AY

www.ringwoodpublishing.com
e-mail: mail@ringwoodpublishing.com

ISBN: 978-1-901514-60-5

British Library Cataloguing-in Publication Data
A catalogue record for this book is available from the British Library

Printed and bound in the UK
by Lonsdale Direct Solutions

Dedication

For Peter McCormack, for forty years
of friendship and Celtic Connections.

It was not the want of employment at home
That caused all the sons of old Ireland to roam,
But those tyrannizing landlords,
They would not let us stay,
So farewell unto ye bonny, bonny Slieve Gallion braes.
But the rents were getting higher,
And we could no longer stay –
So farewell unto ye bonny, bonny Slieve Gallion braes.

[Slieve Gallion Braes, trad.]

Scots steel tempered wi' Irish fire
Is the weapon that I desire.

[Hugh MacDiarmid.]

Part 1

Chapter 1
The Rosses, Co. Donegal, 1911.

Mairead O'Donnell was alone in the house. She was making boxty in the kitchen, and chanting the traditional rhyme:

'Boxty on the griddle, boxty on the pan;
if you can't make boxty, you'll never get a man.'

Her father Pat and brother Eamonn were due back from the tattie-picking in Scotland that afternoon, and she had left the door open to see them coming. Her younger brothers Conal and Tim had gone out on the road to meet them, and her mother Brighid was visiting a neighbour. Mairead, or Peggy as she was known to everyone, was a sixteen-year-old girl, but already showed the tall, erect, slim-bodied figure of the Rosses, with a pale complexion, hair as black as a raven's wing, and blue eyes that danced with the spark of intelligence. A shadow passed over her; she suddenly became aware that there was somebody at the door.

Peggy turned round, her hands covered with flour, and saw Francis Gillespie standing in the doorway. He was watching her, leaning on his blackthorn stick. Gillespie was the rent-collector for Lord Leitrim.

'It's yourself, Peggy,' Gillespie said. 'Where are your ma and da?'

'Me da's coming back from Scotland, and me ma's visiting up the boreen,' Peggy said.

Gillespie was a big man who was very unpopular in the district, as he was a ruthless bully who was quick to use his fists to settle an argument or to facilitate an eviction. Peggy loathed him. She saw his small piggy eyes travel down from her face to her bosom, stopping for a moment, then on down to her bare legs and feet; she felt herself flush with embarrassment.

'Sure, it's the fine big girl you're getting to be,' he said.

Peggy said nothing and continued to stir the mashed potatoes in the bowl with a wooden spoon, keeping her eyes on her work. Gillespie sauntered over to her.

'Is it the boxty you're making?' he said.

'You can see that it is,' Peggy said.

'I'm leaving a note on the table for your da,' Gillespie said. 'It's a Notice of Increase in Rent.'

Peggy stopped stirring and spun round. 'Another one?' she spluttered. 'We've already had one rent rise this year.'

'Well, this is another. And that's a fact.'

'That's ridiculous,' Peggy said. 'It's not fair, hounding poor people for more and more rent. And times are hard. You should be ashamed of yourself, so you should, piling on the misery. Has Leitrim no mercy?'

'Don't act the maggot, Peggy O'Donnell,' Gillespie said. 'You should be ashamed of yourself talking back to your elders and betters.'

'You may be older, but the divil take me if you're better,' Peggy said.

'You're a bold girl, and deserve a good thrashing for your cheek,' Gillespie said, tapping the girl's hip with his stick. Without thinking, Peggy clouted his hand with the wooden spoon she was holding. Gillespie howled and dropped his stick.

'You fecking bitch,' he hissed, bending down and retrieving his stick. 'I'll teach you to …'

Just then, there was the sound of whistling from outside; the tune was *The Rolling Wave*. Eamonn appeared in the doorway. He had the dark wavy hair, broad shoulders, stocky build, strong nose, and square jaw of the O'Donnell men. He saw Gillespie with his raised stick, and thought, that bollocks is about to hit my wee sister. Eamonn dashed forward, grabbed him by the collar, shoved him out of the door, and booted him in the arse. Gillespie went flying.

'You'd dare to raise a stick to my sister, you gobshite, would ye?' Eamonn said. 'Put up your fists like a man.'

But Gillespie picked himself up and scurried away. 'You haven't heard the last of this, Eamonn O'Donnell.' He hurried past Pat, Conal, and Tim, who looked at him with astonishment. That's me fine big brother, Peggy thought, he's just the boyo to sort out the bully.

'What in the name of the wee man does that gobshite want?' Pat said.

When Peggy told him what had happened, Pat was going to go after the rent-collector.

'No, no, don't,' Peggy pleaded. 'It'll only make matters worse. He'll probably evict us on the spot. He was here to serve a Notice of Increase in Rent. There it is on the table.'

Pat picked up the Notice and read it. 'The bastard,' he said. 'There's just no end to their greed.'

'You're right there,' Peggy said, and started stirring the boxty again. 'There's no end to it.'

Just then, Brighid returned from her visit, saw her husband and son, and hugged them joyfully.

Listening to her father, Peggy tightened her shawl round her shoulders as the late autumn wind moaned outside the cottage. A sudden gust bowled down the chimney driving a cloud of smoke up into the thatch and the smell of peat all round the room; the paraffin lamp guttered. That's a cold wind off the Atalantical Ocean, Peggy thought, winter's not far away.

'So when we finished the tattie-hoking, we stayed with me cousin Mick in Glasgow for a couple of days before getting the boat back to Derry,' Pat said. 'And we had a mighty sessiun in the Irish Club, so we did.' He rummaged in his pockets.

'Here you are, missus,' Pat said, shovelling over a fistful of gold coins and banknotes to Brighid.

'How much is here?' said Brighid.

'You count it,' said Pat.

'Wet the tea, will you, girl,' Brighid said to Peggy.

As Peggy swung the kettle on the crane over the turf fire in the open hearth in the gable-end of the kitchen, and blew the flames into life, her mother counted the money. Eamonn winked at her, while Tim and Conal watched with mouths wide open. The glow of the fire gleamed off the crockery on the dresser, flickered over the rough plastered walls, and another puff of smoke trickled into the thatch. Pat and Eamonn had been gone since the beginning of June at the tattie-picking in Scotland; they'd departed with the first boat that came over from Glasgow to Gortnasade pier to collect the workers. Brighid threw her hands over her face, and gasped.

'*A thiarna!* Fifteen pounds!' she said. 'Holy mother o' God.'

'Hard earned, and that's as true as death,' said Pat.

Brighid looked round her family as Peggy made the tea; she made three separate piles of money on the table.

'There's the rent. Then the priest wants a pound towards his new house. And we owe Farley McKeown two pounds,' she said.

'The rent's going up again. From one shilling and sixpence a week to two shillings,' Pat said. 'What doesn't go to the landlord goes to the priest. And what doesn't go to the priest goes to the fecking gombeen man. And we only produce enough spuds to feed ourselves.'

'That's a fierce increase,' Peggy said. 'Sure, I could always go over to Scotland with Da and Eamonn next year.'

'Good God, no,' said Brighid. 'No daughter of mine will ever go across the water with a bunch of men.'

'There's lots of women …' Peggy said.

'You're a sixteen-year-old girl, not a woman,' her mother snapped. 'And look at what happened to poor Norah Ryan when she went to Scotland. Ruined and died in misery in Glasgow, God rest her soul.'

'They're hard times now in The Rosses,' said Pat. 'The people are leaving in droves for Scotland and Americay. I don't see it getting any better.'

As Peggy passed round the bowls of tea, the whole family gazed into the turf fire while the October wind sighed outside. She lifted the heavy iron lid of the Bastible pot on the fire, and the warm, earthy smell of the boxty filled the room. What on earth are we going to do? She thought.

Eventually Brighid said, 'I know you've got to go to Scotland for the tattie-hoking, but I don't like it at all. I don't like the idea of a young lad like Eamonn leaving home.'

'I'm eighteen, Ma,' Eamonn protested. 'And I can do a man's work.'

'He can that, begod,' said Pat.

'Will you look at you,' said Brighid, giving her son an affectionate shove, 'a slip of a boy pretending he's a man. No, we've got to keep the family together. There are too many young ones going abroad, never coming back, and breaking their parents' hearts. And there's too many of the ould ones winding up in the Glenties workhouse. But not this family, not while I can draw breath, so help me God.'

'They're good firm words,' said Pat. 'But do you know what I'm going to tell you?

Whatever we do, we can't earn enough here to make ends meet. That's why the men have to go tattie-hoking every year. The money's in Scotland.'

Brighid poked the fire so that it glowed. 'Well then,' she said, 'better the whole family goes to Scotland than some of us stay and some of us go. And God be with our journey.'

There was a silence in the room. Peggy looked round her family's faces, glowing both in the reflection of the fire, and a sudden excited anticipation; she could hardly believe what her mother had just said. Brighid had never been further than Glenties in her life – and now she was proposing the emigration of the whole family!

'What about Americay?' said Pat. 'John Joe O'Docherty says his son Liam's doing grand over there in Chicago. Sure, the police is all Irish.'

'No,' said Brighid. 'No. I want to be near enough to come back home if things don't work out. And there are plenty of boats to Scotland.'

'Right you are. Get ye a pen and paper,' said Pat to Brighid, 'and we'll write to Mick, so.'

A few weeks later, Brighid and the children watched as Pat slit the envelope with a knife and smoothed out the letter. He coughed, then read out loud.

2 up 3,
917 Neptune Street,
Govan,
LANARKSHIRE.
November 3rd, 1911.

Padraig, a chara,

I have received your letter and am hastening to reply. It is not difficult to find work here in Govan as there are many shipyards that need a plentiful supply of labourers. And there is also work to be found as a docker. But these jobs will be snapped up in jig time come the spring, so if you are coming, come sooner rather than later.

Houses are in great demand here, but I have had a word with the factor and he will do what he can. There are many people from the Rosses in Govan, and you will find it a home from home.

Let me know when you will arrive, and I will meet you off the Derry boat. I hope this finds you as it leaves me; well, thank the Lord. God bless you, Brighid and the childer.

Your cousin,
Michael O'Donnell.

Pat folded the letter, slipped it back into the envelope, and looked slowly round the family. 'We'll be off as soon as we can, so.'

Peggy reached the top of the hill just as the sun was setting and sat on a flat rock. It was her favourite place, for she could see clean over The Rosses from up here, with the peak of Errigal glowing pink in the distance. The lochans sparkled in the soft light, and the whitewashed cottages glowed like strings of pearls strewn over the empty grey-green landscape. It's a fierce hard place, but sometimes its wild beauty would break your heart.

There was the crunch of a footstep, and Eamonn sat down beside her. 'I knew I'd find you up here,' he said.

'Sure, and it's the grand view,' Peggy said. She turned to face her brother. 'What's Glasgow like, Eamonn?'

'Jaysus, it's an enormous, big black city, teeming with people, and fierce noisy. There's miles and miles of fancy shops and big stores, and a pub on every corner. You can criss-cross the city on electrical trams, and also on something called the subway, which is a sort of underground railway.'

'Underground? I don't like the sound of that,' Peggy said. 'But I would like to see the shops with all their fine dresses. McKeown's General Store doesn't stock anything like that. And I wonder if there would be a good job for a girl.'

'Sure, and there would,' Eamonn said. 'It's mainly girls that work in them stores. And some of them are Irish.'

'How do you know that?' Peggy said.

'I met them at the dancing.'

'At the dancing? There's dancing in Glasgow?'

'Sure, there's step-dancing all over the city. They're dancing mad in Glasgow.'

'Ah-ha,' Peggy said. 'Did you get a click?'

A big grin spread over Eamonn's face as he said, 'Me lips are sealed.'

Peggy smiled as she watched red orb of the sun sink below the skyline. 'Glasgow sounds just the job,' she said.

Chapter 2:
Farewell to Erin.

With the lights of Portstewart and Portrush fading away behind them, the boat began to roll in the swell of the open sea. In the saloon, Brighid trembled, drew her shawl tightly about her shoulders, and grasped Pat's arm.

'It's alright,' Pat said. 'Sure, there's nothing to worry about. It's just the waves of the open sea. We'll be sheltered by land soon enough.' But Brighid was not reassured. Peggy could hear her murmuring the words of the Act of Contrition: 'Oh my God, I am heartily sorry for having offended thee …'

Peggy gazed round, fascinated, while the children dozed. The saloon was blue with smoke. Men mobbed the bar, drinking pints of Guinness; several were already drunk and quarrelling. Some people slept sitting upright, jammed side-by-side on the benches. An accordionist, a fiddler, a flute-player, and Eamonn on the tin-whistle belted out reels. A young woman, her hand over her mouth, staggered out of the door retching, and was violently seasick over the rail. Babies gurned, and from below came the constant bellowing of terrified cattle. The stench of vomit and cattle dung hung in Peggy's nose, while the ship creaked and banged. But in spite of the racket, and the lurching of the ship, the exhausted Peggy fell asleep.

As the beat of the ship's engine slowed right down, Peggy gaped as she clutched the rail and scanned the riverbank. The skeletons of ships festooned with wooden scaffolding towered over the Derry boat as it thudded its way slowly up the Clyde. As it passed one shipyard, a wooden roadway sloped right up to the main deck of the ship under construction. Across the river, several warships bristling with guns were moored side by side, while a three-masted sailing ship provided an elegant contrast. Huge cranes with cabins on the end of their booms and high, iron, triangular contraptions punctuated the skyline. In all directions, tall chimneys belched dark fumes. Tugs, ferries, and paddle-steamers bustled past, trailing tendrils of smoke from their funnels.

Even at seven o'clock in the morning, the din from the shipyards was deafening. A metallic cacophony of steam hammers, rivet-guns and clanking chains assailed Peggy's ears from all sides. The cranes whirred large metal plates down to the staging where they were seized by ant-like squads of men, manoeuvred into place and bolted onto steel ribs. Bursts of incandescent sparks lit up the overcast morning as the edges of the plates were welded together by men wearing mask-like helmets. More teams of men rolled red lead onto the fixed plates. Peggy started as the foghorn of a freighter passing slowly downstream gave a single stentorian blast. It was followed by a series of shriller blarps from the numerous small ferries scuttling up and down the river.

A huge cantilever crane loomed out of the thin light, its boom obscured by drifting cloud and smoke. Peggy lent over backwards to stare up at the mammoth, and nearly toppled over; a friendly hand pushed her back upright. A passing seaman grinned and said, 'Aye, lass. The Fairfield Titan crane. Just finished last year, and the highest in the world. A hunner and seventy feet. And it can lift mair than a hunner ton.' Peggy gasped; it could, it could lift a horse-and-cart!

As the boat slid upriver, an elegant park up on the left studded with trees bearing the light green tracery of spring rose up to a long building with a bell tower on the skyline. The friendly seaman told her it was the University of Glasgow. Shortly afterwards, she heard the ship's telegraph clang, and jumped as the foghorn gave a long single blast as it turned in towards the Broomielaw Quay. As seamen prepared the mooring ropes, it was time to join the family; they had to get off here.

As the seamen secured the gangway, Pat pointed over the rail and waved. 'There's yer man, there's Michael himself.' Michael spotted them from the quay and waved back.

'Get your things and keep together,' said Pat, as the crowd of passengers surged towards the gangway. Slipping and slithering down the wet planking, the O'Donnells were soon on the quay to meet a warm welcome from Michael. Tall buildings with dozens of windows towered over the street, while a forest of ships' masts and funnels framed the quayside. There was a constant clatter of hooves and rattle of iron-shod wheels as horse-drawn carts rolled by. Trams zinged along with clanging bells and showers of sparks, while motor-cars and lorries roared past. What a racket, Peggy thought, looking around, mesmerised. The pavements were black with pedestrians – men in suits and bowler hats with rolled umbrellas, women with long skirts and big hats, workers with buttoned collarless shirts and cloth caps, cyclists, boys with barrows, an endless heaving crowd scurrying to and fro. Peggy smiled to herself as she saw a man with a billboard saying: 'REPENT! THE DAY IS AT HAND!'

'Right, so,' said Michael. 'We'll load your boxes on the cart. This is Donnie MacCaskill the carter, a good neighbour. He'll take your stuff to your house for a shilling. Donnie's from the Isle of Skye, and he speaks Gaelic. Sure, it's not that different from our own.'

Donnie, a tall young man of eighteen or so, shook hands all round. The cart was soon loaded, the boxes and crates tied down, and it was decided that Eamonn would accompany Donnie while the rest of the family would go with Michael on the tram to Govan.

Chapter 3:
Govan, Glasgow, 1912.

Peggy, her mother, father, and young brothers sat upstairs at the front of the tram with Michael as it made its way down Paisley Road West towards Govan. Every time the tram swayed, which was frequently, Brighid would gasp, grab a rail, bless herself and mutter a prayer. Stone canyons of four-storey, smoke-blackened tenements towered above the tram. At street level, the tenements were lined with shops, pubs and picture-houses, while cyclists weaved in and out of the traffic, and the pavements crawled with people. Steel wires criss-crossed the street supporting the electric cables for the trams; dozens of pigeons strutted along the ledges above the tenement windows.

'What a racket,' Peggy said. 'Sure, and it's a noisy place, the Glasgow.'

'Would you look at the state of them two, Tim,' Conal whispered, pointing, as the tram stopped. Tim's eyes followed his older brother's finger down to the pavement where two young women swaggered past, swinging their hips. They were wearing skirts well above their ankles, high-heeled shoes, silk blouses with a plunging neckline, broad-brimmed hats, and bright scarlet lipstick. One of them was smoking a cigarette in a long holder. Conal's hands surreptitiously carved the shape of big breasts in the air to Tim, who turned away in disgust. Peggy caught the gesture, and thumped Conal on the shoulder. The tram started with a jolt, and Brighid gasped.

The tram accelerated past a dock where a couple of tugs were fussing around a large cargo ship, manoeuvring it out into the river. Michael nudged Pat. 'That's the Prince's Dock,' he said. 'The big cargo ships come in there, from all round the world. And look, there's the coaling hoist.'

Below them, a hydraulic hoist lifted a railway wagon full of coal over the open bunker of a ship moored alongside the quay. Just as the tram drew level, the hoist tipped the wagon over, and with a thunderous rattle, the coal crashed into the ship's bunker, spewing a large cloud of black dust into the air. Peggy and Pat looked at each other in astonishment.

'And there's the Govan Town Hall,' Michael said, pointing ahead. In front of them, a large, red sandstone building with an ornate pillared portico loomed into view. Just as they reached it, the tram slewed through ninety degrees to the right, and Brighid grabbed the rail again.

'Jesus, Mary and Joseph!' she gasped, 'This is worse than a horse-and-trap race to a wedding at home!'

'Nearly there,' Michael said, as the tram lurched sharply to the left. 'This is the Govan Road.'

As she jumped off the tram, Peggy heard a strange sound. From up the road, there was the rattle of snare drums, the shrill of flutes, and the rhythmic thump of a big drum. She looked up the road and coming towards them was a procession preceded by a band in bright blue tunics and escorted by Police.

'What's all that about?' Peggy said.

'It's an Orange Walk,' Michael said. 'It's the Govan Orangemen and women.'

'Orangemen? And who might they be?' Peggy said.

'They're fierce Prodesans,' Michael said. 'The Orange Order hates us Catholics. And it's strong in Govan because many Ulster Prods came over to work in Harland and Wolf's, and they brought their hatred of us with them. The Orangemen are fierce bigots, so they are, and the Orange Walk is mean to put the fear of God into us Catholics. That's *The Sash My Father Wore* they're playing.'

The O'Donnells watched with expressionless faces as the large band passed; the big drum carried the legend PROTESTANT BOYS GOVAN. The band was followed by dozens of Orangemen and Women marching in step with a curious shuffling stride. The men wore dark suits, bowler hats and orange sashes, while the women were smartly dressed in white, carrying handbags and also wearing orange sashes. The pavements were thronged with raucous and drunken supporters following the walk. A gap between two groups of marchers appeared, and Peggy stepped forward quickly to cross the road. But Michael grabbed her even more quickly and pulled her back.

'Do you want to get yourself killed?' he muttered. 'You never ever cross an Orange Walk. Look ye there.'

Peggy followed his nod. She saw that the Orange stewards were all carrying truncheons of one sort or another and were not bothering to hide them. She gasped with sudden fear as she realised that she might have received a severe beating.

On the cart, Donnie let the reins lie loose on the seat as the horse broke into a trot, and took a chanter out of his inside pocket, wet the reed with his tongue, and gave an experimental blow. Satisfied, he took a deep breath, and began to play, his rigid fingers stopping the holes in a staccato rhythm. Eamonn got the air of the tune quickly and started to lilt it second time round. Donnie nodded his approval as the cart rattled along over the granite setts and finished the tune with a flourish.

'Good man yourself,' Eamonn said. 'What's the name of that tune?'

'*Gun d'dhiùlt am bodach fodar dhomh*,' Donnie replied. 'In English, that would be 'the old man refused me fodder.' But the fiddlers call it *Munlochy Bridge* for some reason. It's a strathspey.'

'We'd call it a Highland in Donegal,' Eamonn said.

'We've rakes of them.'

'It's a Highland right enough,' said Donnie. 'Do you play yourself?'

'I do,' said Eamonn, taking out a tin whistle. 'I also play the uillean pipes. Here's one of ours.' His fingers flew over the whistle in a tune with more of a faster dancing rhythm than the Scottish one.

'That's a grand tune,' Donnie said. 'I've never heard that one before. What's it called?'

'*Gusty's Frolics*,' said Eamonn. 'It's a slip-jig.'

'Do you have your pipes with you?'

'Sure, and I do. They're in the box in the back there.'

'I think we'll be having the odd session together, then.'

'And why wouldn't we?'

The two young men grinned together.

The O'Donnells followed Michael up the stair in Neptune Street. On each landing, there were three doors with names on a brass plate. Peggy noticed that there was also a door on the half-landing and peeped in: it was a toilet.

'It's the jacks,' she whispered to Conal.

'Here we are,' said Michael, unlocking a door on the second floor. 'Your new house.'

The O'Donnells trooped in. There were two empty rooms, each with an inset bed about three feet off the ground. The kitchen boasted a built-in black iron grate with an oven and hot plates. Michael indicated a black cast-iron sink with a brass swan-necked tap and a bunker at the window.

'That's what they call the jaw-box,' he said, bending down to show a cupboard underneath. The floor was covered with grubby linoleum. Jaysus, Peggy thought, it's a kip of a place; everything's really dirty, even the windows. Michael reached under the inset bed and pulled out another bed.

'The hurley bed,' he said. He then showed them a lamp hung from the ceiling on a pulley arrangement so that it could be raised and lowered; Brighid fingered it tentatively.

'It's gas,' said Michael. 'It works on coal-gas. Look.'

He pulled the lamp down, turned the gas on, took out a box of matches, struck one, and lit it. There was a pop! Everyone jumped, and the kitchen was flooded with a warm, soft light. Michael pushed it, and it rose up on the pulley. Peggy peeked out of the window and saw a back court of hard packed earth strewn with rubble, brick-built middens full of bins, and broken-down walls. Good God, not a blade of grass to be seen, and everything seems to be in ruins. They all trooped into the room. It had a tiled fireplace with a mantelpiece and gas fire, a lamp similar to the one in the kitchen, another inset bed with a hurley bed below it, and the window looked out onto the street.

'Sure, it's a grand place,' Pat said.

'There's nothing that a bucket of water and some elbow-grease won't cure,' said Brighid. 'And the rooms are big enough, thanks be to God.'

'Where will we sleep, Ma?' said Tim.

'Right now, let's see,' said Brighid. 'Peggy and meself will sleep in the kitchen. Your da and Eamonn will sleep in that bed there. And Conal and Tim can sleep in here on the hurley bed, so. We'll be as right as rain.'

Peggy noticed her father frown briefly at these arrangements. He opened his mouth to speak, but there was a knock at the front door. Brighid went to answer it and found a small, middle-aged woman with a tartan shawl wrapped round her shoulders. 'Hullo there,' she said, the sound of the sea in her voice. 'I'm Morag MacCaskill, your neighbour, Donnie's mother. *Ceud mile failte gu Govan.*'

'I'm pleased to meet you, Morag,' said Brighid. 'I'm Brighid O'Donnell from The Rosses of Donegal. Come in, come in. This is my husband Pat, his cousin Michael, my daughter Peggy, and my sons Eamonn, Conal and Tim.' The two women went into a huddle, Morag vanished, and reappeared with a mop, bucket, scrubbing-brush, rags and a big bar of green soap.

'Get you men out of here,' said Brighid, 'there's women's work to be done. Here, Peggy, fill this bucket, will you?'

As Peggy filled the bucket with water at the jaw-box, she reflected that it would be a full-time job keeping a two-roomed house clean when it contained two adults and four children. And where on earth would they do their washing?

'Right, so,' said Michael to Pat. 'We'll have a pint in the Irish Club down the road.'

Turning out of the close, Michael led the way down the road. He stopped at a pend into the back court next to a hardware shop and pointed up to the windows on the first floor. Each window was lettered with a word spelling out the legend: THE. GOVAN. IRISH. CLUB.

'Do you know what the Scotchmen call this street?' said Michael.

'How would I know?' Pat said.

'The Irish Channel,' Michael said. Pat laughed out loud.

'Tim and Conal are too young to go in, for there's drink on sale,' said Michael.

'It's alright, Da,' said Conal, 'we'll have a look around.'

'Mind you keep an eye on your young brother,' Pat said to Conal.

'Sure, and I will,' Conal said.

Further down the street, a bunch of young boys were playing football. The ball came sailing through the air towards Conal and Tim. Conal darted forward and trapped it neatly. He dribbled it forward, and body-swerved a couple of the players. They laughed at his skill, and Conal and Tim were drafted into the game.

Pat and Eamonn followed Michael into the pend and up the back stairs into the Club. It was busy even at midday, and loud with the accents of Donegal and Mayo.

'There are men from every townland in Donegal here,'

said Michael. 'From Durnacarrow, Dernaspool, Ballinaboy, Loughbarrow, Dernagriel, Stranasiggart, Cummin, Doochary, everywhere. There are mountainy men and there are islanders. Sure, it's a home from home. And the Guinness comes right off the Dublin boat.'

That evening, with the furniture unloaded and the beds made up, the gas lamp in the kitchen popping softly and a coal fire glowing in the grate, Pat looked round, and nodded.

'Here we all are then, safe in Scotland. We'll say a rosary for our future in the strange land, so.' The O'Donnell family knelt down, taking out their rosary beads.

They had hardly started the first decade when there was the sound of an altercation outside. A man's voice could be heard roaring and a woman screaming. Everyone looked up but Brighid shook her head – ignore it – and they carried on with the rosary.

Peggy lay beside her mother in the bed in the dark kitchen.

'Are you awake?' said Brighid.

'Yes, I can't sleep,' said Peggy.

'No more can I. It's strange, isn't it? You can't hear the sea. Or the mice in the thatch.'

'I know. And there's a funny sooty smell.'

'So there is now. What is it?'

'It's the coal in the grate.'

'Ah, that's what it is, so. I wonder if you could ever get a sod of turf in Glasgow. I miss the smell.'

'Aye.'

'Well, good night now, and God bless.'

'Good night, Ma.'

Her mother turned over, and soon Peggy heard her breathing slow down. From somewhere not too far away, a burst of a metallic rattle wafted down to her, followed by a regular booming clang, one, two, three, and four. A man's disembodied shout could be heard, followed by an indistinct reply. Jaysus, Peggy thought, Glasgow's noisy, even in the middle of the night. Where could you go to get peace and quiet?

Chapter 4:
The Irish Channel, Govan, 1912.

The next morning, as Peggy stepped out of the house onto the landing, Mrs MacCaskill appeared holding something with both hands under her apron. 'Good morning,' said Peggy, but was astonished when her neighbour hurried past and clattered down the stair without responding. A door slammed on the half-landing and there was a gurgle of water as the chain in the toilet was pulled. The door opened, and Mrs MacCaskill came back up the stair carrying a large empty porcelain chamber-pot. She smiled at Peggy as she said, '*Ciamar a tha sibh?*' She held up the chamber-pot.

'How are you, Peggy? I was just emptying the chanty,' she said. Peggy laughed, understanding her neighbour's strange behaviour.

She saw that the back door out to the Green was open and stepped out to have a look. Two wee girls were squatting on a plank, sailing a paper boat on a large puddle. Peggy saw a glint of light beside one of the weans, bent down and picked up a shard of broken glass, the bottom of a beer bottle. She took it over to the midden, and as she tossed it in, shuddered as a brown rat scurried away.

Peggy went back into the close and out into the street. A group of girls about her own age stood on the pavement, shawls wrapped round their shoulders. They turned towards Peggy, who gasped and stepped back.

'Hallo there,' said a girl with bright red hair and freckles. 'You'd be the new people on the second floor, right. I'm Roísín Herron.'

'How are you, Roísín?' said Peggy. 'I'm Peggy

O'Donnell.'

The other girls introduced themselves. They were Mary McGovern, Cissie Ward, and Fionnula O'Docherty, all from Donegal, and Mary Gorman from Belmullet in County Mayo.

'Sure, Peggy's a culchie from Mayo,' Roísín laughed. 'Where are you from yourself?'

'The Rosses,' said Peggy.

'Sure, there's many a family from The Rosses in this street,' said Roísín. 'Do you have a job, Peggy?'

'Not yet,' said Peggy, 'I'll have to find one. What do ye do?'

'We work in the Cooperative Tailoring Factory in Shieldhall,' Fionnula said. 'It's a grand place to work. We'll bring you along on Monday and see if we can get you a start. Can you work a sewing-machine?'

'No,' said Peggy. 'I heard of them right enough, but I've never seen one.'

'Come on round to my place,' said Cissie. 'I'll teach you on me ma's, so.'

It was the noise which astonished Peggy; such a clicking, chattering, clattering, humming and whirring as she'd never heard in her life. She looked round, eyes wide open. Rows of long tables containing sewing-machines stretched the length of the large room, worked by dozens of women. Peggy noticed that most of them were young, in their teens or twenties. The girls had warned her that the forewoman, Miss Carmichael, was a Protestant who not only didn't like Irish Catholics, but also was a strict disciplinarian, so it was important to make a good first impression. Peggy had brushed her hair carefully, parted it neatly in the middle and tied it up at the back in a roll. She wore a long dark skirt and a white blouse, and polished shoes. At home in Donegal, she normally only wore shoes to Sunday Mass.

A voice behind her made her jump. 'So you're the new girl, the friend of Cissie Ward's?'

Peggy turned to see a tall thin woman in her forties, with severe features, rimless spectacles, and her hair scraped back in a bun. She looked as if her face would crack if she smiled.

'Yes, Miss.'

'Well, Cissie's a good worker. Name?'

'Peggy O'Donnell, Miss.'

'Where are you from, O'Donnell?'

'The Rosses of Donegal, Miss.'

'Age?'

'Seventeen, Miss.'

'Can you read?'

'Of course, Miss,' Peggy said, straining to keep the indignation out of her voice. Of course she could read; hadn't she been a monitor back home in the Rosses?

'Address?'

'One-Oh-One-One Neptune Street, Miss.'

'Oh aye. The Irish Channel,' Miss Carmichael said, wrinkling her nose. 'Right, come with me.'

Peggy followed the forewoman into an office. Miss Carmichael filled out a card with the girl's name, age and address, showed her how it was stored in a rack in the wall with alphabetically arranged boxes, and demonstrated how to punch it into the time-clock, and place it in a second rack.

'You start at eight o'clock sharp, and finish at six, with half-an-hour for lunch. Your wages are fifteen shillings a week as a trainee, but your pay is docked if you're late. And it's also docked for faulty or shoddy work. Is that clear?'

'Yes, Miss.'

'Right. I'll sit you next to Cissie so that she can show you the ropes. You'll be on hemming skirts to begin with.'

Cissie winked as Peggy sat down beside her. 'Never mind the ould battle-axe. You'll be grand here. And we'll have good craic.'

Peggy, who had nimble fingers, and was used to needlework and knitting stockings back in Donegal, soon mastered the techniques of the sewing-machine. Initially, Miss Carmichael stopped frequently to inspect her work, but after a couple of days, gave an approving nod, and moved on. And under the expert guidance of Cissie, she began to learn her way round Govan.

One Saturday morning, Cissie took Peggy and Brighid down Neptune Street to Govan Road. They turned right past Govan Cross and the Castle Bar, then down Queen Street onto Summerton Road, to a big building at the corner of Church Street. As Peggy read the sign outside the entrance - PUBLIC BATHS AND WASH-HOUSE - Cissie said, 'The hot baths is for washing yourself, and the wash-house is the 'steamie,' for doing your laundry.' She took Peggy and her mother into the steamie.

Peggy and Brighid stared; they had never seen anything like this in their lives. Skylights in the steamie roof lit up the scene; wraiths of steam drifted everywhere in the humid atmosphere. There were rows of metal washing-stalls, in each of which a woman in headscarf and slip stood on a slatted, square wooden duckboard, slaving away at a scrubbing-board in a large sink. Dirty laundry simmered in huge boilers, and the smell of carbolic soap hung in the air. The newly washed clothes sat in tin basins ready to be run through large hand-cranked mangles. Dripping pipes ran overhead and down to the sinks. A row of large cylindrical drying tanks lined the back wall. It was a vision of Hell, Peggy thought, except the image was belied by the cheerful chatter and laughter of the women as they worked.

Mrs MacCaskill appeared through the steam. 'Och, it's yourself, Brighid,' she said. 'Come here and I'll show you how the steamie works. It's only tuppence an hour.'

'And I'll show you the hot baths,' Cissie said to Peggy. 'It's a penny a bath and you get a towel.'

Peggy had never seen a bath before. At home, the family washed in a basin from the rainwater barrel. Cissie had to show her how the bath worked and how to manipulate the large brass taps to get the water temperature right. Once she became used to the rules, Peggy loved the baths in spite of the ubiquitous smell of chlorine and the echoing yells of weans playing in the swimming pool.

The bath was long and as she floated up and down, she gently swept the water between her legs and over her breasts with her hands. The first time she did this, she was surprised to find that as her fingertips brushed her nipples, they stiffened and stood erect. Her initial reaction was embarrassment, but she soon found the warm, tingling sensation very pleasant. There was an endless supply of hot water and Peggy dozed off, only to be wakened by the attendant banging on the door and shouting, 'Time's up!' – for the Corporation's rules were that each person was only allowed thirty minutes for her bath.

After a couple of weeks, the O'Donnells had settled into a routine in the strange land. Pat went off early every morning with Michael to try and get a start as a docker, but it was casual work, and there were far more men than jobs.

'Yer man the ganger's a black Prodesan, an Orangeman,' Pat said. 'So for us Catholics, it's last in and first out. And if you want a start, you'd better be buying him a couple of jars in the pub. Sure, you can't rely on steady work at all.'

'Aye, bitter Oranges,' Brighid said.

Eamonn had benefited from an introduction by Donnie MacCaskill and had started work with the same firm of carters; his experience with animals stood him in good stead. So he had a weekly wage coming in, as did Peggy from the tailoring factory. Brighid earned some money by helping Mrs MacCaskill in the steamie with the laundry from a big house in the West End where she worked as a cleaner. Conal had got a start as a copy boy on the *Glasgow Catholic Observer* due to an introduction by Father Gallagher, the parish priest, so he too made his contribution. And Tim was still at school. All in all, though hardly affluent, the family got by.

But Peggy could sense that her father was despondent. It was in his nature to be the breadwinner and head of the house, and he resented not having a steady income to maintain his wife and children. So he sulked, and began to spend more time in the Govan Irish Club where he could always be sure of a pint from a fellow countryman. Peggy could also see that her mother was worried about her father's drinking.

One Saturday evening, Pat was late for his tea. He had gone with Michael to watch the Celtic match at Parkhead, and Peggy knew they always went to the Irish Club for a pint afterwards. But he was usually back in the house for his tea by seven. When seven o'clock had come and gone, Brighid served the children with their fish, chips and mushy peas, and put Pat's on a plate in the oven. Shortly afterwards, Pat could be heard coming up the stair roaring out 'The Wearing of the Green.' The boys giggled but Brighid was not amused.

'Peggy, take the boys into the room and shut the door,' Brighid said.

From the room, Peggy could hear Pat fumbling his key in the door which suddenly banged open, and she heard her mother snap, 'Get ye in the kitchen, Patrick O'Donnell.' The kitchen door slammed shut, but Peggy and the boys could hear Brighid giving out to Pat in no uncertain manner.

'He's getting a right bollocking,' Eamonn said.

'He deserves it,' Peggy said. 'Making a fool of himself in the street and shaming the family.'

'Will the Ma be all right if the Da's drunk?' Conal said.

'Oh, she's more than capable of looking after herself,' Peggy said. 'Sure, she's seen it all before. And the Da's harmless when he's drink taken.'

A few days later, Peggy looked up when she heard Miss Carmichael spluttering.

'You stupid girl,' she hissed at Fionnula O'Docherty. 'You've ruined that jacket. You call these buttonholes? You stupid taig. Stand up.'

Fionnula stood up. Miss Carmichael held up the jacket and addressed the girls in a loud voice.

'Look at what this stupid taig has done. She's done the buttonholes vertically instead of horizontally. You may have vertical buttonholes in Ireland, but we don't in Scotland. We're civilised.' She hit Fionnula in the face with the jacket. The girl grabbed the jacket and threw it on the floor at Miss Carmichael's feet.

'*Póg mo thóin*, you stupid Prod,' Fionnula said. Kiss my arse. The many Irish-speaking girls in the workshop giggled.

'What? What did you say?' Miss Carmichael screeched. She slapped Fionnula on the face. A horrified gasp rippled round the room. 'Get out of here, you insolent toe-rag. You're fired.'

'*Póg mo thóin*, you gobshite,' Fionnula said as she picked up her coat and stormed out. The girls' laughter evaporated as Miss Carmichael spun on her heel to see who found it funny. Peggy couldn't believe it. You can't treat people like that. That's not fair. Fionnula made a mistake but sure anyone can make a mistake. And you can't go around hitting people for making a mistake. Peggy stopped her machine and looked round the room for support. But the other girls looked down at their work and avoided her gaze.

'That's not fair,' Peggy said. 'She only made a wee mistake, that's all.'

'*Bí i do thost*, Peggy!' Cissie whispered. Be quiet!

As Miss Carmichael's face went livid, Peggy stood up and faced her. 'You've no call to be using that kind of bad language,' she said. 'Sure, anyone can make a mistake. And you've certainly no right to be hitting anyone.'

Miss Carmichael gasped. You could have heard a pin drop in the workshop. She grasped the edge of a table so tightly that her knuckles turned white.

'Get out of here, you brazen Irish hussy,' she hissed. 'You're fired too.'

Peggy gathered her things and stalked out, her feet echoing on the wooden floor. When she reached the door, she stopped and said, 'Who would want to work for a crabbit ould gulpin like you anyway? You're as twisted as the divil.'

There was an audible titter in the workroom as Peggy slammed the door behind her.

As the family sat round the fire that evening, Peggy explained why she had been fired. 'She called Fionnula O'Docherty a stupid taig and an insolent toe-rag because she'd done the button-holes up-and-down instead of across. So Fionnula said, '*Póg mo thóin*,' and the Carmichael woman fired her on the spot. So, I sez, sure it's only a wee mistake she made, so she ups and fires me too.'

Brighid shook her head and said, 'Why do they hate us so much?'

Pat took the tongs and threw another lump of coal on the fire. 'Arra, that's all they're good for,' he said. 'Dirty black Prods.' He spat in the fire.

'Still and all,' Brighid said, 'you be careful over here with that quick temper of yours, Peggy O'Donnell. Sure, that mouth of yours could get you into big trouble. These Scotch people aren't the same as us.'

'That's a fact,' Pat said.

There was silence for a second, then Eamonn said, 'Let's have a tune, so.'

He took his uillean pipes out of their case while Pat took his fiddle down from the hook on the wall.

'*The Pinch of Snuff* and *Bean an Tigh ar Lar*,' Eamonn said. A moment later, there was a happier atmosphere as the reels rang round the kitchen. Peggy soon forgot that she was jobless; tomorrow would look after itself.

Chapter 5:
Eviction.

A few days later, Brighid and Peggy were woken early by shouting and screaming and banging and clattering from the house across the landing. They were not surprised because the family that lived there, the Walshs from County Mayo, were frequently at loggerheads. The father, Mick Walsh, was a heavy drinker and when he staggered home from the Irish Club on a Saturday night, he would frequently beat his wife Gráinne mercilessly while their six screaming children tried to drag him off. Peggy and Brighid had been appalled when Gráinne appeared one Sunday morning with a black eye, a split lip, and a bruised face. What Peggy found even more appalling was that Gráinne seemed resigned to the violence; it seemed to her to be a normal part of married life. But Peggy knew that her mother had had a quiet word in the ear of the parish priest.

Brighid and Peggy opened their door to see two burly Sheriff Officers haul the Walshs' pathetic sticks of furniture down the stairs. Gráinne Walsh was weeping loudly, wringing her hands, while the children howled. Mick was nowhere to be seen.

'What's going on, Gráinne?' Brighid said.

'They're evicting us for arrears of rent,' Gráinne sobbed. 'Mick drank the rent money, and now they're putting us out on the street. What are we going to do?'

Peggy dressed quickly and hurried down the stairs. Mick was sitting on the kerb, his head in his hands, still drunk. The furniture was heaped on the pavement in a pile, while a small crowd of women neighbours watched, muttering their anger and helplessness. The two Sheriff Officers came out carrying the double bedstead, and tossed it on the pile.

'Youse have no shame,' Peggy said. 'You should be ashamed of yourself doing dirty work like that,'

'Mind your own bloody business, you Irish whore,' one of the Officers snarled. 'You want to …'

'You want to mind your language, you Scotch bollocks,' Peggy said.

The Sheriff Officer swung his hand back to slap Peggy when his wrist was grabbed and his arm twisted up behind his back.

'What did you call my sister?' Eamonn said. He forced the man's arm further up his back, eliciting a yelp. The other Sheriff Officer pushed Eamonn back and waved a paper in his face.

'This is a Writ,' he said. 'It's a legal document issued by the Sheriff Court authorising this eviction. You're obstructing officers of the Court in the legal execution of their duties, for which you can go to jail. Now back off, Paddy, if you know what's good for you.'

Eamonn had no option but to release the Sheriff Officer and step back.

'That's outrageous,' Peggy said, 'treating people worse than animals.'

A voice beside her said, 'It is that, but it happens at least once a week somewhere in Govan.'

Peggy turned to see Mrs MacCaskill standing beside her.

'And they're not officers of the Court at all. That's just lies to frighten people. They're just paramasites. But what's even worse are the warrant sales,' Morag said.

'What's a warrant sale?' Peggy said.

'That's when someone gets in debt so bad that the Sheriff Officers sell off all their belongings in public to pay off the debts,' Morag said. 'It's like an auction of all their worldly possessions.'

'Sure, and that's criminal,' Peggy said. 'It's waging war on poor people, so it is.'

'You're right there,' Morag said. 'But we have our ways of fighting back.'

'How do ye do that?' Peggy said.

'There's one tomorrow at the end of the street,' Morag said. 'I'll come for you about a quarter-to-ten, and I'll show you what we're after doing.'

By the evening, all the Walsh's furniture on the street had vanished, except for a few rags of clothes; Peggy saw locals helping themselves. The Walshs had also vanished. Peggy asked Morag what had become of them. Morag told her that Gráinne had relatives in the East End and had probably gone there. She thought that Mick would wind up in a dosshouse.

'No better than he deserves, the *drongair*,' Morag said, her eyes glinting with anger.

The next morning, Morag took Peggy down to the far end of Neptune Street; Morag's shawl was pinned tightly across her shoulders and chest. A table had been set up at the close mouth, with household items – crockery, cutlery, pots and pans, vases, wally dogs, pictures, clothes, and curtains – on top of it. The same two Sheriff Officers stood behind the table, muttering to each other and consulting their fob watches. A small crowd of women had gathered, among whom Peggy recognised several of her neighbours.

Morag nudged Peggy. 'See them two?' she said, gesturing at two large women with big handbags at the front of the crowd. 'They're hawkers from the old clothes market in Greendyke Street, professional bloody vultures. They read the news of the Warrant Sales in the papers and attend as many as they can.'

One of the Sheriff Officers stepped forward. 'Right, let's start,' he said. He held up a large vase ornamented with

Chinese motifs. 'What am I bid for this?'

'A ha'-penny,' one woman shouted.

'Three-farthings,' another yelled.

The two hawkers exchanged angry looks at these ridiculously low bids. One of them turned to the Sheriff Officer, took a deep breath, and let out a strangled scream. Morag shook with silent laughter as the second hawker asked the first what had happened. The woman indicated her backside, rubbing it, and gasping.

'Sold to the woman in the black shawl for three-farthings,' the Sheriff Officer said.

While his colleague handed over the vase, he held up a stack of plates and bowls.

'What am I bid for this crockery set?' he said.

'A ha'-penny,' a local woman shouted. There was a silence.

'Going for a half-penny,' the Sheriff Officer said, with a disgusted look on his face. 'Going, going ...'

One of the hawker women put up her hand, preparing to shout a bid. The Sheriff Officer turned towards her, but all that came out of her was a loud squawk, as she jumped forward. She turned angrily to the women behind her, rubbing her backside, but they all looked as if butter wouldn't melt in their mouth.

'Sold for a ha'-penny,' the Sheriff Officer said.

Peggy could feel Morag quaking with silent mirth beside her. She shook her head in enquiry. Morag glanced round, slid a large hatpin out of her shawl, palmed it and showed it to Peggy. As Peggy grinned her understanding, Morag slipped forward through the crowd to behind where the two hawkers stood and nodded subliminally to another neighbour woman.

The Sheriff Officer held up a faded canteen of matching, but stained, cutlery.

'What am I bid for this matching set of cutlery?' he said.

'A ha'-penny,' a woman called.

The Sheriff Officer scowled. 'Come on, ladies,' he cried. 'This is a six-piece matching set in good condition. Who'll offer me sixpence?'

One of the hawkers raised her hand and just as she was about to call her bid, she screamed and jumped in the air. As her friend turned to help her, she too suddenly yelled loudly. Morag appeared beside Peggy, sliding the hatpin back into her shawl, and winking. It was Peggy's turn to be overcome with silent laughter. The two hawkers left the scene hurriedly, followed by the catcalls and threats of the neighbourhood women.

Peggy watched as the warrant sale ended. Practically everything was bought by local women at knockdown prices. The moment the disgusted Sheriff Officers departed, the women gave everything they had bought back to the woman from whom it had been seized. She thanked her neighbours profusely, tears streaming down her cheeks.

As Morag and Peggy strolled back down the street to their close, Morag said, 'We can't stop the Warrant Sales, but we can stop most of the stuff from leaving the street.'

Peggy nodded. 'That's grand, so. Fair play to ye.' There's more to these Govan women than meets the eye. They may be poor, but they're not stupid – and they're brave. I'm on their side. We've got to stand up for ourselves against the landlords and Sheriff Officers who can put poor people out on the street just like that.

Chapter 6:
Partickhill.

'Look, Peggy,' Mrs MacCaskill said, 'I've an idea. You know I work every morning from Monday to Friday as a maid in a big house in Partickhill. Well, I'm getting a bit old for that now, and I said so to the people I work for. They were thinking of employing a live-in maid, and a big strong lassie like you would be ideal for the job. It's nothing you couldn't handle – a bit of cleaning, going the messages, simple cooking, and helping when they have a dinner party. They're very nice, kind people, two sisters, both school teachers, the Misses MacDonald, real ladies. I could have a word with them if you like. What do you think?'

'Oh, I'd like that fine,' Peggy said.

A few days later, Mrs MacCaskill told Peggy that the Misses MacDonald would like to see her that afternoon. So with her hair brushed and tied up neatly, and wearing her Sunday best, Peggy accompanied her neighbour to Govan Subway Station. She had never been on the subway before, so looked around with interest as they went down the steps to the platform. Peggy inhaled; there was an earthy smell in the station.

Suddenly, there was a rattling roar and a small brown train erupted out of the tunnel and whined to a halt at the platform. She laughed out loud as the latticed gates slid open.

'Sure, it's like a toy train,' Peggy said to Mrs MacCaskill.

'Maybe, but it's after being very handy for getting you about the city,' her neighbour said.

The gates slid shut and the train took off, swaying as it roared through the tunnel;

Peggy had an impression of great speed. Mrs MacCaskill shook Peggy's arm.

'We're going under the River Clyde now,' she said. Peggy looked around in panic and grabbed the rail, her mouth open, and gasped, 'Jesus, Mary and Joseph.'

The train began to climb an incline; there was a sudden blaze of light and it whined to a stop at Merkland Street station.

'Here we are,' Mrs MacCaskill said.

The two women dodged the trams crossing Dumbarton Road and turned into a street which led to a canyon-like steep hill with tenements on both sides all the way to the top; the road-sign said: 'Gardner Street.'

'This hill is getting too much for me,' Mrs MacCaskill said, 'twice a day, five days a week.'

They climbed to the top of the hill and turned left into Partickhill Road. Mrs MacCaskill paused, panting, and held onto the cast-iron railing. 'See what I mean?' Peggy nodded. She could also see that the local tenements were much bigger and more ornate than those in Neptune Street, and the entrance stair was both more commodious and better lit than hers.

As Mrs MacCaskill introduced Peggy to the two MacDonald sisters, Maggie and Catherine, Maggie said, 'Oh my, what a lovely girl. You must sit for me.'

Seeing the confusion on Peggy's face, Catherine laughed. 'She means she would like to paint you, Peggy. Maggie is a painter.'

Peggy still hadn't a clue what they were talking about, but smiled and nodded as Catherine gestured to a chair. The sisters were impressive ladies in their thirties, tall, striking looking, and smartly dressed. Catherine was the older, with a commanding presence, while Maggie appeared friendlier.

As Maggie poured the tea, Peggy was aware she was

being scrutinised, but she tried to stay calm. She looked round the sitting-room. It was huge, with large bay windows overlooking a bowling-green. Two walls were covered with paintings, and Peggy did a double-take at one of Maggie without a stitch of clothing on her. A third wall ran the length of the room and was completely full of books; Peggy had never seen so many books in one place in her life. Could they have read them all?

'Sugar, Peggy?' Maggie said.

'Yes, please,' Peggy said. 'One.'

Maggie passed the teacup and saucer over. 'A scone? Home-made this very morning.'

'Thank you,' Peggy said.

'Now, Peggy,' Catherine said, 'what is your position on the Home Rule for Ireland question?'

Jaysus, Peggy thought, taking a mouthful of scone to win a moment's respite – whatever next?

'Me father is a fierce man for Home Rule, Miss Catherine,' Peggy said. 'A Home Ruler entirely.'

Peggy noticed the two sisters exchanging an approving glance; well, well, Scotch Home Rulers.

'And how is your reading and writing?' Maggie said.

'Oh, they're good, Miss Maggie. I was a monitor – a pupil-teacher – in The Rosses, looking after the First and Second Infants. The schoolmaster was Francis O'Neill, and he gave me many novels to read – I love reading – and got me to write compositions on them.'

'I see,' Catherine said. 'And what did you read?'

'Lady Morgan's *The Wild Irish Girl*, *O'Donnell*, Carleton's *Traits and Stories of the Irish Peasantry*, and Banim's *The Nowlans*,' Peggy said.

'O'Donnell?' Maggie said with a laugh. 'It's your very own surname.'

Peggy smiled. 'Yes, it is. I like stories about our own people.'

'Right,' Maggie said. 'Let me show you the house.'

Peggy put her cup and saucer down on the coffee table, stood up, and followed Maggie to the door. She sneaked a glance at the painting to make sure; yes, it was of Maggie, and no, she didn't have a stitch on. Maggie noticed the glance, and said, 'Yes, that's me. Painted by John Duncan Ferguson. I was younger then, of course.' She patted her hips and laughed. 'And I've put on a bit of weight since then.'

As Peggy followed her out of the room, she could feel her cheeks burning. And who was John Duncan Ferguson?

'I modelled for several paintings for John,' Maggie said, 'but only the one nude.' Peggy didn't know where to look.

'And this is the kitchen,' Maggie said.

Peggy looked round the large room. Most of one wall was occupied by a complicated black metal range with a grate, where Mrs MacCaskill was busy. A warm smell of baking permeated the room. The opposite wall was lined with shelves containing crockery, pots and pans, a wine-rack, wine glasses and cookery books. A large table stood in the middle of the floor; a drawer was open showing a rake of cutlery. Maggie pointed out the window. 'We've a splendid view.'

Peggy looked out. Way down below was a large sports ground. 'That's the West of Scotland cricket ground,' Maggie said. 'And do you see these cranes?'

'Yes,' Peggy said.

'That's the Fairfield Shipyard in Govan. Where you and Morag live. So, it's not so far away as the crow flies. Now. If we come to an agreement, this is where you would sleep.'

She took Peggy to the wall opposite the kitchen window and pulled back a curtain to expose a large recess containing an iron-framed bed. On the wall was a series of bells marked 'Sitting-Room,' 'Bedroom 1,' 'Bedroom 2,' and 'Study.'

'If we want you, we'd ring, and all you have to do is look at the bell to know from which room we're ringing,' Maggie said.

She went to the kitchen door and called, 'Catherine, ring the bell, please.'

As Peggy watched, the bell marked 'Sitting-Room' jangled; it's all organised down to the last detail in this house, she thought.

'And you can store your things in this chest-of-drawers,' Maggie said.

Peggy followed Maggie out into the hall and noticed again that the walls were covered with paintings and drawings.

'The bathroom,' Maggie said. Peggy saw a long room with a large bath, sink and toilet, racks with bath-towels and shelves with soap, shampoos and unknown lotions and potions. God o' Gods, thought Peggy, and we don't even have a jacks in our house, let alone a bath.

'This is my bedroom,' Maggie said.

She opened the door, and Peggy glimpsed a double-bed with a brightly coloured silk throw on it, a tailor's dummy with a black cocktail dress with a plunging neckline and short skirt, a large wardrobe with mirrored doors, and a dressing-table containing all sorts of small bottles of perfume and cologne, and boxes of make-up. Strings of pearls and amber necklaces hung from a hook. And there was a framed black-and-white print of a dark-haired woman with bare breasts and her skirt low down on her hips exposing her bellybutton, with some kind of ugly leprechaun playing the guitar at her feet, facing the bed. Peggy gulped and glanced away; this house is full of paintings of women in their bare buff. That's very bold.

'Catherine's bedroom,' Maggie said, pointing, without opening the door. 'And this is the study-cum-studio.'

Peggy's eyes opened wide as she saw even more books. There were two desks at opposite ends of the room and an easel with a canvas on it at the window. An artist's palette, brushes, and tubes of paint lay on a table nearby. And there were yet more paintings on the walls. Peggy glanced at the painting on the easel and recoiled. Jesus, Mary and Joseph. The painting was of a naked man, looking out at the artist; you could see the hair round his thing and all. Has Miss Maggie no shame at all?

Maggie saw Peggy gazing at it, and said, 'That's a life painting of my friend Charlie. I've still to finish his legs. I'll do that on his next visit.'

Peggy gulped, averted her eyes, and followed Maggie out into the hall. 'And this is the cleaning press,' she said, opening a door to reveal brooms, brushes, mops, ash-pans, buckets, an ironing-board, and boxes and shelves of cleaning materials.

'And the linen cupboard,' Maggie said, opening another door to show shelves of sheets, pillow-slips, blankets, quilts and towels.

Catherine smiled at Peggy as she and Maggie sat down again in the sitting-room.

'How do you like our house, Peggy?' Catherine said.

'Oh, it's grand, it's lovely,' Peggy said.

'Well,' Maggie said. 'If you'd like the job, we'll offer you ten shillings a week for the first couple of weeks, and you can learn where everything is, and the daily routine, from Morag. Then she'd leave and you would be on your own. We would then offer you twelve shillings and sixpence a week for the next four weeks to see how you cope. Then, if we're happy, and you're happy, we'd then raise that to fifteen shillings a week. After that, we'll see. You'd live in Mondays to Fridays, with Saturday afternoon and Sunday off. You don't have to sleep here on weekend nights, but you do have to be back by seven on Monday mornings to have the range on, the kettle boiling and the porridge ready. Sometimes we have a dinner-party on a Saturday night, and we'd ask you to help out. We'd pay you extra for that and supply you with a maid's outfit. Otherwise, through the week, you can wear your own clothes and we'll give you several aprons. I think that's it.'

Maggie glanced at Catherine, who nodded, and said, 'It's not that hard once you've mastered the routine, Peggy. And if you're interested in learning to cook, we'd help you. So. What do you think?'

'I think I'd like it fine,' Peggy said, 'and I'd be rarin' to learn to cook, so.'

'Good,' Maggie said. 'You can start next Monday. Ten shillings for the first two weeks, and twelve shillings-and-sixpence for the next four weeks. And then we'll review the situation. Agreed?'

'Agreed,' Peggy said. To her surprise, both Maggie and Catherine stood up and shook her hand. Back home in Donegal, women didn't shake hands like men.

As Mrs MacCaskill was helping the sisters with a party that evening, Peggy went back to Govan on the subway alone. She picked up an abandoned *Glasgow Herald* newspaper and read SITUATIONS VACANT on the front page. She saw that the average weekly wage for a maid was ten shillings, plus a meal a day. Boys oh boys, she thought, if I keep me nose clean, I could be earning fifteen bob a week in a month's time!

That evening, as Peggy explained her new situation to her parents, she said, 'You should see their house. It's huge, like something out of a fairy story. And they're going to teach me to cook.'

'God bless the mark,' Brighid said. 'It's a great start you have there.'

But Pat scowled. 'I don't like the idea of me daughter working as a skivvy for the gentry. They're …'

'They're not gentry, Da,' Peggy said. 'They're not land-owners like back home in Donegal. They're, they're educated ladies, school teachers. I think I could learn a lot from them.'

Pat scowled again and stared into the fire. 'Well, a job's a job's and that's a fact. But don't you be getting any fancy ideas from them educated ladies now.'

'Oh thanks, Da,' Peggy said, giving her father a hug.

Chapter 7:
Forward!

Peggy shut the bolt on the door of the outside toilet, lifted her skirt, slid down her knickers and sat. Her eye was caught by the toilet-paper hanging by a string from a nail; it was a newspaper cut into squares. She pulled off a square and read the title: ***FORWARD***. She then saw a column headed: 'Catholic Socialist Notes,' by the Catholic Socialist Society. She read:

> *We repeat that the Catholic Socialist Society stands foursquare behind the Independent Labour party and its goals. It is not a separate entity, stands for the same principles as the socialist bodies of Scotland, and seeks to propagate these principles amongst the Catholic population.*

Peggy wasn't sure what socialism was, although she had heard the term, and she hadn't a clue what the Independent Labour Party was. She read that the Society had socials every Sunday afternoon, and organised summer rambles. Hmm, just like the jig *The Ramblin' Pitchfork* me Da plays. Sounds interesting. She was just reaching for another sheet to read when the door rattled, and a male voice said, 'Hurry up in there.' Mortified, Peggy used the paper – as intended – adjusted her clothes, pulled the chain and left.

Outside, it was Donnie MacCaskill's turn to be embarrassed. 'Och, it's yourself, Peggy, sorry about that,' he said.

'Not a bit of it,' Peggy said.

The next Saturday afternoon, Peggy went with Cissie to the Rialto café on Govan Road. It was a meeting place for young people, mainly Irish, and the Italian owners kept up a steady supply of coffee, tea, hot chocolate, and ice-creams. The boys sat at one end of the café, the girls at the other, and the craic flew back and forth.

'Would you look at the bould Liam Sharkey,' Cissie said, 'making eyes at me, so he is. I hope he gives me a dance at the Club tonight. Are you going?'

'I didn't know there was a dance tonight,' Peggy said.

'Sure, there's step-dancing every Saturday night,' Cissie said. 'It's great craic.'

'I'll have to ask me Da. I don't know if he'll let me.'

'Oh for Jaysus' sake, girl, it's only a dance.'

'I know. But he can be fierce close-minded.'

'Tell him there's no harm in it at all, at all. Sure, Father Gallagher himself looks in.'

'Alright, Cissie. I'll ask him, so.'

But when Peggy arrived home a little later, she found Father Gallagher in the house sharing a glass of whiskey with her father.

'How's about you, Peggy?' Father Gallagher said. 'I hear you've got a start as a maid up in the West End.'

'Yes, Father,' Peggy said. 'In Partickhill.'

'But your employers are Protestants.'

'They are, Father.'

'Well, there's nothing wrong with that, but keep your wits about ye, and be prepared to defend your faith.'

'I will, Father, I will,' Peggy said. She watched as the priest took a sip of his whiskey, and said, 'Da. What's socialism?'

The priest exchanged a sharp glance with Pat, and said, 'Where did you learn about that?'

'I read it on a bit of old newspaper in the jacks,' Peggy said. 'The *Forward*.'

Father Gallagher scowled. 'That socialist rag! Socialism is the enemy of the Catholic Church, Peggy. It's an evil doctrine which thrives off the poor man's envy of the rich. The socialists and the communists want to take people's land and property away from them, but the right to own property is a God-given right. It's a divine right, do you understand? God put property-owners on earth to run things.'

Peggy nodded, even although she wasn't sure she did understand. But then, Father Gallagher was the parish priest, educated at Maynooth College. He knew what was right and what was wrong; he knew what was what.

'The issue is not to think of seizing property, but to spread the influence of Holy Mother Church so that we can create a fairer relationship between employers and employees, 'a fair day's wage for a fair day's work,' do you see?' Father Gallagher said.

Peggy nodded again. Father Gallagher turned to Pat. 'Them socialists send their children to Socialist Sunday Schools to learn atheism,' the priest said. 'They should be banned entirely.'

'Amen to that,' Pat said.

Father Gallagher stood up. 'Thanks for the drink, Pat. I'll be off to look in at the dancing at the Club, so.'

Peggy said quickly, 'Da, could I go to the dance? Just for a while?'

Pat frowned and Peggy could sense he was going to say no, but Father Gallagher put his hand on her father's shoulder and said, 'Lookit, there's no harm in it for an hour or two, Pat. I'll be there myself. Why don't you come yourself and bring your fiddle? We could use a dacent fiddler in the band.'

'Sure and why wouldn't I?' said Pat, and reached for his fiddle.

The air was blue with smoke from pipes and cigarettes, but Peggy didn't mind as she whirled around. On the stand were

Pat and another fiddler, Eamonn with his uillean pipes, a flute-player, and a man with a bodhrán. Peggy, a head taller than most of the other young women, was dancing for Donegal, her face flushed, eyes sparkling, hair flying, feet battering out the percussive rhythm on the floor while her upper body remained erect. The set finished to cheers and applause. Peggy sat beside Cissie, who had a big smile on her face.

'You look like the cat that's got the cream,' Peggy said. 'What are ye so pleased about?'

'Liam Sharkey asked me if he could walk me home,' Cissie said.

'Get along with you,' Peggy said. 'You're codding me.'

'As God is my witness.'

'Have you said yes?'

'Oh Jaysus, no. I'll play him along for a wee while more.'

Peggy laughed. 'You're a divil, Cissie Ward.'

After the next set, it was eleven o'clock, and Father Gallagher told the younger girls it was time to be on their way. As Peggy walked along the Irish Channel with her friends, she thought that she had not felt so happy for a long time. Maybe Glasgow was going to be good for her.

Pat was yet again not selected from the throng of dockers clamouring for work. As the gates of the dock closed, Pat spat, and made his way to a derelict pier. He sat on a bollard and lit his pipe, watching the filthy waters of the Clyde flow downstream. West, west, where home is, where Donegal is, where there's clean fresh water in the rivers and lochans; where the air is pure, and there is peace and quiet instead of the incessant din of Glasgow and the bitterness of the Orangemen and the Prodesans.

The song *The Hills of Donegal* came into Pat's head, and he softly sang:

Oh gran machree I long to see
my own native hills again,
On a foreign shore my heart is sore
with exile's longing pain.
Could I but see those mountains free
'twould compensate for all,
And I'd live as my poor fathers
lived in the hills of Donegal.

Peggy sat as still as she knew how while Maggie sketched.

'They're called pastels, Peggy,' she said. 'It's a sort of soft crayon which gives a light effect on the paper. I think it suits a sketch of you, for you've a lovely skin tone, and there are hints of navy blue in your hair.'

Would you listen to herself, Peggy thought, navy blue me arse; me hair is coal black, so it is.

'There you go,' Maggie said. 'What do you think?'

Peggy studied the sketch. It showed the head of a girl with a pale face, black hair, with shades of navy blue right enough, and striking dark blue eyes, looking calmly and directly at the artist. Peggy gasped.

'Is that what I look like?'

Maggie stood up and touched Peggy's cheek with her fingertips. 'My dear girl, you don't know how beautiful you are.'

There was the rattle of a key in the front door, and it opened and closed.

'Cooee,' Catherine called, 'I'm back.'

'Now, Peggy, Catherine wants to speak to you about an extra Saturday night,'

Maggie said.

Maggie and Peggy went into the kitchen where Catherine heaved several heavy shopping-bags onto the table. 'I'm dying for a cup of tea,' she said. 'Be a darling, Peggy, and put the kettle on. Lipton's was packed and I couldn't find a boy to carry the messages up Gardner Street. I'm knackered.'

Later, Catherine explained to Peggy that they were having a dinner-party two weeks on Saturday, in the evening, and would like her to help. 'There will be six people in all – us, our brother Archie, Elpseth Mavor – she's an almoner in the Western Infirmary, and very sweet on Archie – and Jack and Patricia Ritchie. Jack's a doctor in the Corporation Public Health Department and Pat's a music-teacher. Our Archie teaches history at Hillhead High School – you'll like him, he's a live wire. He's very active in the ILP and might even stand for parliament. Anyway, if you'd help us prepare and serve the dinner, and clear up afterwards, we'll of course pay you extra, and give you a maid's outfit for the evening. Could you do that?'

'Of course I could,' Peggy said.

A few days later, Catherine passed a sheet of notepaper to Peggy. The girl read it:

Oysters with champagne-vinegar mignonette

Poached salmon with Hollandaise sauce

Roast saddle of venison with red wine sauce

Lemon syllabub

'Well, what do you think?' Catherine said.

Peggy felt her cheeks flush with embarrassment. 'I've never heard of any of them, Miss Catherine.'

'Really? Never?'

Peggy shook her head and handed the sheet of paper back, mortified. Catherine laughed.

'Well, we'll teach you. It'll be good fun, you'll see.'

The next couple of weeks were a whirl. The sisters taught Peggy how to shuck oysters, prepare the mignonette, poach the salmon, roast the venison, make red wine and Hollandaise sauces, and create a frothy syllabub. Peggy worked with a will because she was keen to learn, on the one hand, and wanted to please Maggie and Catherine, on the other. The sisters sent her uptown on the subway to Fraser's with a shopping-list for a maid's costume. Peggy wandered through the store, spellbound by the fancy clothes and furniture. She eventually found the right department and handed over the list. The saleswoman kitted Peggy out with a maid's uniform: a black dress and stockings, a white pinafore with lace trimming, and a white mop cap, also with a lace trim. She handed Peggy a large paper bag containing the uniform. As Peggy left, she had to pass through the lingerie department. She saw a plastic mannequin dressed in nothing but a frilly bra and knickers and, mortally embarrassed, averted her gaze as she hurried past.

On the evening of the dinner, Peggy, wearing her brand-new maid's outfit, took the guests' coats and hung them on the hall stand. She noticed that Miss Mavor did not address a word to her, while Dr and Mrs Ritchie merely thanked her. Catherine said her brother Archie would probably be late because of his endless political meetings. Peggy was heating up the mignonette when the doorbell rang. She hurried down the hall and opened the door to see a tall and handsome young man with piercing eyes, high cheekbones, and a quiff of dark hair falling over his forehead. He smiled and said, 'Ah! You must be Peggy. I've heard a lot about you. How do you do?'

He stretched out his hand and Peggy shook it. As he took off his coat, he studied Peggy's face and smiled.

'Aye,' he said. 'You're every bit as pretty as my sisters say you are. A lovely Irish colleen right enough.'

Peggy blushed and took his coat and hung it up to hide her embarrassment. As no man had ever paid her a compliment in her whole life, she didn't know where to look. And Archie was so good-looking.

'Ah, there you are, Archie,' Maggie said behind her. 'We

were wondering where you were.'

'Sorry, Maggie,' Archie said, 'I was held up at the Ward Committee meeting.'

In the kitchen, Peggy turned the gas down under the mignonette and sliced some seedless red grapes. A little later, the dining-room bell rang. Peggy spooned a little mignonette over each oyster and sprinkled them with the grape slices. She lifted the tray and, tongue between her teeth, carried it into the dining-room where the guests were opening their table-napkins. Archie smiled at her again, and said, 'There she is, Kathleen Mavourneen herself – except she's called Peggy!'

Everyone laughed, but Peggy glimpsed a frown crossing Miss Mavor's face.

Peggy opened the kitchen door a crack so she could listen. Someone was playing the piano in the sitting-room, and everyone was singing in a language Peggy did not recognise.

Au clair de la lune
Mon ami Pierrot
Prete-moi ta plume
Pour écrire un mot.

Ma chandelle est morte
Je n'ai plus de feu
Ouvre-moi ta porte
Pour l'amour de Dieu.

Archie's voice could be heard indistinctly making some comment, and there was a burst of laughter. The dining-room bell clanged, and Peggy jumped.

She opened the sitting-room door to see everyone with a glass in their hand, and Archie sitting at the piano, turning the pages of a music-book.

'You can bring the coffee in now, Peggy,' Maggie said.

As Peggy turned to go, Archie said, 'A girl from Donegal

must know some good songs. How about an Irish song, everyone?'

There was a murmur of assent, and Catherine smiled encouragement. Peggy twisted her hands behind her back and shifted her feet, flustered at being the centre of attention, and said, 'Oh no, I …'

'Something in Irish, maybe?' Archie said.

Peggy looked round the company. Everyone smiled encouragement, except Miss Mavor whose smile did not reach her eyes. Bad cess to you, missus, Peggy thought; what have I done to deserve the evil eye?

'Right, so,' Peggy said. 'I'll sing *Bheir Mí Ó*.' She interlaced her fingers in front of her and began the haunting song.

Bheir mi óró 'bhean ó
Bheir mi óró, ó 'bhean í
Bheir mi óró ó hó
'S mé tá brónach 's tú im dhíth

'S iomaí oíche fliuch is fuar
Thug mé cuairt is mé liom féin
Nó go ráinig mé san áit
Mar a raibh grá geal mo chléibh

I mo chláirseach ní raibh ceol
I mo mheoraibh ní raibh brí
No gur luaigh tú do rún
'S fuair mé eolas ar mo dhán.

After a few bars, Archie began a soft accompaniment on the piano, and to Peggy's surprise, Maggie and Catherine joined in on the chorus, except that they sang it in English. When she came to the end, everyone clapped loudly – except Elpseth, who had eyes only for Archie. Archie turned to his sisters and said, 'A beautiful girl with a beautiful voice. You *are* lucky!'

Peggy didn't know where to look, so she half-curtsied

and fled to the kitchen for the coffee things.

Later, as the guests left, Peggy handed them their coats. Archie was last, talking about some ILP meeting with his sisters, while Miss Mavor waited at the door. He finished his discussion and took his coat from Peggy.

'Thank you for the song, Peggy,' he said. 'It was a lovely end to a lovely evening. Goodnight.' He put out his hand, and Peggy shook it, feeling something hard pressed into her fingers.

'Goodnight, girls,' he said to his sisters. 'Thank you for a memorable evening.' As she closed the storm doors, Peggy noticed that Miss Mavor took his arm.

'A perfect evening, Peggy,' Maggie said. 'You did a grand job.'

'Yes,' said Catherine, 'you did. Thank you very much. Put the coffee things in the kitchen, and you can do the dishes in the morning. Night-night.'

In the sitting-room, Peggy unclenched her hand. In it was a gold half-sovereign.

Good Lord, why has he given me so much money? It's a week's wages. What can Mr Archie be thinking of at all, at all?

Chapter 8:
Celtic Park.

As Pat, Michael, Eamonn and Conal came up out of St. Enoch subway station and turned into Argyle Street, they encountered hordes of football fans all heading east for the League Cup game between Celtic and Rangers at Parkhead. At fifteen years of age, Conal had never seen such dense crowds of people. Sure, he had been to the fairs at Ardara and Glenties several times with his Da, and they were crowded, but they simply did not compare with the mob of football fans. While looking around with fascination, he made sure he stayed close to his sturdy big brother, Eamonn.

Just as they approached Glasgow Cross, they saw a statue of a man in Roman costume on a horse in the middle of the road. A jam-packed tram clanged past with Celtic fans hanging from the platform, an empty beer bottle whizzed through the air, smashed against the head of the statue, and an exultant yell went up from the crowd. Pat turned to Michael in surprise.

'Yer man's King Billy,' Michael said. 'The statue's of King Billy.' Pat and his sons burst out laughing.

Going along London Road towards Parkhead, the crowds grew even thicker and all the trams were packed as tight as cattle on the Derry boat. Each of the many pubs along the way had a huddle of men at the door, drinking pints and smoking. A troop of mounted Police trotted past. Nearing Parkhead, Pat, Eamonn and Conal were astonished; they had never seen so many people in the one place in their lives. Conal clung onto Eamonn's arm as they approached the entrance. The crowd heaved and shoved its way towards the turnstiles, and Conal was being swept away until Eamonn grabbed him and pulled him back.

Conal gasped as he felt himself being pushed to one side. A mounted policeman towered above him, backing his horse into the mob to form a rudimentary queue. When they reached the turnstile, they paid their sixpence entry and climbed the steps to the terracing to be greeted with an ear-splitting din. A sea of emerald-green contained thousands upon thousands of men and boys in cloth caps standing waiting for the kick-off, many of them with bottles of beer in their hands. Clouds of blue tobacco smoke hung in the windless air and sparks flared continuously through the smoke as men struck matches to light their pipes and cigarettes.

'It holds well over fifty thousand,' Michael told the gobsmacked boy. 'And Michael Davitt himself laid the first sod of turf, from County Donegal, in 1892.'

'Michael Davitt!' Eamonn exclaimed.

Michael led the way, fighting his way down the terracing to the very front. 'It's the only place where the wee fellah will get a sight of the game,' he said.

Suddenly, a mighty roar shook the stadium. The Celtic players in their green and white hoops ran out onto the park, and the supporters burst into song spontaneously.

God save Ireland, said the heroes
God save Ireland, said they all
Whether on the scaffold high
Or the battlefield we die
Oh, what matter when for Erin dear we fall.

'Here you are, Son,' Pat said, handing a programme to Conal. The boy read it quickly. The team was: Mulrooney; McNair and Dodds; Young, Loney and Johnstone; McAtee, McMenemy, Quinn, Travers, and Brown. There was another loud roar as the Rangers players ran out onto the park in their blue strips.

Rangers won the toss, the referee blew his whistle, and the

Light Blues immediately attacked down the left wing. The game raged backwards and forwards, then suddenly Reid of Rangers dummied the Celtic back McNair, cut inside, shot, and hit the crossbar. There was a collective gasp from the Celtic fans, and sustained applause from the Rangers fans.

But thirty minutes into the first half, there was a roar from the Celtic fans as Loney broke away, slid the ball into the path of Quinn, who struck it right into the back of the Rangers net. Pandemonium broke out on the Celtic terracing as the fans danced up and down; there was a deafening silence from the Rangers fans. Conal was swept off his feet and the breath crushed out of him as the crowd swayed and surged, but again, Eamonn grabbed him in the nick of time.

Celtic were still one goal ahead when the half-time whistle blew. The Celtic fans celebrated by singing *The Wearing of the Green*.

Not long into the second half, Quinn fired another shot directly at goal which hit the crossbar and dropped into the hands of Lock, the Rangers goalie. But shortly afterwards, Quinn scored a second goal with a spectacular volley which left Lock with no chance. Rangers did their best, but Celtic were all over them, and ten minutes later, Quinn scored a third goal to complete his hat-trick. The referee blew the final whistle and the Celtic fans gave a triumphant roar: Celtic – 3; Rangers – 0!

'A grand win for the Bhoys, sure,' Michael said.

'And James Quinn is yer only man,' Pat said.

Struggling towards the exit through the throng of excited fans, Conal felt his shoes dampen. He looked down and saw a torrent of yellow piss cascading down the terracing, which was littered with empty beer and stout bottles and cigarette packets. Jaysus, that's a bloody liberty, he thought, so it is.

As they made their way back down London Road towards Glasgow Cross, Pat was all for stopping for a pint, but Michael was dead against it.

'Sure, we're better amongst our own people in the Irish Club,' he said. 'You never know who's who in these uptown pubs. And you know what they call the Rangers?'

'No,' Pat said.

'The Huns. They're all black Prodesans. They hate us.'

'Jaysus,' Pat said. 'There's an awful lot of hatred in Glasgow, so.'

Peggy could sense the triumphant atmosphere in the Irish Club that evening, as the famous victory was replayed again and again and dissected in forensic detail. Then the band formed up with Pat on the fiddle, and the session began. They played a rake of tunes, many with a Donegal slant: *The Swallow's Tail* and *The Sligo Maid*; *The Policeman's Holiday* and *Drowsy Maggy; Farewell to Erin and The Foxhunter's; O'Rourke's and The Wild Irishman; The Boy in the Gap* and *Toss the Feathers*; and *The Gold Ring*.

There was a cry for a song, and Peggy was pushed forward. Pat led the cry of '*Ciúnas! Ciúnas!*' and the din died down. Peggy said, 'I'll sing *Slieve Gallion Braes*, so,' and there was a murmur of appreciation. She composed herself, shut her eyes and launched into the song.

As I went a-walking one morning in May
To view your fair valleys and your mountains so gay
I was thinking of your flowers all going to decay
That grow around ye bonny, bonny Slieve Gallon Braes.

Oft times have I wandered with my dog and my gun
And travelled your valleys for joy and for fun
But those days are gone forever and I can no longer stay
So farewell unto ye bonny, bonny Slieve Gallon Braes.

Oft times in the evenings and the sun in the west
I roamed hand in hand with the one I love best
But the dreams of youth have vanished and I am far away

So farewell unto ye bonny, bonny Slieve Gallon Braes.

Peggy paused, took a deep breath, and put her heart into the key verse.

It was not the want of employment at home
That caused the poor sons of old Ireland to roam
But those tyrannising landlords
They would not let us stay
So farewell unto ye bonny, bonny Slieve Gallon Braes
But the rents are getting higher and I can no longer pay
So farewell unto ye bonny, bonny Slieve Gallon Braes.

There was silence for a second when the girl finished, then a storm of applause; there were many people in that room who knew all about tyrannising landlords and higher rents.

Nevertheless, the evening ended on a lighter note, for when 'Last Orders' were shouted, the well-oiled Pat brought the house down when he yelled, 'James Quinn for Pope!'

Chapter 9:
Glasgow Green.

Peggy hurried down the stairs. She was wearing a white silk blouse with a high collar and long sleeves, an ankle-length navy-blue gored skirt, a jacket with pleats at the back and faux lace cuffs, and flat shoes. She was hatless, but her shoulder-length hair was tied back with a red ribbon. Roísín, Mary and Cissie, looking equally smart, were waiting for her outside the close on a warm, sunny, spring Sunday.

'The Number 26 tram will take us all the way to Glasgow Green,' Roísín said.

'Tell me again, what's the craic on the Green?' Peggy said.

'Sure, there's a bit of everything,' Cissie said, 'shows, all the fun of the fair, bands playing music, fellas spouting politics, others spouting religion, and ...'

'– and lots of fellas!' Mary said.

The girls laughed as they made their way to Govan Cross.

Peggy stared around her as they made their way onto Glasgow Green past Monteith Row. Throngs of people, all dressed in their Sunday best, strolled along the paths to the People's Palace, while speakers in booths and on soap-boxes filled the Green. The girls paused at a booth with the legend: LOYAL ORANGE INSTITUTION OF SCOTLAND.

A man in a black bowler hat and an Orange sash held up a piece of wood before an audience of several dozen men and women.

'Do you know whit the Papists say this is?' he bawled.

'They say this is a piece of the wid of the true cross on which Christ wis crucified. Do you know whit ah say? Ah say there are mair than enough bits of the true cross in Europe to build an ocean-going liner!'

As the crowd roared its approval, the girls hurried away, Cissie muttering, 'Bitter oranges, bitter oranges.' Peggy didn't say anything, but she thought what the Orangeman was saying was actually quite funny. Her eye was then caught by a large poster reading:

WOMEN'S FREEDOM LEAGUE:

SCOTTISH CAMPAIGN:

VOTES FOR WOMEN.

A tall, elegant woman wearing a large hat and a purple, green and white pendant was speaking.

'Ladies and gentlemen,' she said, 'and particularly ladies. My name is Anna Munro and I am a suffragette.' She lifted the pendant. 'And these are our colours. That means that I campaign for equal voting rights for women. We say no taxation without representation, as our American cousins did in their War of Independence, and that is why we boycotted last year's Census. It's an utter scandal that we're now twelve years into the twentieth century, and women are still treated as second-class citizens.'

'Quite right too,' a man yelled.

'With brains like yours, who needs men?' Anna Munro retorted. Peggy laughed out loud, but Cissie pulled her away. 'Sufferagettes? Suffering Jaysus more likely,' she muttered.

The next stall bore the legend: ANCIENT ORDER OF RECHABITES.

'What on earth's a Rechabite?' Peggy said.

'Sure, they're them eejits that give up the gargle,' Cissie said.

'Just like the Pioneers in Ireland,' Roísín added.

'The No-Fun Brigade,' Mary said.

A bell clanged, and a cyclist shot past the girls and turned into the next stall which displayed a banner: CLARION CYCLING CLUB & SCOUTS. Posters showed cheerful young people camping, rambling, and cycling in the Scottish countryside. That looks interesting, thought Peggy, and picked up a couple of pamphlets. She wouldn't mind a bicycle herself.

As they strolled along through the throng, Peggy saw hawkers selling broadsheet ballads, buskers playing the fiddle, gamblers doing card-tricks, jugglers keeping Indian Clubs in the air, and men on stilts. A slight breeze carried a blast of music and, in the distance, Peggy saw an Army band playing in the bandstand, with crowds of people sitting or lying on the grass listening. Suddenly, she did a double-take. She saw Archie MacDonald mounting a platform bearing the legend INDEPENDENT LABOUR PARTY, where a stout man wearing round glasses stood waiting.

'Come on,' she said to the girls. 'I want to hear this.'

'Aw Jaysus, Peggy,' Cissie said, 'not bleeding politics.'

'I know him,' Peggy said, 'I know him, he's the brother of me gaffers.'

Behind her, Peggy heard a man with an Irish accent, ask, 'Who's the stout fellah?'

'Councillor John Wheatley of the ILP. He's a Waterford man.'

Wheatley stepped forward and introduced Archie MacDonald as the prospective ILP parliamentary candidate in South Side Ward. Archie lambasted the Tories both at local and national level for perpetuating the shocking working and living conditions of the Glasgow working-class.

'According to last year's Census,' he said, 'thirteen-point-eight per cent of the population of Glasgow live in single-ends. And forty-eight per cent live in rooms-and-kitchens. Add them together and what do you get?'

A murmur ran through the crowd. Peggy shut her eyes

and did some rapid mental arithmetic. 'Sixty-two-point-one per cent,' she shouted.

'Correct. Go to the top of the class, comrade,' Archie said. 'Sixty-two-point-one per cent. That means that nearly two-thirds of the population of this city live in houses of not more than two rooms. Now. Have they got inside toilets?'

'No!' roared the crowd.

'Not bloody likely,' Roísín shouted.

'That's exactly right, comrade,' Archie said. 'Not bloody likely. The ruling class in Glasgow, the fat cats who own the shipyards and the engineering works, don't give a tuppenny damn about how their workers live. Do you know what I call the housing situation in Glasgow? Death by tenement.'

The crowd roared its approval again as Peggy watched, entranced.

'Well, you're the lucky girl,' Cissie said. 'Yer man's dead good-looking.' The girls watched as Archie held the crowd spellbound.

'The only way we can achieve equality in this country and improve the material conditions of existence of the working-class,' Archie concluded, 'is by the common ownership of the means of production, distribution and exchange. That's the programme of the Independent Labour Party. And that, comrades, is why we ask all workers, by hand or by brain, to join the ILP. Thank you all very much for listening.'

A wave of applause swept through the crowd, joined by Peggy and the girls. He's the great talker, Peggy thought, but she wished she knew what he was talking about. What the bejaysus is the "material conditions of existence" and the "means of production?"

Several young men and women came through the crowd handing out pamphlets. Peggy took one with the title, 'The Irish Home Rule Question' thinking she knew what that's about, but just as she was about to open it, a voice said, 'Peggy, I thought it was you I spotted from the platform.

How are you? It's good to see you here.' It was Archie.

Peggy felt herself blushing as she said, 'Good morning, Mister MacDonald.'

'Mister MacDonald nothing,' Archie said. 'My name's Archie. And who's this charming collection of colleens?'

'These are my neighbours – Roísín Herron, Mary McGovern and Cissie Ward,' Peggy said, introducing each of the girls in turn. Archie shook their hands.

'I'm very pleased to meet all of you,' Archie said. 'Let me treat you to a cup of coffee in the People's Palace. It's not every day I have the luck to meet such a collection of lovely Irish colleens.'

'We'll be off, so, Peggy,' Cissie said later with a knowing wink, putting down her empty coffee cup. 'See you back home.'

As the girls left, Peggy looked round the Winter Gardens, trying to think of something to say. The sun streamed down through the glass and it was warm in the café.

'They're a lively collection of girls,' Archie said.

'They are that,' Peggy said. 'They're great craic altogether.'

'So how are you enjoying working with my sisters?'

'Oh, it's grand,' Peggy said. 'They're lovely ladies, very kind. I enjoy working for them. They're so, so educated – and smart.'

Archie laughed. 'You're right there. They're as smart as they come. But you're smart too, Peggy.'

Peggy didn't know where to look. 'I don't think so, sir – Archie, I mean.'

'Maggie and Catherine have the advantage of an advanced education. But there's nothing wrong with your brain. Maggie said you were some kind of teacher in Donegal. Is that right?'

'I was a monitor. That is, I helped the teacher looking

after the very young ones. And, and if we hadn't come to Scotland, I might have gone on to Teacher Training College. But we came to Scotland.'

'Would you like to train to be a teacher?' Archie said.

'Oh, indeed I would,' Peggy said. 'But there's no chance of that.'

Archie looked thoughtful. 'We'll see about that.'

He stood up. 'Come on. Let's go for a walk while the sun is shining.'

As they strolled past the nearby Templeton Carpet Factory, Archie explained that it was modelled on the Doge's Palace in Venice.

'What's a Doge?' Peggy said.

'The city boss,' Archie said. 'Like the Lord Provost here in Glasgow.'

'I see,' Peggy said. 'So, the Independent Labour Party is all for socialism, is that it?'

'That's correct,' Archie said.

'And what is this socialism?' Peggy said.

'That's a good question,' Archie said. 'The key thing is the abolition of capitalism and the private ownership of property; only the working class can do that. The next thing is common ownership. All these rich capitalists who own the shipyards and the engineering works and the tenements in Glasgow would be abolished, and the working people would own them. Socialism will abolish profit and free the people.'

'Chance would be a fine thing,' Peggy laughed.

'Well, we've got to make it happen,' Archie said. 'The key idea in socialism is that everybody would be involved in deciding what was important to produce, and how they would be distributed. For example, we might decide to not produce any more weapons of war – guns and warships – but use our skills to build decent affordable housing for the workers. We'd only produce things that people really need. So, we socialists say, "from each according to his ability, to each according to his need."'

'I see,' Peggy said. 'But our parish priest says the right to own property is a God-given right, and socialism is greed and envy of that right.'

Archie snorted. 'Well, he would say that, wouldn't he? The Vatican is one of the richest institutions in the world while in Italy, the workers and peasants live in dire poverty. The Catholic Church doesn't want to give any of its property away to the poor, does it? It has forgotten what Christ said.'

'What did Christ say?' Peggy said.

'"It is easier for a camel to pass through the eye of a needle, than for a rich man to enter into the kingdom of God,"' Archie said. 'You see, Peggy, the ownership of property and riches confer power, and socialism is against that power, because the powerful use it against the powerless. The rich use it to keep the poor in their place.'

'Uh-huh,' Peggy said, by now hopelessly confused.

A smart woman wearing a large bonnet, a fur coat, and a long string of beads approached; she stopped.

'Hello, Archie,' she said, 'it's a lovely day.'

'Hello, Helen, it is that. This is Peggy O'Donnell who works for my sisters. Peggy, this is Mrs Helen Crawfurd,' Archie said.

The two women shook hands. 'You'll have to excuse me,' Helen said, 'but I'm speaking on the suffragette platform in five minutes. See you at the Ward meeting, Archie. Good to meet you, Peggy. Cheerio.' She hurried off. Peggy and Archie resumed their stroll.

'Mr MacDonald – sorry, Archie.' Peggy paused. 'I find it hard to call you Archie, you know.'

'Why is that?' Archie said.

'Well, lookit,' Peggy said. 'You're an educated gentleman and, and I'm just a simple girleen from The Rosses.'

'Och nonsense, girl,' Archie said. 'It's true I went to university. But that's formal education. But you're as sharp as a tack, you've got your wits about you.'

Peggy wasn't at all convinced, so to change the topic said, 'So Mrs Crawfurd's a sufferagette?'

'Yes, she is,' Archie said. 'Helen Crawfurd is one of Glasgow's leading suffragettes. They are very brave women, and many have gone to prison and go on hunger strike for their beliefs.'

Well, if it's not one thing, it's another, Peggy thought. Everybody seems to be rared up about something in Glasgow. But on the other hand, why shouldn't women have the right to vote? After all, they're much more sensible than men.

Chapter 10:
The Kinning Park Co-Operative Guild.

'Now Peggy,' Catherine said, 'I'm going to a meeting of the Kinning Park Co-operative Guild tonight. It's for women. You should come; I think you might be interested. Do you know what a Co-op is?'

'Sure and I do,' Peggy said. 'Paddy the Cope founded one in Cleendra near us in the Rosses. It was a grand idea. My mother and father were members, so they were. But the gombeen men and the priest were dead against it.'

'What on earth is a gombeen man?' Catherine said.

'He's a fella who might have a shop now, and lets the poor people have credit for their messages, but he charges a rake of interest which the people can never pay off. There's a poem about the 'Gombeen Man' by Joseph Campbell.'

'Do you know the words?' Catherine said.

Peggy closed her eyes, muttered to herself, and then declaimed,

'Behind a web of bottles, bales,
Tobacco, sugar, coffin nails,
The gombeen like a spider sits,
Surfeited; and, for all his wits,
As meagre as the tally-board,
On which his usuries are scored.'

'Ah,' Catherine said. 'A money lender.'

'Yes,' Peggy said, 'the very divil of a money lender.'

As Catherine ushered Peggy into the Co-op hall, she said, 'There's the very woman you should meet, Peggy – Mary

Barbour. She also lives in Govan.'

Peggy saw a woman in her thirties, medium-built, with a pleasant, open face and dark hair. When she saw Catherine, the woman's face lit up with a smile and she hurried over.

'Hello, Catherine,' she said, 'good to see you, I'm glad you could come tonight.'

'Hello, Mary,' Catherine said. 'I'd like you to meet a fellow Govanite, Peggy O'Donnell from County Donegal. Peggy looks after Maggie and me, very well it must be said. Peggy, this is Mrs Mary Barbour.'

Mary smiled at Peggy as she shook her hand. 'It's good to meet you, Peggy. There's a lot of Donegal people in Govan as I'm sure you know. From which part of the County do you come?'

'The Rosses,' Peggy said.

'Well then,' Mary said, 'how would you like to give the ladies a talk on The Rosses? I'm sure they would appreciate it.'

'Oh no, I couldn't do that,' Peggy said, flustered. 'I wouldn't know how to give a talk at all, at all. I've never done anything like that before.'

'I can help you,' Mary said. 'It's simpler than you think. Come on, let's have a cup of tea and I'll show you how to do it.'

Later, Mary slid a sheet of paper with headings on it over to Peggy. 'Here you are. It's easier than you think. You say what you are going to say – and use these headings: Geography, History, Culture, Language, and Economy. Then you say it following these headings, and finally you sum up by saying you've said what you said you were going to say. And then you ask: any questions? Do you think you can do it? It's important that our members know about the situation in Ireland with so many Irish people in Govan these days, and you've had hard times over there.'

'That's the very truth,' Peggy said.

'You said you were a monitor, Peggy?' The girl nodded. 'Well,' Mary continued, 'just think of the ladies as a class of pupils and give them a lesson. Keep it simple, that's the thing. We'll put three quarters of an hour aside next week for you. If you talk for about half an hour, we'll have questions for about fifteen minutes, and then we'll all have a nice cup of tea. Agreed?'

'I'll do my best,' Peggy said.

'Good girl!'

Peggy found it easier than she had anticipated, for she had prepared her talk carefully according to the headings Mrs Barbour has suggested, and after all, it was something she knew about from personal experience. The room was packed with Guild women who were obviously interested in her talk, and paid rapt attention as she described the barren, rocky landscape of the Rosses, punctuated by sea-lochs and lochans.

'The land is poor,' Peggy said, 'because being so near the sea, the air is full of salt. So, the most people can hope for is to grow some potatoes, while the luckier people have a milk cow, and can churn butter. The women can make a little money from knitting, but the pay is very poor so in general, there's not a lot of money about. Yet the landlords rack-rent the people and have no hesitation in evicting them for arrears of rent. The big problem in Donegal is that most of these landlords are absentees who live in London, and their big estates are managed by ruthless agents. And that's why there's a strong Home Rule movement in the county.'

Peggy continued by talking about the Gweedore riots of 1889 and how her own grandfather was jailed for participating. And she talked about the rich musical tradition of the area, the fiddle-playing and the sean-nós singing – and concluded by saying that these tunes and songs could be heard every weekend in the Govan Irish Club, if the ladies were interested.

There were many questions, and Mrs MacCaskill generated a storm of applause when she argued that the Land Wars in Ireland were about the same issues as the Highland Clearances, pointing out that her family had been driven off the land in the Isle of Skye in the same way that Peggy's family had been driven off the land in The Rosses. So many women came up to Peggy afterwards at tea and congratulated her on her talk that she blushed and didn't know where to look.

Mrs Barbour took her aside and said, 'That was a great talk, Peggy. I knew you could do it. All you've got to remember is that when you're leading a meeting, you must take charge. You must be prepared, and not let anyone put you off or interrupt you until you have finished. Well done, lass!'

But the highlight of her evening was when she travelled back to Partickhill in the subway with Catherine after the close of the meeting.

'You know, Peggy,' Catherine said, 'you've great natural intelligence. That was a very effective talk. You've got to do something with that brain of yours. I can't see you as a maid for the rest of your life. You can do better than that. I'm going to talk to Archie and see if he has any ideas.'

Peggy blushed for the second time that evening. But later, as she lay in her bed in the kitchen, the phrase: "great natural intelligence" revolved in her head. She recalled that Mr O'Neill also said she was a bright girl, so maybe she could do something with herself, she thought, as she turned and went to sleep.

Peggy hovered outside Miss Cranston's Willow Tearooms in Sauchiehall Street, where Archie had asked her to meet him. She glanced in, but he wasn't there. Intimidated by the posh, well-dressed women holding their bone-china teacups with extended pinkies, and prattling in Kelvinsayde accents, she retreated outside. A minute later, Archie hurried up.

'Sorry I'm late, Peggy,' he said, 'but I met a comrade and we had a quick discussion about tonight's meeting.'

They went inside and Peggy noticed he was greeted like a long-lost friend by the woman who seemed to be in charge. Her glance swept over Peggy but did not linger.

Another stuck-up gobshite, Peggy thought, as the woman ushered them to a table by a window.

'Now you said you were in this monitor scheme back in Donegal,' Archie said as he unfolded his table-napkin. 'Tell me how it worked.'

'Well,' Peggy said, 'most of the children leave school when they are twelve. But the master would select one or two of the older pupils to help him teach the infants, the First and Second Babies. And they would stay on the school for another four or five years.'

'How were they selected?'

'Oh, you had to be quite good at your lessons.'

'Quite bright?'

'Yes, I suppose so,' Peggy said, colouring.

'And what did you teach them?'

'Reading, writing and 'rithmetic. And hymns.'

'Hymns. Of course. And what did *you* learn?'

'That depended on the teacher,' Peggy said. 'But Mr O'Neill was a great man for the learning, a grand scholar, so I did Irish, English, drawing, history, geography, and a lady came in once a week to teach needlework. Sure, it was great craic altogether. I really enjoyed it.'

'Quite a curriculum, then?' Archie said.

'Curr ... "curriculum?"' Peggy stuttered.

Archie laughed. '"Curriculum." It means the list of subjects you studied. Did you get any form of certification for this curriculum? A leaving certificate, for example?'

'No,' Peggy said. 'There was nothing like that. But if you had been a monitor for four or five years, and you got a good reference from the master, you could be accepted for teacher training at Carysfort College in Dublin. I would have liked that. I wanted to do it.' Peggy waved her hands in the air. 'But … but we came here. To Scotland.'

Archie thought for a moment, cutting his cake into tiny pieces. 'So, in Ireland, four or five years' experience as a monitor is accepted as qualifying you for formal primary teacher-training?'

'Yes,' Peggy said, 'as long as you had a good reference from the master.'

'Did you get a reference from Mr O'Neill?'

'I did.'

'Do you still have it?'

'I do.'

'What did it say?'

Peggy blushed again. 'Oh, it said some nice things about me. He said I'd make a good teacher.'

'Would you let me see it?' Archie said.

'Of course,' Peggy said. 'Em. Em, can I ask why?'

Archie smiled. 'I've an idea, Peggy. I have the beginnings of an idea.'

Chapter 11:
Painting from Life.

Maggie looked at Peggy, and said, 'Are you comfortable?'

'I am,' Peggy said, adjusting her position in the chair and smoothing her skirt down over her knees.

'Now, could you look over your shoulder at me?'

Peggy half-turned and looked at Maggie.

'Can you hold that position? Tell me if you need a break.'

Peggy nodded as Maggie slipped on a smock and picked up a palette and several brushes. 'That's good. That's just right,' she said as she started painting.

As Maggie squeezed some oil paint out of a tube onto her palette, Peggy gazed at the painting behind her. It was an unfinished self-portrait of Maggie down to the waist, with no clothes on, her full naked breasts facing the viewer squarely. She wondered why there were so many paintings and drawings of women with no clothes on in this house. It's - it's dirty, and it's an occasion of sin, for the body is the temple of the Holy Ghost. And neither of the sisters is even married! Has Maggie no sense of shame, she thought, to be flaunting her titties so boldly? But Maggie was so polite and charming that Peggy could not believe she was shameless. Maggie caught the girl staring at the self-portrait, turned, and looked at it.

'Do you like it?' Maggie said.

Peggy blushed, embarrassed to be found out.

'Oh, it's grand,' she said. 'It's just like you. But, but ...'

'But what, Peggy?'

Peggy didn't know where to look. 'But, but you've no clothes on. It's very bold to paint yourself with no clothes on.'

Maggie laughed out loud. 'Bold? You *are* a funny girl. I don't think it's bold at all. I think it's natural. Women have breasts. You have breasts. Men like them. Men have been painting them for centuries. So why shouldn't I paint my own breasts?'

Peggy couldn't think of an answer.

'I don't think anyone has the right to tell us what we can and cannot paint,' Maggie said. 'The naked human body, of both men and women, has preoccupied artists from the beginning of time. It's perfectly natural. It's what we look like without clothes. Look.'

To Peggy's horror, Maggie took off her smock, then her blouse, then her slip, then her bra, and exposed her large full breasts. She cupped them in her hands and bounced them up and down, smiling as she did so. 'These are my tits, Peggy.' She ran her hands down over her hips. 'This is my body. No one else's.' She came up to the girl and traced her breasts through her blouse with a fingertip. 'And these are your breasts.'

Peggy blushed and shrunk back as Maggie said, 'They're beautiful, Peggy.' She patted Peggy's shoulder. 'And this your body. No one else's. You decide what you want to do with it. And don't let anyone tell you any different. Especially not a man.' Maggie grinned. 'And most especially not priests. Or ministers. Repressed bloody perverts, all of them. Now relax for a moment.'

Peggy swivelled in her chair and watched Maggie as she put her clothes back on, thinking she's told me I'm beautiful several times. But what does it mean? Nobody else has ever said that to me.

Maggie went up to the bookcase and took out a large book. 'Look,' she said to Peggy, thumbing through the pages. There were dozens of pictures of nude men and women.

'Look,' Maggie said, pointing to a photograph. 'The

Venus de Milo. The sculptor knew she was beautiful. And here – Renoir knew it too. She's lovely, isn't she?' Peggy nodded assent; she could see that she was.

'It's not bold to celebrate naked beauty. The ancient Greeks did it. The Romans did it. They did it in medieval times. And during the Renaissance. The Impressionists did it – look. And we're still doing it. And we will continue to do it in the future. Take this book and study the pictures. Now. Can you sit up straight again for me?'

Peggy did so, looking over her shoulder at Maggie as she started painting again. But her mind was in a whirl; so many pictures of nudes in one book. There was silence for a while as Maggie concentrated, her tongue between her teeth.

'You've lovely skin tone, Peggy,' said Maggie. 'You really are quite beautiful. Did you have a beau back in Donegal?'

Seeing the girl frown at the unfamiliar word, Maggie laughed. 'A man. An admirer. A suitor. A boyfriend.'

'Oh no, miss,' Peggy gasped.

'What about here? In Govan? In the Irish Club?'

Peggy shook her head; not a bit of it. Maggie continued painting, an enigmatic smile playing on her lips. 'Well, I suspect you might have an admirer in the West End.' Peggy didn't know what she was talking about; she didn't know any men in the West End, where they were all toffs anyway.

Later, back in the kitchen, Peggy slowly leafed through the book Maggie had given her. She stared at a picture. It was of a naked young man holding a sling over his shoulder and a rock in his other hand. So that's what his thing looks like, she thought, peering closely; it's not very big. She turned the pages and found a painting called *La Maja Desnuda.* She looks very bold, very bold indeed, just looking right at you without a stitch on, without a care in the world. Peggy leaned forward, and gasped. And you could … you could see her hair, down there. She leaned back and studied the painting. Hmm – but she looks very relaxed. I wonder how she can be so relaxed just lying there looking at a man staring at her naked body. And painting it. I wonder if he touches her, if he arranges the way – the doorbell clanged and interrupted her reverie.

Peggy ran to the door, still clutching the book. She opened it and there was Archie smiling on the doorstep.

'Hello, Peggy,' he said. 'May I come in?'

'Of course,' Peggy said. 'But Miss Catherine and Miss Maggie are out.'

'Never mind,' Archie said. 'I could murder a cup of tea. What's that you're reading?'

As Archie took the book from her hands, her finger still in the page of *La Maja Desnuda*, Peggy wished the ground would open up and swallow her.

'Ah, Goya,' Archie said, studying the print. '*La Maja Desnuda.* It's magnificent, isn't it? She's gorgeous; I always think she looks so proud, so natural. It's as if she is saying: this is me. Take it or leave it. Wouldn't you agree?'

Peggy nodded. Archie looked up, spotted her embarrassment, closed the book, and said, 'Let's put the kettle on, shall we?' Peggy agreed, happy to have something to do.

As she poured his tea in the kitchen, Archie said, 'To tell you the truth, Peggy, I actually came in to see you. John Wheatley is giving a talk at the Catholic Socialist Society on Saturday evening called 'Catholics and Socialism: The Present Position.' I thought you might be interested. You're a Catholic, and so is John. Do you think you'd like to go?'

'Oh yes,' Peggy said. 'I'd like to know what this socialism is all about.'

'Well,' Archie said, 'it's in the Pearce Institute at Govan Cross at half-past seven. I'll see you there.'

'Right, so,' Peggy said.

Peggy watched with interest as Wheatley began to speak. He was a portly man wearing a well-cut suit, and round spectacles. His voice wasn't very powerful, but there was something about the way he spoke which impressed her. He believes in what he's saying, he believes in it passionately.

'So, to say it yet again,' Wheatley said, 'the socialism I am advocating is not the revolutionary socialism of the likes of Rosa Luxembourg in Germany. It is a socialism which believes in the brotherhood of man, which remembers that the early church, the church of Jesus and the Apostles, was the church of the poor, people like simple fishermen who owned no property and had no power. Our socialism here on the Clyde advocates a living wage, and decent working and living conditions. That is the birth-right of every Catholic man, woman and child. We need to stop the murder of our children in rotten slums owned by grasping landlords, and that is not a revolutionary demand, but the reasonable political demand of any sane person who calls himself a Christian. To oppose this is to interfere with basic human rights. And we should all remember that the great Daniel O'Connell himself said that the Church should not dictate political decisions. That is the basic civil liberty of all adult men – and, may I say it? – women. Let me conclude by stating that the socialism of the Independent Labour Party is no barrier to the task of Holy Mother Church in looking after our spiritual welfare. What *we* are concerned with is our material welfare, both in the workplace, and at home. Thank you all very much.'

Peggy and Archie both joined in the enthusiastic applause which followed Wheatley's talk. 'What did you think?' Archie said.

'He's a man who talks a lot of sense,' Peggy replied.

'He talks extraordinarily good sense,' Archie said. 'He's a most capable man. He's standing as an ILP Councillor for the Corporation, you know.'

‘More power to his elbow,’ Peggy said. ‘If I had a vote, and if he stood in my Ward, he’d certainly get it. But, women can’t vote.’

‘Not yet they can’t,’ Archie said, ‘but we’ll see if we can’t change all that.’

Peggy glanced at him. I hope he means that, she thought. Wheatley talked about the brotherhood of man. But what about the sisterhood of women? Archie speaks with the same burning intensity as Wheatley. It was as if socialism was their religion. But there was one big difference between Archie MacDonald and John Wheatley; Archie was handsome.

Chapter 12:
Square Go!

Peggy came up out of the subway station at Govan Cross, went along Govan Road, and turned into Neptune Street. As she approached her close, she saw a stooshie on the pavement outside. People were milling about, there was an excited hubbub, a lot of pushing and shoving, and suddenly, they all rushed into the close. Peggy accelerated and bumped into Eamonn.

'What on earth's going on?' she said. 'What's the hullabaloo all about?'

'It's the Da,' Eamonn said. 'He's going to have a square go with Sammy McKee. He called Da a Fenian bastard, so the Da says, "Right, ye Orange hoor, out the back".'

'Oh my God,' Peggy said. Sammy McKee, a virulent Orangeman from north County Down and a stalwart of the Lorne Street Govan Orange Band, lived at the foot of Neptune Street. He was also a big man, noted for brawling and picking fights with Catholics, especially when he was drunk, which was every Saturday night.

'He'll kill the Da,' Peggy said, for Pat was much smaller than McKee.

'I wouldn't bet on that,' Eamonn said. 'I saw Da knocking seven bells out of a big man at the Glenties Fair once. Sure he's not big, but he's fast.'

They hurried into the back court, where a large, excited crowd was already forming and a couple of freelance bookies were doing a roaring trade in bets, offering odds-on of one to three on Sammy, and ten to one against Pat. Pat gave his jacket to Michael, rolled up his sleeves, and undid the front stud of his collarless shirt. Michael gave him something which Pat slipped into his hip pocket. McKee took off his jacket and indulged in a quick display of shadow-boxing, roaring, 'Croppies lie down.' Pat grinned, and chanted, 'O, the French are in the bay, they'll be here without delay, And the Orange will decay, you gobshite.'

Ritual insults having been exchanged, the fight started. McKee rushed at Pat, who stepped aside smartly and planted a right hook into McKee's ribs. The Orangeman grunted and threw a haymaker which Pat ducked easily. Floating round, Pat slammed a couple of hooks into McKee's belly. The big man roared and lumbered after Pat, who skipped in a circle round him. But McKee closed in and belted the smaller man on the side of the head. Peggy winced as Pat shook his head and staggered back. McKee bored in, hit Pat a straight right in the face, and his nose began to trickle blood. The crowd roared. What a bunch of savages, Peggy thought, they want to see me da destroyed entirely. Pat back-pedalled, wiping his nose with his forearm as the bigger man came after him. McKee dummied with his left, hit Pat under the jaw with an uppercut which lifted him right off his feet and knocked him to the ground on his back. The crowd gasped as McKee swung his foot back and lashed out at Pat's groin with his hobnailed boot. Peggy's heart jumped into her mouth. But Pat caught the foot in both hands, twisted it, and heaved with all his strength. The big man staggered sideways and in an instant, Pat was on his feet, landing several punches on McKee's head as he straightened up.

The fight raged up and down the back court, with dozens of neighbours hanging out of their windows watching. The crowd of spectators grew bigger by the minute, yelling encouragement to one or other of the fighters. But both men were slowing down now, each with battered faces. One of Pat's eyes was puffed and closing, his nose was still leaking blood, while McKee had a bad cut in an eyebrow. But still they slugged it out. McKee caught Pat again on the jaw with a wild hook and it took all the wee man's strength to stay on his feet, while shaking his head. But he bored in again, hitting McKee in his large beer-belly with a flurry of punches. The big man staggered back, with a midden close behind him. But McKee suddenly rushed forward, lashing out with his foot at Pat's leg. But Pat dodged aside and as McKee stumbled, trying to regain his balance, hit him in the mouth with a powerful right cross. The big man fell backwards into the midden, his split lip spraying blood. There was a resounding clang as he stumbled into a waste bin, his head falling forwards. Pat palmed something out of his hip-pocket, stepped up smartly and hooked McKee in the jaw again. The big man toppled over amongst the metal bins and passed out. There was a roar from the crowd, Pat was hoisted onto the shoulders of his supporters, and carried in triumph round the back court. As the jubilant crowd reached McKee's close, they stopped and chanted *The Soldier's Song*:

Sinne Fianna Fáil,
Atá faoi gheall ag Eirinn,
Buíonn dár slua, thar toinn do ráinig chugainn,
Faoi mhóid bheith saor, seantír ár sinsear feasta
Ní fhágfar faoin tíorán ná faoin tráill;
Anocht a théam sa Bhearna Baoil
Le gean ar Ghaeil chun báis nó saoil,
Seo dhíbh canáigh, Amhrán na bhFiann.

Enraged by the Republican song, Mrs McKee launched several dinner plates at Pat from her first-floor window, but they missed by a country mile and smashed to smithereens at Peggy's feet. She glimpsed Conal beside her drawing his arm back. He fired a stone from a home-made catapult, and Mrs McKee shrieked as her window shattered. Conal winked at Peggy as he stuffed the catapult up his jersey.

Brighid nearly collapsed when she saw Pat's face. One eye was puffed and closed and already purple, while his nose was swollen and bloody, and the rest of face covered with weals and bruises. But Peggy quickly made a solution of Epsom Salt in a basin, Brighid soaked a clean tea-towel in it, and they gently mopped Pat's facial injuries. Peggy noticed a trickle of blood coming from her father's still clenched fist. She prised his fingers open to expose a shipyard rivet. Pat grinned as he said, 'A wee surprise for the Sammy fella,' putting his swollen hands in the basin. Eamonn rushed in and pushed a sheaf of banknotes into Brighid's hands. 'Ten pounds, Ma,' he said. 'I put my full wage-packet on the Da at ten to one, so I got eleven quid back – a tenner plus my pound wager.'

Later, the kitchen was full of Irish neighbours celebrating the famous victory. Bottles of Guinness and glasses of whiskey were passed around. But Pat brought the house down when he started to sing:

As down the glen one Easter morn
To a city fair rode I.
There armed lines of marching men
In squadrons passed me by.
No pipe did hum, no battle drum
Did sound its loud tattoo
But the Angelus bell o'er the Liffey's swell
Rang out in the foggy dew.

Right proudly high over Dublin town
They hung out that flag of war.
'Twas better to die beneath an Irish sky
Than at Suvla or Sud el Bar.
And from the plains of Royal Meath
Strong men came hurrying through;
While Britannia's sons with their long-range guns
Poured hell through the foggy dew.

Part 2.

Chapter 13:
Things Get Better – and Then Worse.

It was early summer 1913, a year since the O'Donnell family had come to Glasgow. Peggy felt that things were really looking up for the family. Pat had joined a squad of dockers who were all Irish Catholics, with a Catholic ganger. They secured the contract for unloading and loading the regular Derry boats at the Broomielaw, so her father was seldom out of work. Brighid continued to do the MacDonald sisters' laundry – along with that of a couple of their Partickhill neighbour – with Morag MacCaskill in the steamie. Peggy, now eighteen, still worked as a maid for them and she loved her job. Catherine and Maggie taught her fancy cooking and encouraged her to read by lending her books. In fact, they treated her more like a young sister than a maid. Peggy was also becoming more and more interested in the Cooperative Women's' Guild and the ILP, and attended as many meetings as she could, although she kept this from her father. Pat was a good man, but he couldn't see past the nationalism of the United Irish League, and attended their meetings in Govan.

Eamonn had landed on his feet, for he used his father's connection with the Derry boats to secure work in his job as a carter taking Irish immigrants and their luggage all-round the city, and delivering Irish produce to Lipton's stores. He and Donny and a couple of friends had formed a band called *Ceoltori Clyde*, they played for ceilidhs and dances, and this made them some extra money. Conal had moved up from being a copy boy at the *Catholic Observer* to a cub reporter at the *Forward* and was improving his chances by attending night-classes in Pitman's Shorthand and English Composition at the Athenaeum. Tim, a bookish boy, was still at St. Anthony's School, where the teachers were urging him to try for his Intermediate Certificate, an opportunity which Brighid encouraged, for she could see that education was the key to success in the big city. Tim also seemed interested in the priesthood and discussed this with Father Gallagher from time to time.

One Saturday evening, they were all sitting down to their tea before going out for the night. 'Where's the Ma?' Peggy said.

'She's at the Factor's paying the rent,' Eamonn said. 'She said she had something she wanted to discuss with him.'

'Discuss with that fat gobshite?' Pat said. 'Sure, he hasn't enough brains to hold a discussion.' The family laughed, for Brawn, the well-overweight Factor, was universally loathed in Govan as a bully for his rapacity and readiness to prosecute tenants in arrears of rent. The front door opened and Brighid swept into the room, barely able to contain her excitement.

'What's up, Ma?' Peggy said.

Brighid took off her hat, sat down, and poured herself a cup of tea, so beside herself that the tea splashed into the saucer. 'Lookit,' she said. 'The Storeys down the road are moving to the East End as Seán has got a new job at the Parkhead Forge. Now their house is two-rooms and a kitchen. With an inside toilet. It's time Peggy had a room of her own, for she's a growing girl. So, I spoke with the Brawn fellah.'

There was a brief silence in the kitchen. Two-rooms-and-a-kitchen? Peggy thought. With an inside toilet? Unimaginable luxury.

'And?' Peggy said.

'And he said we could have it when the Storeys move out

'No wonder the Labour leaders Jim Larkin and James Connolly want to do something about it,' Archie said. 'That's an intolerable situation in a capital city in the twentieth century.'

'Connolly and Larkin are nothing but damn Communists,' Pat said. 'Trying to ship out Catholic children to England to be looked after by Prodesans and lose their faith.'

'It says the children of the Dublin strikers are starving, Da,' Peggy said. 'They're earning no money at all. How can they feed their own weans? The English trade-unionists are only offering to help.'

'Don't talk nonsense, girl,' Pat said. 'The Church won't let these children starve. Sure, there's the Saint Vincent de Paul Society which collects money for the poor.'

'But there's hundreds of them, Da,' Peggy said. 'The Saint Vincent de Paul can't feed them all.'

'They can try,' her father said. 'And Rome can help.'

Rome? Chance would be a fine thing.

'No, the problem is them fecking socialists and communists wanting to form trade-unions,' Pat said. 'What for? Sure, William Murphy who owns the Dublin United Tramways Company is one of us – a Catholic and a good Home Ruler. He looks after his workers.'

'He makes them work long hours for poor pay – fourteen-hour days, and fires anyone who joins the Irish Transport and General Workers Union, that's what he does,' Peggy said. 'And the Church backs him up.'

'Not a bit of it,' Pat said. 'That's all socialist lies, that's what it is.'

'I'll put the kettle on for a cup of tea, so,' Brighid said, frowning. 'Enough of this political argy-bargy.' The problem is there's not enough of this political argy-bargy in this house, Peggy thought to herself. The Da tells everyone what to think, and that's that.

A few days later, Peggy, Pat, Eamonn and Conal sat round the kitchen table discussing the Home Rule controversy. Peggy listened intently as her father gave out again. 'Sure, Home Rule's in the bag now,' Pat said. 'The Gladstone fella has promised it and it's going through the British parliament.'

'That's right,' Eamonn said, 'and then we'll have our own parliament in Dublin.'

'But England will still be in charge,' Conal said. 'We'll still be a part of Great Britain. What use is that? We need an independent Ireland.'

'That's all my eye and sour porter,' Pat said. 'That's never going to happen. Home Rule will be good for Ireland. We can control the landlords and the rents and stop evictions.'

'And pass our own laws to suit Irish circumstances,' Eamonn said.

'But England will still control defence and foreign affairs,' Conal said. 'That means Ireland will still be under British control.'

'But we'll still be sending MPs to the British parliament as well as having our own,' Pat said, 'and sure, they'll speak up for us.'

This is hellish complicated, Peggy thought, but young Conal's got a point. What happens if Britain decides on a foreign policy which is against Irish interests?

'Are they going to speak up against absentee British landlords?' Conal said. 'In fact, I bet these Irish MPs at Westminster will be these same absentee jackeens looking after their own interests.'

'Don't act the maggot, young man,' Pat said. 'Talk is cheap. Sure, it's the Irish who would elect them Irish MPs. They're not going to elect MPS who would exploit them.'

'But …' Conal said.

'But me no buts,' Pat said. 'Shut your gob.'

Conal stood up and stormed out of the room, muttering. Eamonn winked at Peggy.

Hmm, she thought, the Da's laying down the law as usual, but Conal's definitely got a point. Home Rule sounds like a clever way for Britain to keep ultimate control of Ireland.

'What do you think, Peggy?' Eamonn said.

'Why ask her? She's a girl,' Pat said. 'What do girls know about politics?'

'I think if you want to be free, you have to be totally free. Being half-free is meaningless,' Peggy said.

'You see, Da,' Eamonn said. 'She has a point. She may be a girl, but she's a clever girl.'

Pat harrumphed.

Chapter 14:
Riot!

As she poured Peggy a cup of coffee in the kitchen, Catherine said, 'What we suffragettes believe in are equal rights for men and women. For example, women can vote in the municipal elections, for the Corporation of Glasgow, but they can't vote in parliamentary elections. What kind of nonsense is that in the twentieth century? That's why we decided to boycott the 1911 Census. If women aren't equal citizens, why should we agree to be counted?'

'I can see that,' Peggy said. 'But I've read in the newspapers about suffragettes attacking pillar-boxes with acid. That seems very bold.'

'Look, Peggy,' Catherine said. 'Many women believe in campaigning for equal rights with men, but don't believe in militant tactics. These women are called suffragists. They believe they'll eventually achieve equal rights by constitutional methods. We socialist women in the ILP do not believe women will ever be granted equal rights simply by asking for them. We believe we have to take direct action to *force* men to give us those equal rights. The more the press prints stories about this direct action, the more questions will be asked about what we actually want, and this in turn generates public debate about our demands.'

'I see,' Peggy said.

'And another thing,' Catherine said. 'We also demand equal rights over our own bodies. Within marriages in this country, the husband owns his wife's body. She has no control over the number of children they have, and no say in limiting family size.'

That's true enough, Peggy thought. There were numerous very large families in the Irish Channel. One woman in the next close had fourteen children.

'And in Glasgow,' Catherine continued, 'the amount of wife-battering that goes on is quite outrageous. And the Police and the Courts won't do anything about. It's a "domestic" they say, and we shouldn't interfere between a man and his wife. Fiddlesticks! Men who beat up their wives should be locked up. Simple as that.' Catherine snorted with anger.

That's the truth, Peggy thought. There wasn't a woman in Govan who didn't know a neighbour woman who wasn't routinely beaten, like Gráinne Walsh – especially when the pubs closed on a Saturday night, or after a football match, especially if the home side had been beaten.

'Anyway,' Catherine continued. 'Next month, Mrs Emmeline Pankhurst is going to address a suffragette meeting in the St. Andrew's Halls. And Helen Crawfurd will also be speaking. Maggie and I are going. Would you like to come with us?'

'Yes,' said Peggy, 'I would.' It's about time I learned what this sufferagette thing is all about, Peggy thought.

It was a sunny, if chilly, March day as Peggy, Maggie and Catherine walked towards the St. Andrew's Halls. Dozens of smartly dressed women were headed in the same direction.

'It looks like the whole of the West End has turned out,' Catherine said.

'Well, there are flyers everywhere, and the streets were chalked with the details last night,' Maggie said. 'I didn't get home till after eleven. I'm sure we'll get a big turnout.'

'But won't the police be there to arrest Mrs Pankhurst?' Peggy said.

'Oh, they'll be there,' Maggie said, 'dozens of them. But there's a plan to smuggle her in, and we will protect her.'

'How on earth will you do that?' Peggy said.

Maggie grinned as she unbuttoned her coat. 'Psst!' she said. As she flicked her coat open, Peggy glimpsed a wooden club with a spherical head hanging from a loop over her shoulder, before Maggie closed her coat and buttoned it up again.

'It's an Indian Club,' Maggie said. 'Helen Crawfurd and I are in charge of the platform party, and we've taken precautions.'

Catherine smiled at Peggy. 'Maggie's not just a pretty face, you know.'

Bejaysus, that's as true as God, Peggy thought. But the nearer they got to the Halls, the more policemen were to be seen on the streets, scrutinising the faces of the approaching women. At the doors to the Hall, male stewards wearing the suffragette badge in their lapels examined Peggy's and Catherine's tickets carefully before permitting entrance. Maggie had gone round to the Kent Road entrance.

Peggy looked round, fascinated; she and Catherine were sitting near the front. The hall was packed with women, hundreds of them, chatting in an expectant manner. The front of the platform was decorated with material displaying the suffragette colours of purple, white and green, and pots of palms, ferns and flowers; the whole hall had a carnival atmosphere. There was only one senior police officer to be seen, standing at the back of the hall. The platform party of about a dozen women marched onto the stage to tumultuous applause. Peggy recognised Maggie, Helen Crawfurd and Janie Allan. As Lady Isabel Margessen, the Chair, stepped forward to address the meeting, Peggy saw a woman in a long fur coat and a big hat slip onto the platform and sit down. Catherine nudged her. 'Mrs Pankhurst,' she whispered.

As Lady Isabel introduced Mrs Pankhurst, there was a sudden yell from one of the male stewards at the back of the hall: 'Look out!' Peggy turned and saw dozens of policemen with batons drawn rush forwards towards the platform. More poured in from a side door. Oh my God, Peggy thought, they're going to batter the women. But the women on the platform jumped to their feet as the policemen tried to storm it and attacked them with Indian clubs. Peggy saw the policemen rip the suffragette colours apart to reveal several strands of barbed wire, which they tore down. As several policemen made it onto the platform, lashing out indiscriminately with their batons, Peggy saw Helen Crawfurd launch a flowerpot at one which knocked him flying. The platform was a seething mass of fighting policemen and women. Peggy saw several of the latter knocked to the ground, while the women in the audience screamed and yelled, 'Shame!'

Suddenly, a couple of shots rang out, but they didn't stop the fighting, and Peggy saw Maggie on the platform ram a chair at a big policeman who hit her a glancing blow on the head with a baton. She collapsed to the floor. Peggy screamed and tried to rush forward but was trapped in the mass of shouting and gesticulating women. She saw a policeman grab Mrs Pankhurst and drag her bodily off the platform. In front of her, another policeman with baton drawn pushed Catherine aside so violently that she staggered and fell to the ground. To Peggy's horror, the policeman raised his baton to strike her. Paralysed for a second, Peggy suddenly pushed the policeman in the back as hard as she could; he tripped over Catherine and went sprawling on the floor, his baton sliding away. Peggy pulled Catherine to her feet and towed her to the side entrance which was now wide open, with women streaming out.

They found Maggie outside on Kent Road, dazed and hatless, with an egg-shaped lump on her forehead but otherwise all right. 'They've taken Mrs Pankhurst to the Central Police Station,' she gasped. 'Tell the women to gather there as soon as possible.'

Hundreds of angry women made their way to St. Andrew's Square, but the main gate of the police station was guarded by dozens of policemen with a troop of mounted police in reserve. Peggy looked round; there was a huge crowd of women, which surged backwards and forwards. As the church bell rang ten o'clock, the mounted police moved slowly into the crowd, dispersing them.

'It's all over bar the shouting,' Catherine said. 'And Maggie has a splitting headache. Time to go home.'

That night, it took Peggy a long time to drift off into sleep. She could still hear the din in the Hall and see images of struggling men and women in her mind's eye. The Peelers are just like the Royal Irish Constabulary at home – gobshites. Attacking a bunch of women deliberately, the cowardly bastards. Still, she thought, smiling to herself, I saved Catherine from being cracked on the head. Me, pushing a policeman? I wonder what the Da would say to that. There's no going back now. The only way is forward. That's why the ILP newspaper is called *Forward.*

Chapter 15:
1914 – War on Two Fronts.

'Mornin, Missus Hannavy,' Peggy said, as she passed her neighbour locking her door.

'Morning, Peggy,' Missus Hannavy said. 'Is that you off up the West End again?'

'That's where me work is,' Peggy replied.

Missus Hannavy managed a sniff and a frown, as if to imply the West End was a den of iniquity. Sure, she's a pathetic old shawleen, Peggy thought, up at the crack of dawn every day and off to the first mass. She's never out of the chapel and sucks up to the priests. In a way, Peggy felt sorry for the older woman. Her husband had been killed with the Dublin Fusiliers in the Boer War and, childless, she survived on a pittance of a pension. But she had turned into a dried-up, bitter ould widow and busybody, suspicious and critical of anybody and everybody in the close and the street. Faith, hope and charity, all three, Peggy thought, but the greatest of these is charity. But Missus Hannavy wouldn't know what charity was if it came in and slapped her on the face with a cold mackerel.

Peggy bought a *Glasgow Herald* at Govan subway station and scanned it as she waited for the train. There was nothing but frightening talk of war with Germany. God forbid, thought Peggy, for Eamonn and Donnie had been discussing joining up if war was declared. She had already had a furious row with Eamonn about it.

Up in Partickhill Road, Peggy laid out the breakfast and the newspaper on the kitchen table for the sisters.

'There's going to be war,' Catherine said to Maggie. 'The

Herald's full of it.'

'Men,' Maggie said. 'I despair of men. The working-class of Britain, France and Germany rushing to slaughter each other for the profit of the capitalist class. It's sickening.'

'We women must oppose it from a principled pacifist stance,' Catherine said. 'We must hold out for peace.'

'I agree,' Maggie said. 'We will. But it's time for school right now. We'll see you this evening, Peggy.'

Peggy looked at Eamonn in his Highland Light Infantry uniform, come to say goodbye to the family on his embarkation-leave. He looked smart, no doubt about that, and stronger, more self-confident, Peggy thought. But Brighid couldn't contain her tears, while Pat couldn't hide his confusion. What was a young Irishman doing fighting for the Sassenach?

'Look, Da,' Eamonn said. 'There are lots of our people in the British Army. Half the lads in the parish have joined up already. And there's thousands from the Ould Sod in the Dublin Fusiliers, the Munster Fusiliers and the Connaught Rangers. Sure, half the British Army is Irish. And Redmond himself has said that it's our duty to join up and fight, to convince the English that we're loyal to the Empire – even if we want Home Rule. And look at what the Germans are doing to Catholic nuns in Belgium. We can't have that. It's as simple as that.'

Would to God that were true, Peggy thought. It's not simple at all. There were some Irish people – like the Sinn Feiners – who argued that England's problem was Ireland's opportunity. But her parents were so upset at Eamonn's imminent departure that she decided to say nothing. And she herself was confused by her employers' argument that women should oppose the war utterly. How could she oppose the war if her own brother was a soldier? There was a knock at the door. Peggy opened it to find Donnie MacCaskill, also in uniform, on the doorstep.

'Time to go,' Donnie said. 'We've got to get up to the barracks in Maryhill Road.' Seeing Brighid in tears, Donnie patted her on the shoulder.

'Don't you worry, Missus O'Donnell. We'll have the Boche on the run in jig-time, and we'll be home for Christmas.'

As the two pals shouldered their kitbags and strode up Neptune Street towards Govan Cross, Brighid and Peggy burst into tears.

Several weeks later, Peggy read the newspaper on the tram as she headed for an anti-war meeting. The paper was full of news about a major German offensive which was driving British and French troops back towards Mons. I don't think the bhoys will be home for Christmas at this rate, Peggy thought, as the tram halted at Glasgow Green.

Peggy arrived at the meeting just in time to hear a soldier yell, 'Fuck off back to Ireland, you Fenian scum,' a couple of his mates shouting support. But on the ILP platform, John Wheatley carried on speaking, supported by Archie and Helen Crawfurd.

'We've no quarrel with the German working-class,' Wheatley said. 'Our quarrel is with the capitalist class of both Britain and Germany who wage war for their profits with the blood of British and German workers. We say the war should be halted and a peace negotiated between the two countries before there's any more bloodshed.'

Peggy could see that the majority of the audience on Glasgow Green was hostile to Wheatley, as they whistled, booed and shouted abuse. A couple of policemen began to try and calm the soldiers down, while a Sergeant mounted the platform and remonstrated with Wheatley. He was obviously asking Wheatley to call the meeting off, but was being refused. A hand grasped Peggy's elbow. She whirled round to see Archie's anxious face.

'Leave at once, Peggy, and go home. It's getting ugly here and there may well be trouble. Go home, please. At once.'

'No,' Peggy said. 'I'm staying. You need all the support you can get.'

Just then, a kilted soldier confronted Archie.

'You're wan o' they Conchies. You were on the platform wi' that Wheatley bastard, weren't you?' Without warning, the soldier punched Archie in the face, and he went reeling backwards. Peggy gasped with horror, then swung her handbag with full force at the soldier's head. He ducked and aimed a punch at her, but his hand was seized by Archie who threw the soldier over his hip to the ground. A wholesale melee erupted, and within minutes, Peggy found herself being frog-marched to the police-station along with Archie and several of the demonstrators.

'Full name?' the desk Sergeant said.

'Mairead O'Donnell,' Peggy said.

'Maw-rade?' the Sergeant said. 'What kind of a name is that?'

'It's Irish,' Peggy said. 'Irish Gaelic.'

'I should have known,' the Sergeant said. 'How do you spell it?'

'M–a–i–r–e–a-d,' Peggy said. 'But I'm known as Peggy.'

As the Sergeant wrote her up, Archie appeared, his collar and tie awry, holding a handkerchief to a cut on his cheek leaking blood.

'What's the charge, Sergeant?' Archie said.

'Same as yours, Mister MacDonald: Breach of the Peace.'

As the Sergeant wrote down Peggy's address, he cautioned her to appear at the Magistrate's court at ten o'clock the next morning and dismissed her. Outside, Peggy examined the cut on Archie's face. 'That's a bad cut,' she said, as she dabbed at the wound with Archie's blood-stained handkerchief.

'He was wearing a signet ring,' Archie said. 'It's nothing a sticking-plaster won't cure.'

As they walked towards the tram-stop, Peggy vented her anger. 'It's not fair, us being charged. It was the soldiers who attacked us.'

'I know,' Archie said, taking Peggy's arm. 'I saw you try to clout that soldier with your handbag. The fighting Irish right enough. But the anti-war movement is in a tiny minority. The Government has successfully stirred up a jingoistic sentiment right across the country.'

'What does 'jingoistic' mean?'

'It means a war fever,' Archie said. 'The Germans are all evil and the British are all angels. Anybody who challenges that can be called a traitor – traitors to want such a thing, especially when there's a war on.'

'I see,' Peggy said as they boarded the tram. 'Sure, they've got us every which way.'

Back in the sisters' house, Peggy sat Archie on a chair in the kitchen, poured some Dettol into a basin of water, dampened a rag and patted the cut on his cheek. As she dried it and carefully peeled an Elastoplast over the wound, she became aware of Archie's eyes close to her own and his breath on her face.

'You've a very soft touch, Peggy,' he said.

Peggy found that her eyes were riveted to Archie's lips. As his head slowly approached hers, Peggy suddenly felt faint and closed her eyes; she heard the front door opening. She jumped to her feet in a panic as Maggie came into the room.

'I heard there was trouble at the …' Maggie said. 'Oh my God, Archie, what on earth …?'

'It's alright, Maggie,' Archie said. 'There was a scuffle with some soldiers on the Green, that's all. It's just a scratch and Peggy has patched me up. She has a very gentle touch.'

'I'm sure she has,' Maggie said, suppressing a smile. 'She's a very gentle girl, Archie.'

Peggy didn't know where to look.

Chapter 16:
Eamonn's Letter.

As Peggy came into the house with a bag full of messages, Brighid said, 'Ah, there you are. We've been waiting for you.' She waved a letter in the air. 'It's from Eamonn.' Pat, Conal and Tim sat waiting to hear the news from Flanders.

Peggy put her shopping bag on the kitchen table, sat down, and said, 'Let's hear what the bould soldier boy has to say, so.'

Brighid slit the envelope open with a knife and took out the letter. She scanned it quickly, cleared her throat, and read out loud.

Dear Ma & Pa

I'm writing to you from a village in France, but we're not allowed to name it. We've been training here for a couple of weeks and move up to the front line tomorrow. But don't worry, we'll soon have the Boche on the run and be home for Christmas.

'That's the spirit,' Pat said. Brighid continued.

The lads are all in good form and raring to go. Sure, there's no stopping the Highland Light Infantry! There's an estaminet in the village, which is a sort of pub, and we gather there of an evening for a sing-song and a few tunes. I have me tin whistle, Donny has his chanter, and one of the lads has his melodion, so the craic is mighty. They sell a gargle called red wine here which is all right when you get used to it – although it's more like Red Biddy to me!

Brighid paused and laughed, as did Pat, Peggy, Conal and Tim.

It's fine summer weather at the moment, and the fields is full of ripening wheat, a grand sight to see for they are very big, not like the small fields of Donegal. So, it's yellow for miles.

'That must be a rare sight,' Peggy said. 'I'd like to see that, so I would. Miles of yellow.'

Donnie and me have been talking. We've decided to set up our own carting business when we come home. We've got the contacts, Donnie, with the Highland people and me with the Irish. So, it would be better working for ourselves than for someone else. We'd have to find a stable for a couple of horses and we'd have to buy another cart, but that won't be a problem.

'Now that's a grand idea,' Pat said. 'Good on ye.'

Well, that's it for now. I'm off for a jar of the Red Biddy as it will be the last for a while. I hope this letter finds you all in as good a form as it leaves me. God bless you all.

Your loving son,

Eamonn.

Brighid folded the letter and put it back in the envelope. 'Well, he sounds in great form, so he does,' she said.

'Aye,' Pat said, 'and that idea of a carter business of their own is a first-class one.'

'Sure, we'll be rolling in money,' Peggy said.

The whole family laughed.

Chapter 17:
1914: Disaster.

Towards the end of August, Peggy looked up from chopping onions in the kitchen in Partickhill as Archie shook his *Glasgow Herald* and said to Catherine and Maggie, 'Could you believe it? The Germans have destroyed a whole Russian Army at Lake Tannenberg, wherever that is. They've killed thousands of Russians and taken more than a hundred thousand prisoners.'

'My God,' Maggie said. 'A whole army? What a fearful slaughter.'

'Yes,' Archie said. 'A catastrophe for the Russians.'

'Thank God our lads aren't involved,' Catherine said.

As Peggy continued her chopping, she thought: it's a pity for the poor Russians, but at least Eamonn will be safe.

In mid-September, Peggy herself read in the *Herald* that although inflicting heavy losses on the Germans, the British Army was forced to retreat from Mons to cover the withdrawal of the French. She couldn't understand the strategy of it all, but she knew a retreat was a retreat, and it seemed to be going on day after day. That can't be good news for our lads, she thought.

Coming up out of the subway station at Govan Cross, Peggy went into St Anthony's Church, lit a candle for the safe return of Eamonn, and said a prayer for him before hurrying home to Neptune Street.

Peggy knew there was something wrong the minute

she opened the door, for there was a deathly silence in the house. She hurried into the kitchen to see Brighid rocking backwards and forwards in her chair, her teeth clenched. Her white-faced father handed her a telegram. Peggy opened it and read:

> **SIR, IT IS MY PAINFUL DUTY TO INFORM YOU THAT A REPORT HAS THIS DAY BEEN RECEIVED FROM THE WAR OFFICE NOTIFYING THE DEATH OF 524562 PRIVATE EAMONN O'DONNELL, 2nd HIGHLAND LIGHT INFANTRY, WHICH OCCURRED ON THE RETREAT FROM MONS ON THE 25TH OF AUGUST 1914, AND I AM TO EXPRESS THE SYMPATHY AND REGRET OF THE ARMY COUNCIL AT YOUR LOSS.**

There was more, something about personal effects, but Peggy collapsed into a chair, tears welling from her eyes. It wasn't possible – big, gentle Eamonn, the boy who was always smiling, who was so good with animals, who was such a good piper, the apple of his mother's eye, a boy who never had an enemy in his life, who was a grand big brother. Peggy howled and went over to try and comfort her mother. Pat got up, muttering angrily, barged out, and slammed the door so hard the house rocked.

At the Requiem Mass, Peggy and her family sat in the front row listening to Father Gallagher. Brighid sobbed quietly under a black veil.

'These young Catholic men did their duty for their comrades-in-arms, their Regiment and their King and country,' the priest said. 'They also paid the ultimate sacrifice. But their death wasn't in vain, for the British Army's stand at the Marne has stopped the German Army at the gates of Paris. Our young heroes are now in a better place, in Heaven, in the hands of Our Lord, where they can suffer no more. Eternal rest grant unto them, oh Lord, and let perpetual light shine upon them, for ever and ever.'

'Amen,' the congregation murmured. What about us here on earth? Peggy thought; what about me mother and her broken heart?

Several weeks later, Donnie MacCaskill came to visit the O'Donnells while on leave after the Battle of the Marne. Twisting his cup of tea round and round in his hands, he stared at the floor for a long time before he spoke.

'Eamonn never knew a thing, Missus O'Donnell. Our platoon was attacking a German machine-gun post. We charged it, and Eamonn copped it right in the head. He never knew a thing, honest. One minute he was there, and the next.' His hand waved helplessly in the air. 'We gave him a good send-off. I … I played the pipes for him – *The Flo'ors o' the Forest.'* The whole Company was there, Major Lawrie, the Company Commander, made a speech saying what a good soldier he was, and the Padre done the service.'

'Thank you, Donnie,' Brighid said. 'Thank you for coming to see us. I appreciate that. It's some comfort to know that Eamonn knew no suffering, thank the Lord.'

'Aye,' Donnie said, draining his tea. What he didn't tell Brighid was that his platoon had been attacking the German machine-gun post at the run with fixed bayonets, shouting and yelling, when a burst of fire decapitated Eamonn. His headless body had carried on running for several paces before collapsing, blood still spurting out of his neck. Donnie also didn't say that he had had nightmares about this every single night since the battle.

Chapter 18:
A Second Disaster.

It was a crisp, but bright winter's Sunday morning as Peggy and Archie strolled up through the Kelvingrove Park after visiting the Art Gallery and Museum. They had been to the Glasgow Boys' exhibition, and Peggy was fascinated to learn that Archie and his sisters knew some of these painters. Without thinking, Peggy took Archie's arm as he explained how the artists wanted a return to a simple form of painting nature and people, real people in real places around Glasgow, a style which had been influenced by the French Impressionists.

Archie suggested they go into the University Café in Byres Road for a cup of coffee, and Peggy was happy to agree. She loved the bustling atmosphere of the café, with the smell of bacon, beans and coffee, customers jammed next to each other in the booths, and the owner and his assistants cheerfully yelling at each other in Italian. As she and Archie turned into Byres Road, neither of them saw Mrs Hannavy staring at them from a passing tram.

After their coffee, they stopped outside Archie's flat in Havelock Street. 'That was a lovely day, Peggy,' Archie said. 'Thank you for your company.' He leaned forward and gently kissed her cheek.

Half an hour later, as she climbed the stair to the family home in Neptune Street, all Peggy could think about was that kiss. She went weak at the knees thinking about it, but her mind was still racing with elation. As she opened the door and blessed herself from the font of holy water, she could smell the Irish stew simmering in a pot on the grate; the fire crackled occasionally as the coal settled. Tim sat at the table doing his homework as Brighid peeled more spuds. Pat sat opposite Tim, scowling, his fingers drumming on the table; Peggy could smell the drink off him. Brighid glanced at him from time to time, trying to work out what was on his mind.

'God bless all here,' Peggy said. 'God bless all in this house.'

'Ye bloody hypocrite!' Pat snarled.

'Pat!' Brighid exclaimed.

Peggy paused in the act of taking her coat off.

'Da,' she said, 'whatever is the matter?'

'You've turned your back on your God, and the faith of your fathers, ye hypocrite,' Pat said.

'What on earth are you talking about, Da?' Peggy replied.

'I'm talking about the fact that you're keeping company with a bloody Prod!'

'Ah! That's what this is all about,' Peggy said, taking her coat off and hanging it up, her heart sinking.

'And don't give me any of your lip, ye young hussy.'

'For God's sake, Pat,' Brighid whispered.

'Sure, your daughter's been seen cavorting round the streets of Glasgow with a black Prodesan, Missus. Do you expect me to keep silent? It's a bloody disgrace, that's what it is. Me own daughter turned into a trollop.'

'Da,' Peggy said, 'that's ridiculous and you know it.'

'I know that I'm the laughing-stock of Neptune Street, that's what I know. Me own daughter a scarlet woman.'

'There's no need to insult me,' Peggy said. 'Meself and Archie have done nothing to be ashamed of.'

'Oh, so it's Archie, is it? Who's this feckin' Prod Archie when he's at home?'

'Archie MacDonald is a school-teacher, a graduate of the University of Glasgow. He's from a perfectly respectable crofting family on the Isle of Skye, from a Gaeltacht, like us.'

'He's not like us, you turncoat! He's a bloody Prod, the people who put us out of house and home.'

'That's just ridiculous,' Peggy said. 'Archie's own family was evicted during the Highland Clearances.'

'I don't give a tinker's curse,' Pat roared, 'he's a bloody Prod. He's the enemy. He's the type who put us Catholics through dungeon, fire and sword. What on earth is Father Gallagher going to say when he hears this? I'll never live it down.'

'I don't give a damn about Father Gallagher,' Peggy retorted.

Pat jumped to his feet; his chair crashed to the floor. 'Hark at her! She's turned against her own priests now. That's it, Peggy O'Donnell. I forbid you to see this black Prod ever again. We'll have no turncoats in this family.'

'Da. I am nineteen years of age, nearly twenty. I earn a living. You can't forbid me to do anything. It's nineteen-hundred-and-fourteen, for God's sake. We're in the twentieth century. You can't keep up those bigoted ideas anymore. They're irrelevant over here.'

'Be the holy man!' Pat exclaimed. 'First, she whores around with a Prod. And then she calls her own father a bigot. Don't you dare talk to me like that, young woman.'

Peggy fought back her tears. 'I am not a whore! You have no right to speak to me like that.'

'Patrick! Patrick!' Brighid cried. 'She's your own daughter.'

'It's no daughter of mine that whores around with Prods. It's …'

'You're an ignorant, bigoted, foul-mouthed man,' Peggy retorted, 'who …'

The kitchen echoed to the crack as Pat slapped Peggy hard across the face. She staggered backwards and collapsed on the floor. There was dead silence.

Her head reeling, Peggy lurched to her feet, a red weal already blossoming on her cheek. Tim was frozen at his books. Peggy stood up, white-faced, and nearly fell over again. She swayed, but steadied herself by holding on to the edge of the table. She took a couple of deep, rasping breaths, turned on her heel, went into her bedroom and locked the door. She sat on the bed, her head in her hands, her cheek smarting, her brain still spinning as she stared out of the window into the dark. Tears blurred her vision. She took a series of deep breaths, and the spinning slowed down. Well, Kitty's Da hit her back home right enough but to be hit in me own house by me own da who had never raised a hand to me in my whole life unbelievable fathers are supposed to protect their daughters keep them safe fathers of religion fathers of the nation fathers of children he'll never apologise and me head's ringing and outside the church bells are ringing too I'm not having that I'm out of here yes but what to take a couple of changes of clothes some toilet things oh yes and me portrait it'll break me ma's heart I can hear her crying in the kitchen …

She pulled her suitcase down from the top of the wardrobe.

But I can't stay here if he hit me once he'd hit me again yes better make a clean break of it. I'll miss the boys but what about this dress it needs washing, but I'll wash it later …

In the kitchen, Brighid collapsed back into her chair sobbing her disbelief. Tim was petrified with shock. Pat stood erect. There were two loud clicks from the bedroom, and the key turned in the lock. Peggy came back into the kitchen carrying her suitcase, and her pastel portrait under her arm. She looked her father right in the eye, an expression of utter contempt on her face, then turned and strode out of the door, her head held high and body erect. As the door slammed shut, Brighid threw her apron over her head abruptly and burst into tears. She'd lost her eldest son and was now losing her only daughter. Pat glared at the door, pretending indifference. Tim coughed nervously. The stew bubbled away on the grate.

Chapter 19:
1915: The Glasgow Rent Strike.

Catherine, Maggie and Peggy sat round the kitchen table in Partickhill. Maggie poured the tea.

'Look, Peggy,' Catherine said, 'you can stay here. That's not a problem – you're practically one of the family now anyway.'

'That's right,' Maggie said, 'that's the least of your worries.'

Peggy wiped away a tear as she said, 'Thank you. Thank you.'

'But what will we do about your father?' Maggie said.

'Nothing,' Peggy said. 'That's for me to handle. But I'm not going to speak to Da until he apologises for hitting me. Which he won't. He's as stubborn as a donkey.'

'Won't he come looking for you?' Catherine said.

'No,' Peggy said, 'not a bit of it.' How to explain it to the sisters?

'I know it's hard for you to understand,' Peggy continued, 'but all he ever had in his life was a few acres of bog, like his father before him. And he didn't even own that, he rented it from an absentee landlord. And the rent kept going up. And he always owed money to the gombeen man.'

Peggy took a sip of her tea. 'Me da never had any power. The only power he had was over his family. So, he can't be seen to be challenged by me, his only daughter. It's like he's been made a laughing-stock. It doesn't matter that I never had any intention of raring up against him. He thinks I did, and that's that. He's not a bad man, the Da, but he's an old-fashioned Irishman, so he can't abide any attack on what he sees as his only bit of power – especially by a woman. And then he blames everything that's wrong on the Protestants. So, when someone told him I had been seen walking out with Archie, it was as if I was a traitor to the Cause.'

'The Cause? What do you mean "The Cause"? What Cause?' Catherine said.

'Oh, Home Rule for Ireland, of course,' Peggy said.

'What a lot of baloney,' Maggie said.

'I know,' Peggy said, 'but it's Irish baloney. I understand how it works. So please leave it to me.'

Catherine and Maggie exchanged a glance. Catherine took Peggy's hand. 'Of course, my dear, of course.'

'You've got be joking!' Archie said.

'No,' Catherine said, 'I'm not joking. That girl's father hit her because she was seen going out with you by some interfering besom. And you're a Protestant. Therefore, you're the enemy, as far as Peggy's father is concerned. So, you're responsible for this mess. I think you have to review your attitude to that girl, Archie. She's an innocent country girl of nineteen.'

'Huh! I seem to remember you going out with Iain Mavor when you were seventeen.'

'That's different. We were …'

'Oh, stop it, you two,' Maggie said. 'Archie, what have you been up to with Peggy? Are you courting her?'

'No! We went to the exhibition at the Kelvingrove Art Gallery, walked home and had a coffee at the University Café on the way.'

'Archie,' Maggie said. 'Have you kissed that girl?'

Archie looked round the sitting-room for respite; there was none.

'Yes,' he said. 'Yes, I have. But only on the cheek.'

'Oh dear,' Catherine said. 'Archie MacDonald. Are you in love with Peggy?'

'No. Yes. I don't know,' Archie said.

Catherine sighed as she addressed Maggie. 'He's in love.'

'I know,' Maggie said. 'Mind you, I don't blame him. Peggy is a beautiful as well as intelligent girl.'

'She is,' Catherine said. 'But that's not the point. The point is, it's our job to protect her.'

'So, what do you propose, oh wise one?' Archie said.

'I'm thinking about it,' Catherine said.

Mary Barbour rapped the end of her pencil on the table.

'Order, ladies, order,' she said.

Peggy listened intently as Mrs Barbour outlined the position. 'As you all know, the city, and particularly Govan and Partick, have been flooded with munitions workers from the Woolwich Arsenal in London. Consequently, and quite opportunistically, the landlords and their factors have put up rents as demand far exceeds supply. But for a lot of sitting tenants, with their men away at the Front, they can't afford these hikes in the rent. Andrew McBride of the Glasgow Labour Housing Association asked for a meeting with the Glasgow Property-Owners and Factors Association, but this was refused. The landlords now propose taking action for eviction in the Small Debts Court for tenants in arrears of these increases. One of these tenants is Missus Ferguson whose husband is serving with the Highland Light Infantry on the Western Front. We say that such action against the wife of a serving soldier is both illegal and immoral, so we propose, first, an immediate rent strike, and second, the establishment of committees of women in each neighbourhood to resist eviction. I put these two proposals to the meeting. All in favour raise their hand and say 'Aye'.'

Peggy looked round as a thunderous response of 'Aye' echoed round the room; it seemed as if every single woman present had raised her hand. Mrs Barbour handed out flyers that read:

GLASGOW LABOUR HOUSING ASSOCIATION
RENT STRIKE
AGAINST INCREASES
WE ARE
NOT REMOVING

'I want to see these in the windows of every street in Govan,' Mrs Barbour said. Peggy took a handful and distributed them to women from Neptune Street. A hand plucked at her elbow. 'Can I have one?' a familiar voice said. Peggy turned to see her mother. She hugged Brighid and gave her a couple of flyers. 'Good on ye, Ma,' she said.

'Will you not come home, girleen?' Brighid said. 'Sure, the house isn't the same without you. And your father's breaking his heart that you won't speak to him.'

'Bad cess to him, Ma,' Peggy said. 'It's his own fault. And to tell you the truth, this Rent Strike is more important than me Da's finer feelings.'

'Oh Peggy, you're turning into a hard, hard woman.'

'It's hard, hard times that are in it,' Peggy said. 'Ma, I have no quarrel with ye. You know that. I'll be in touch to be sure.' She kissed her mother and continued to distribute the flyers.

Mrs Barbour quickly organised a Govan Committee with a representative from every main street, and asked Peggy to represent Neptune Street along with Mrs MacCaskill.

They decided to hold the Govan district meeting immediately after the main meeting.

'The thing is,' Mrs Barbour said, 'how do we alert the women when the factors arrive?'

'How about a hand bell – like a school-bell?' Peggy said.

'The very dab, Peggy,' Mrs Barbour said. 'Could you find a brass-moulder and get a price for a dozen bells?'

'Sure, and I will,' Peggy said.

'Right,' Mrs Barbour said. 'When we spot the factors, we'll ring the bells, and jam-pack the close of the tenant to be evicted with women. It would be a brave man who would fight his way through a close full of angry Govan women! And I think we should have something to throw at them, something which will make them think twice about coming back.'

'We threw stones at them in Skye,' Mrs MacCaskill said.

'I don't think that's a good idea, Morag,' Mrs Barbour said. 'Someone will get injured and we'd wind up in Duke Street Jail – and that's not a good place for women.'

'What about peasemeal?' Peggy said.

'Yes,' Mrs Barbour said, 'that's a great idea. Every woman should make sure she has a spare bag of peasemeal to give to the factors!'

The committee women fell about laughing.

Peggy spotted the factors as they turned into Neptune Street: three of them, Brawn himself and two of his Clerks. She grabbed her handbell and began clanging. Women poured out of the closes and gathered outside Mrs Ferguson's close at Number 852. Mrs Barbour organised them to jam-pack the entrance to the close and right up to the first-floor landing where Mrs Ferguson's house was. All of the women had bags of peasemeal and, Peggy noticed, some had bags of soot while others had rotten fish. Mrs Barbour had placed some of the biggest women – Mrs McGinlay, Mrs Hanrahan and Mrs O'Docherty – at the very entrance to the close, and Peggy saw that women were also hanging out of every window above the close-mouth. A big poster hung above the entrance to the close, and several Union Jacks and an Irish tricolour flew from adjacent windows. The poster read:

NO SURRENDER.
GOD HELP THE SHERIFF OFFICER
WHO ENTERS HERE.

Peggy joined Mrs Barbour in the second row of women as Brawn and his men approached. Missus Ferguson's six-year-old son, Jamesie, joined the front rank of women, carrying a placard that read:

MY FATHER IS FIGHTING
IN FRANCE.
WE ARE FIGHTING
THE HUNS AT HOME.

'Good lad yourself, Jamesie,' Peggy said, and the boy grinned. Then she spotted Conal across the road, clutching his reporter's notebook, and accompanied by a photographer; at eighteen, Conal was now a trainee reporter for *Forward.* Peggy saw her brother point out Jamesie to the photographer, who took several pictures of the boy and the crowd of women. When Brawn saw the close-mouth packed with women, he stopped in his tracks.

'Now you women get out of the way,' he bawled, taking a document out an inside pocket. 'I've a warrant for an eviction here.'

'There'll be no eviction in this close, you fat gobshite,' Mrs Hanrahan said, to a chorus of approval by the other women.

'Willie Ferguson is away fighting the Prussians on the Western Front,' Mrs O'Docherty said. 'And you've the bloody nerve to try and evict a sodger's wife, you miserable gett.'

Brawn breenged forward, shouting, 'Get out of the way there.' There was a resounding crack, and the factor staggered backwards, holding his cheek.

'The dirty bastard grabbed me bosoms,' Mrs McGinlay cried. There was a yell of outrage, a paper bag of peasemeal flew through the air and burst on Brawn's head, knocking his bowler hat off, which Jamesie promptly booted out into the street. A hail of bags of peasemeal and soot and fish rained down on the three men as well as a torrent of water as the women above emptied their chamber-pots over them. Spluttering and cursing, Brawn took to his heels, followed by his two clerks, and the jeers of the women.

'That was a real Donnybrook,' Peggy said.

'It was,' Mrs Barbour said. 'But they'll be back, this time with Sheriff Officers and the Polis. So, we've got to be ready.'

On November 17th, Peggy was one of hundreds of women in Mrs Barbour's Army packed outside the Sheriff Court in Ingram Street. The Rent Strike had now taken a firm hold all over the city, and the 'We Are Not Removing' placards were to be seen in the windows of every working-class neighbourhood in the city. The factors and Sheriff Officers had found it impossible to evict anyone; the resistance was too strong. After the women had torn off the trousers off one aggressive Sheriff Officer, they had given up even trying, and had gone to the Small Debts Court seeking arrestment of wages to pay off arrears of rent. Eighteen munitions workers were to go on trial today in front of Sheriff Lee for arrears, and a huge demonstration was planned.

Peggy heard them before she saw them. In the distance she heard the rhythmic thud of a big drum, the shrill of tin-whistles and the tramp of marching feet. Suddenly, crowds of men with the blackened faces and bonnets of shipyard workers poured out of Royal Exchange Square and into Ingram Street to join the women. Peggy read their numerous placards:

RENT STRIKERS.

WE ARE NOT REMOVING.

She recognised John Maclean amongst the marchers as she heard a delegation of workers from Beardmore's shipyard in Dalmuir demand a meeting with the Sheriff from the Inspector in charge of the Policemen in front of the Court building. The white-faced Inspector hurried inside as a group of workers hoisted John Maclean onto their shoulders, standing on a poster-board taken from the front of a nearby newsagent's. The crowd roared approval as Maclean detailed the greed of the factors and property-owners in increasing the rent of small houses while the householders were away fighting in the Army in Flanders, or which were already over-crowded with munitions workers.

'Will we let them get away with this?' Maclean cried.

'Never!' the workers and women thundered.

'Will we allow the factors to attack our wages?'

'Never!'

The Police Inspector re-appeared and ushered the delegation inside as the speeches continued; Peggy saw Helen Crawfurd addressing the crowd from the top of a beer barrel. Shortly afterwards, the delegation came out of the Courthouse and announced that the Sheriff had persuaded the factor to drop the cases in the face of a threat of a strike. Sheriff Lee had telephoned Lloyd George to inform him of the gravity of the situation. A huge cheer went up. John Maclean then proposed a motion that a telegram be sent to the Government demanding that any rent increases for the duration of the War be forbidden. This was carried by acclaim and Maclean hurried off to the Post Office in George Square to send the telegram.

As Peggy left the city centre with the crowd of women, the air of jubilation was palpable.

'We showed them what we're made of,' Mary Barbour said.

'Sure, and we did,' Peggy said.

The party in Partickhill to celebrate the famous victory went on into the wee small hours. There were so many people crowded into Maggie's and Catherine's flat that Peggy was run off her feet supplying drinks and making pots of tea. Archie and a couple of men had been dispatched to the licensed grocer's in Hyndland to buy more drink as they were about to run out.

Mary Barbour grabbed Peggy's arm as a man wearing a pair of dungarees with a joiner's rule sticking out of a side pocket and a cloth cap began speaking.

'Listen to this, Peggy,' Mary said. 'That's Jock Strain from Beardmore's. He was in the delegation that spoke to the Sheriff.'

'The Sheriff wanted tae continue the cases,' Jock said. 'So, I sez tae him, 'We're no here tae negotiate wi' you. We're here tae tell you that if these cases are continued, there'll be a hunner thoosan men out on strike the morra. And if you want a general strike, you kin have it. Know wit ah mean?' Aye. He got the message kinna quick.'

Peggy laughed out loud.

Chapter 20:
John Maclean.

Peggy had heard John Maclean speak out against the War on his Sunday night meetings in Bath Street, and had read his articles in *Vanguard*, the British Socialist Party's newspaper. She admired his pacifist courage profoundly, especially at a time of national jingoism, so she decided to go and hear him speak on Glasgow Green in January 1916.

The weather was unusually mild, so there was a large crowd surrounding Maclean's soapbox. Peggy squeezed her way to the front and listened intently.

'They don't need conscription,' Maclean said. 'They already have plenty of soldiers and plenty of munitions. So why are they talking about conscription? First, because it means that all young men, whether as soldiers or workers in controlled factories, would then come under the control of the military authorities, because these factories come directly under military discipline. So, we would have both military and industrial conscription. Second, at the end of the War, there will be so many discharged soldiers looking for work that they can be used as cheap labour. The workers are being made military slaves to suit the bloody British capitalists, which is pure Kaiserism. Now, we socialists have no objection to the capitalists going to war and killing each other. That is their affair, not ours. In fact, we would encourage it, for it might well accelerate the path to socialism!'

There was a ripple of laughter among the crowd, but also quite a few catcalls. Peggy noticed that a man near her had a peculiar posture. She moved nearer and saw that he was holding a notebook close to his chest and was writing rapidly in it. When he realised that he was being watched, he turned and glared at Peggy.

'Mind your own business, Miss,' he snarled, 'if you know what's good for you.'

From his hostile tone, Peggy realised that the man might be a plain-clothes policeman, backed away and turned to hear Maclean finish his speech. Just then there was a shout from the crowd, 'Away and enlist!'

John Maclean turned to face the heckler and said, 'I've been enlisted for fifteen years in the socialist army. It's the only army worth fighting for. God damn all other armies.' There was scattered applause from the listeners, but a barrage of abuse from people whose men were soldiers at the Front.

Undaunted, Maclean continued, 'If British soldiers laid down their arms, so would the Germans and those of the other nations, as they were all war-weary long ago. So, the best advice I can give you workers is to sell your alarm-clocks, sleep-in in the morning, and not go to work. The only weapon we have as the working-class is the strike, and we must use that weapon relentlessly against conscription. Comrades, be armed and ready!'

There was a smattering of applause from the crowd mixed with much more hostile shouting. John Maclean is one brave man, Peggy thought, as she left Glasgow Green.

The next evening, Peggy discussed John Maclean's speech with Catherine and Maggie in their sitting-room.

'John is a courageous and principled socialist,' Catherine said. 'But he is a diehard, who is prepared to give his life for the cause, and …'

'And he probably will,' Maggie said. 'John's problem is that he's a zealot, he doesn't realise that ordinary workers do not share his principles to the extent that he does. He demands too much, he asks for too much sacrifice – losing your job like he did, going to jail, going on hunger strike. Ordinary workers want to stay free in order to work and support their families.'

'But everybody agrees this War's pointless and is now just endless slaughter,' Peggy said. 'And John points out that the capitalists who own the munitions factories and the shipyards which build warships are the only people who profit.'

'And he's right,' Catherine said. 'But workers still have to make a living, war or no war. Pacifism is a courageous calling.'

'Then Helen Crawfurd and Agnes Dollan and Mary Barbour are courageous,' Peggy said.

'Yes, they are,' Maggie said. 'But their campaign is for a negotiated peace settlement, which is at least sensible if it can galvanise enough public opinion in the country as a whole. But John would probably see that as a gradualist sell-out.'

'So, what does he propose?' Peggy said.

'I think he wants some kind of spontaneous general strike which would bring the Government crashing down, and lead to immediate peace talks,' Catherine said.

'Fat chance,' Peggy said.

'Exactly,' Maggie said.

Shortly afterwards, John Maclean was arrested, charged with sedition, and imprisoned in Edinburgh Castle, while awaiting trial under the Defence of the Realm Act. He went to the High Court in Edinburgh on April 11th, and to the horror of his supporters, including Peggy, was sentenced to three years imprisonment with hard labour.

Chapter 21:
A Terrible Beauty is Born.

In early 1916, Sinn Fein held a meeting about the Irish Home Rule issue in the Hibernian Hall in Govan Road. Peggy decided to attend as she was confused about the relationship between socialism and home rule. The hall was packed when she arrived, and she spotted Conal sitting at the back with some of the Irish lads from Neptune Street. He was doing well as a reporter, his articles were lucid and interesting; he had a mind of his own and was showing considerable maturity for a young man of only eighteen.

The debate was passionate. The old-fashioned Home Rulers, men like her father, held to the line that the British Liberal Party had promised Home Rule, the War had intervened, so it was suspended, but would be granted when the War ended. The more radical speakers, usually those from Sinn Fein, argued that they should demand Home Rule now. Peggy was surprised when Conal jumped to his feet and said that patriotic Irish people should not wait for Britain's pleasure in granting Home Rule, but should seize it now, and proclaim an independent republic. 'England's difficulty is Ireland's opportunity,' he argued. Peggy could see that there was no one line that was dominant, and noted that the more pragmatic speakers emphasised the problem with the Protestant counties of Northern Ireland that would flatly refuse to join any Republic.

At the end of the meeting, Peggy had a cup of tea with Conal, and was impressed with how vehemently her younger brother argued for the declaration of an Irish Republic. 'Sure, you're quite the Sinn Feiner,' she said.

'I am that,' Conal said. 'I joined the Govan branch at the end of last year, after Eamonn was killed.'

'Well, you'll not get your Republic while this war is on,'

Peggy said. 'And there are thousands of Irishmen in the British Army. The point isn't simply the Republic, but what kind of Republic it is going to be.'

'We'll sort that out afterwards,' Conal said. 'But I'm sure we would both agree that we want an Irish Workers' Republic.'

'Amen to that,' Peggy said. 'But the Irish workers didn't do so well out of the Dublin lockout. It was defeated entirely.'

Peggy sat in Archie's kitchen with a cup of tea as he read her reference. He looked up.

'That's a brilliant reference,' he said. 'Mr O'Neill has a way with words. And every word of it true.' Peggy blushed.

'Look, Peggy, I think you should apply for the Junior Student's Certificate,' Archie said. 'It's a system here in Scotland whereby if you have a school Intermediate Certificate, you can be accepted for three years training as a teacher in a school which is recognised as a Junior Student Centre. My school, Hillhead Secondary, is such a Centre.'

'But I don't have an Intermediate Certificate,' Peggy said.

'True, but you do have appropriate experience – nearly four years as a monitor in Ireland – plus this reference. I think I can guarantee you would be accepted in my school.

Would you like to give it a go?'

'Oh yes,' Peggy said, 'I would, so. What would I be doing?'

'Well, it's hard work. You would do reading, writing, arithmetic, music, phonetics, needlework, science and drawing.'

'Janey Mac,' Peggy said. 'Busy-busy-busy.'

'Aye. But nothing you couldn't handle – and I would help you. And it's interesting. And we need good teachers.'

'What happens at the end of the three years?'

'Well,' Archie said, 'you do an exam. And if you pass, you can then go onto Teacher Training College for two years for a professional teacher's course. Or you could apply for entrance to the university.'

'My goodness,' Peggy said. 'University?'

'Yes.'

Peggy laughed.

'What's the joke?' Archie said.

'I was just thinking, the Da would go raging.'

'Why?'

'Hillhead Secondary is a Protestant school!'

Peggy arranged to go and see her mother at home on Saturday night when she knew her father would be playing his fiddle at the Irish Club. As she approached her close, she saw Conal and a couple of his mates loading a horse-drawn cart with heavy boxes in a pend. As her heels clicked on the pavement, Conal spun round to see who it was.

'Arrah, it's yourself, Peggy,' Conal said.

Peggy could see clearly the stencilled marking on the box he was carrying. It read:

BRITISH DYNAMITE COMPANY.
ARDEER, AYRSHIRE, N.B.
HIGH EXPLOSIVES - DANGEROUS.

'In the name of the wee man,' Peggy said, 'what on earth are you doing with that geliganite?'

Conal glanced round. 'It's going across the water to where it will be useful. And you didn't see a thing. Right?'

'Right,' Peggy said.

The news of the Easter Rising in Dublin came as a complete shock to Peggy. The first she heard about it was on the morning of the Wednesday of Easter Week, when she learned from a telegram from Conal that he had been sent to Dublin by *Forward* to report on events. In the house, the MacDonald sisters had several newspapers spread out on the kitchen table.

'I don't believe it,' Catherine said. 'What's a socialist like James Connolly doing in an armed insurrection? No socialist can support that kind of violence.'

'I don't know the answer to that,' Maggie said. 'But I do know that the Rising is real. The papers say the rebels have seized several places in the centre of Dublin. Have you any news, Peggy?'

'No,' Peggy said, 'but it's important enough for *Forward* to have sent Conal to Dublin.'

'Ah yes,' Maggie said. 'He's the reporter, isn't he?'

'Yes, he is.' Peggy didn't say that she also suspected that Conal might be involved.

Within the next twenty-four hours, a clearer picture of events in Dublin emerged. Groups of Rebels had seized key points in the city centre including the General Post Office, the Four Courts, Boland's Mill and the South Dublin Union. The British Military were taken completely by surprise, but brought in reinforcements rapidly, including artillery and a gunboat. They bombarded the Rebel positions and soon the city centre in Sackville Street was rubble. Peggy scanned the newspapers and haunted the *Forward* office looking for news of Conal, but couldn't find anything; Brighid was demented at the lack of news about her son.

The following Sunday, April 29th, the Rebels formally surrendered. On the Monday, Conal was back in Glasgow. He got off the Dublin boat at Merkland Street, took the subway to Govan to assure his parents he was alive and well, then filed his copy. He phoned Peggy in Partickhill to say he would be round in half-an-hour, and to put the kettle on.

As Peggy poured the excited Conal another cup of tea, Maggie and Catherine hung on his every word.

'You want to have seen it,' Conal said. 'Bullets were flying everywhere, Sackville Street and Abbey Street were on fire, and a gunboat anchored in the Liffey was shelling Liberty

Hall. But the worst fighting I saw was at Northumberland Road at the Mount Street Bridge. The British soldiers kept charging at the bridge – and I saw an officer leading the charge with a drawn sword! But a couple of our lads in a house shot them down, and the street was littered with dead and wounded soldiers – in the gutters, on the steps up to the houses, beside the canal, everywhere – dozens of them. There was blood everywhere. It was a slaughter.'

'Good God,' Maggie said.

'When the Rebels surrendered,' Conal said, 'there were a lot of the Dubs giving out at them. Sure, a lot of the shawleens' husbands and sons are fighting in the British Army in Flanders. It was ugly.'

'Where is it all going to end?' Catherine said.

It sounds as if it's just beginning, Peggy thought.

Peggy read in the newspapers of the start of the executions a few days after the Rebels' surrender. But when she read of the execution of James Connolly, so badly wounded that he could not stand up and had to be tied to a chair, she gasped in disbelief and turned to the sisters.

'The Brits must be mad,' Peggy said. 'Don't they know that what they're doing will turn every man, woman and child in Ireland into a Republican?'

Chapter 22:
Teacher Training.

Peggy rang the doorbell at Archie's flat. He opened it and said, 'Ah, there you are. Come in, come in, and I'll put the kettle on.'

They took their coffee into the sitting-room and sat down. 'There's no need to be nervous, Peggy,' Archie said. 'Mr Maxwell, the Hiedie, is a very nice, warm man. You'll like him. He's nobody's fool. I've given him your reference from Mr O'Neill. All you have to do is be yourself and you'll be fine.'

Peggy nodded assent, thinking, easier said than done.

'Tell him a bit about where you come from in Ireland, tell him a good bit about your experience as a monitor,' Archie continued, 'and tell him what kind of teacher you want to be. I've already told him a bit about you, so you're in with a shout.'

On the following Saturday, as Peggy cleaned the ashes out of the fireplace in the sitting-room in Partickhill Road, she thought about what Archie had said, and made a mental note of things to say about her teaching of the Infants back in the Rosses. The front door opened and Catherine and Maggie came in.

'Finished for the day?' Catherine said.

'Nearly,' Peggy said. 'I'll be done in a minute.'

'Any plans for the weekend?' Maggie said.

'I'm going to the ILP Social tonight,' Peggy said. 'Mrs Barbour has asked me to sing a couple of Irish songs. And this afternoon I'm going to the Mitchell Library to make some notes for my interview at Hillhead School and look at the syllabub.'

Catherine and Maggie laughed out loud.

'Syllabus, Peggy,' Catherine said. 'Syllabub is what you eat.' As Peggy blushed, the sisters glanced at each other.

'Sit down, Peggy,' Maggie said, 'there's something we'd like to discuss with you.'

'Now we both know you're excited about the idea of teacher training,' Catherine said, 'and you couldn't do it in a better school than Hillhead. But we wondered if that might not cause a problem.'

'What kind of a problem?' Peggy said.

'Well, my dear,' Maggie said, 'you're a Catholic, and Hillhead is a Protestant school. And you're Irish, and the Easter Rising in Dublin has caused quite a lot of anti-Irish feeling in this country. You might encounter some hostility.'

'So, we wondered if you mightn't be better doing your training in a Catholic school, where you'd feel more at home,' Catherine said. 'It's a big step for you to undertake your training in a Protestant school. Do you see what we mean?'

'I do,' Peggy said.

'You'd have to feel quite confident in yourself in going to Hillhead,' Maggie said. 'Do you feel up to the challenge?'

Peggy thought for a moment. 'It would be a lie if I didn't say that the thought's a bit frightening. But it would also be frightening in a Catholic school.' She paused.

'I'd prefer to go to Hillhead because to tell you the truth, I'm sick of the Father Gallaghers of the Catholic Church. The man's an ignorant bollocks who thinks he's a cut above. I'm sick of being told what to think. I'd like to get away from the likes of him and think for meself.'

Catherine and Maggie laughed, 'Oh you can think for yourself all right, Peggy,' Catherine said.

'What about your family?' Maggie said. 'Wouldn't it cause trouble if you went to Hillhead School?'

'Well, I'm in enough trouble with the Da already,' Peggy said. 'So a bit more won't do much harm.'

'Good for you, girl,' Maggie said.

'But I was thinking …' Peggy said.

'What?' Catherine said.

'What am I going to do about my job here?'

'We've thought about that,' Maggie said. 'We think it would be best if you continued to stay here until you finish your training. You can help us in the house and we'll help you with your lessons. And we'll continue to pay you. If you find it is all too much, then we can discuss other options. How does that sound?'

'It sounds grand,' Peggy said. 'That's very generous of ye. Thank you.'

'It's a pleasure,' Catherine said. 'That's that sorted, then. Now. How about a nice cup of tea?'

'I think a touch of scarlet lipstick would be good for the interview,' Catherine said to Peggy. 'It will offset your pale complexion, black hair and a white blouse.'

'I agree,' Maggie said. 'And how about a black neck-band?'

'The very dab,' Catherine said.

A little later, Peggy looked at herself in the mirror. She gasped with surprise as she saw a tall, smartly dressed young woman of twenty, her hair neatly pinned-up with a middle-parting. She wore a white sheer silk blouse, a black neckband with a pearl pendant, a black skirt, matte stockings, heels, and a coat which reached halfway down her calves. She applied a touch of the dark-red lipstick which Catherine had lent her. She then put on a broad-brimmed hat and pinned it in place. She turned sideways and studied her profile in the mirror. Well, well, well, she thought, I can barely recognise myself. You don't see smart women like that in The Rosses every day.

Archie met her at the door to Hillhead School, a big grey four-storey stone building at the foot of Cecil Street, with Greek columns framing the main entrance door. His eyes opened wide with astonishment as he looked her up and down. 'My goodness, Peggy,' he said. 'You look absolutely stunning.'

'Thank you,' Peggy said. 'I feel a bit like a scarlet woman, to tell you the truth.'

Archie laughed. 'Don't be daft. Come on, I'll take you to Mr Maxwell's office. Remember. Just be yourself.'

'I'll try,' Peggy said.

Archie knocked at a door with HEADMASTER on it. A voice from within said,'Come.'

Archie opened the door and ushered Peggy into a well-lit room lined with books.

'This is Miss Peggy O'Donnell, Mr Maxwell. Peggy, this is Mr Maxwell, the Headmaster.'

Peggy saw a well-built, middle-aged man with an open, friendly face. He got up immediately, smiled and held out his hand. 'I'm pleased to meet you, Miss O'Donnell. I've heard a lot about you from Mr MacDonald. Please. Sit down. Thank you, Mr MacDonald.'

As Archie turned to leave, he winked, and Peggy had to clench her jaw in order not to laugh. Mr Maxwell picked up a couple of sheets of paper.

'I understand that you were a Monitor in Ireland, Miss O'Donnell,' he said. 'Perhaps you could tell me a bit about that. It's not a system with which I am acquainted.'

'Well, sir,' Peggy said, 'the National Schools in Ireland have very big classes, particularly in the countryside, like where I come from. And there's usually only the one teacher. So, he selects a few of the brighter, older pupils to help him as

Monitors with the youngest ones, and they stay on at school past the age of twelve. The teacher teaches the Monitors, and they've an annual examination. If ye stayed on as a Monitor, passed your annual examinations, and satisfied the teacher, you could go on to Teacher Training College and become a professional teacher.'

'So, it's like an apprenticeship?' Mr Maxwell said.

'Exactly,' Peggy said.

'And for how long did you do this?'

'For one term short of four years, sir.'

'And do the Monitors get paid?'

'Yes, sir, they do,' Peggy said. 'But it's buttons. I'd say it's a form of cheap labour.'

Mr Maxwell laughed. 'I'm afraid that's the lot of apprentices everywhere. Now I've read your reference from your teacher, Mr O'Neill. It's a long time since I've read such a positive reference. 'Consistently high marks in her exams.' 'An inspired teacher of young children.' 'A gifted communicator.' It seems that you're a natural, Miss O'Donnell.'

Peggy felt her cheeks burning. 'I just do my best, sir.'

'Your best seems to be outstanding. Now, have you read the curriculum for the Junior Students' Certificate?'

'Yes, sir. I have.'

'Do you anticipate having any problems with any part of it?'

'Well, we didn't do any Science at my school, so I'd have to read up on that. And I'm not much good at drawing. And we didn't do much Physical Training. But that was because everybody played Hurley or Camogie.'

'Hurley or Camogie?'

'Yes sir. Hurley is like Shinty in Scotland. And Camogie is women's Hurley.'

'I see. I take it you'll be acquainted with the Domestic Arts?'

Peggy laughed. 'Oh yes sir. Every woman and girl in Donegal knits, and knows needlework and sewing.'

'Good, good,' Mr Maxwell said. 'What about foreign languages?'

'There were no foreign languages taught at our school, sir. But I speak, read, and write Irish and English. And I know a bit of Latin from Mr O'Neill.'

Mr Maxwell leaned back and studied Peggy. 'What kind of teacher would you like to be, all things being equal?'

Peggy stared out of the window for a moment, then turned and looked back at Mr Maxwell. 'I think I'd like to teach girls, sir. Teenage girls.'

'Why is that, Miss O'Donnell?'

'I'd like to show girls that there's more to life that being a slavey and having lots of babies.'

'Indeed, Miss O'Donnell, indeed. Now, here's what I am going to do. I'm going to recommend to the School Board that you be accepted as a candidate for the Junior Students' Certificate in this school, on the basis of your experience as a Monitor in Ireland, your consistently high marks in your examinations, and Mr O'Neil's reference.'

Peggy felt her heart leap; God o' Gods.

'But I should warn you of one thing. The decision about your acceptance is the School Board's, not mine. It's not automatic. But you'll be informed of their decision in writing in a few weeks. If you're accepted, you'd start here in the autumn term. Is that clear?'

'Yes, sir.'

'I may tell you that I'd be very pleased if you were accepted for this school, Miss O'Donnell. It was a pleasure to meet you. And I wish you good luck.' Mr Maxwell stood up. 'I will have your reference copied by the school secretary and will return it to you by post within the week. Good day, Miss O'Donnell.'

'Good day, sir.'

In the University Café, over a cup of coffee, Archie snapped his fingers.

'You're in, Peggy, you're in!' he said. 'Mr Maxwell told me he was most impressed by you. It would be unheard of for the Board to turn down a headmaster's recommendation. Well done.'

Two weeks later, Peggy received a letter from the School Board informing her that she had been accepted for the Junior Students' Certificate at Hillhead School. As she showed the letter to Catherine and Maggie, she thought it must be the happiest day in her life. Her only regret was that her father wouldn't be able to share her happiness.

Chapter 23:
Men and Women.

As Peggy came in the front door, she heard a noise from Maggie's bedroom, even although the door was shut. There was a rhythmic creaking which accelerated in pace, and Maggie could be heard gasping loudly. Peggy crept past on tiptoe, slipped into the kitchen, shut the door, and unpacked the shopping.

A little later, Maggie swept in bare-footed, tying up a dressing-gown, and started when she saw Peggy. 'Oh, Peggy,' she said, 'I didn't hear you come in.'

'I'm just back from the shopping,' Peggy said, busying herself putting things on shelves, not wanting to meet Maggie's eye.

'When you're ready, be a darling and bring a pot of coffee for two to the sitting-room,' Maggie said. 'And some shortbread.'

'Right you are,' Peggy said.

Peggy balanced a tray with the coffee-pot, milk and sugar, two cups, saucers and plates, and some shortbread, and knocked at the sitting-room door.

'Come in, Peggy, come in,' Maggie called, 'there's no need to knock.'

Peggy carried the tray in. Maggie was sitting on the sofa, bare legs crossed and exposed to the thigh, beside a man, also wearing a dressing-gown, who rested his hand on the inside of her naked thigh. Peggy felt herself blushing as she placed the tray on the coffee-table. Has Maggie no shame to be indulging in such bold behaviour?

'Thank you,' Maggie said. 'Peggy, this is my friend

Charlie. Charlie, this is Peggy O'Donnell.'

'How do you do, Peggy?' Charlie said, extending his hand. 'I've heard a lot about you from Maggie and Catherine.'

Thinking about where it had just been, Peggy shook Charlie's hand as quickly as she could. She saw a handsome man of about fifty, with dark hair and a dark moustache. His dark eyes burned with a fierce intensity as he smiled at Peggy, who realised that he was the man in the nude painting. He turned to Maggie.

'I can see why you wanted to paint her,' he said. 'She's lovely. Such natural beauty.'

You condescending bollocks, Peggy thought. But she literally didn't know where to look as she could see that both Maggie and Charlie were naked under their dressing-gowns, and they didn't seem the slightest bit bothered about it.

'Charlie's an architect and designer, Peggy,' Maggie said. 'But unfortunately, he lives in England now. A prophet without honour in his own country.'

As Peggy closed the door behind her, she could hear Maggie and Charlie laughing. She hoped they weren't laughing at her.

Later, Peggy watched as Maggie, now fully clothed, hummed as she arranged a bunch of yellow roses in a vase. Her eyes sparkled and her face wore a happy smile.

'Charlie brought them for me,' Maggie said. 'Aren't they lovely? I do love roses.'

Peggy steeled herself. 'Can I ask you something, Maggie?'

'Of course. Why don't you sit down and spit it out?' They both sat.

'Is Charlie … is Charlie your fiancé?' Peggy said.

Maggie laughed out loud. 'Goodness gracious me, no. Charlie's married, Peggy. We're just very good friends.'

'I see,' Peggy said. Except she didn't.

'Charlie and I are lovers, part-time lovers,' Maggie said. 'We only see each other occasionally these days. But we still like to go to bed with each other.'

'Oh,' Peggy said. 'But, but what about his wife?'

'What about his wife?' Maggie said. 'She knows about us. It's only sex, Peggy. Charlie and I are not going to run away together.'

Peggy studied Maggie's face. She seemed very nonchalant about the whole affair.

'But … but marriage is a sacrament,' Peggy said. 'For life. The gospel says, 'what God hath joined together, let no man put asunder'.'

'That's Christian gobbledygook,' Maggie said.

'Gobbledygook?' Peggy said.

'Mumbo-Jumbo,' Maggie said. 'I'm not a Christian, Peggy, I'm an atheist. I don't believe in God. I believe that all the Christian teaching about marriage is a way of keeping women under the thumb of men. I believe men and women are born free and should be able to choose their partners freely, without interference from churches, ministers or priests.'

'Do you mean …?' Peggy said.

'I mean you should be able to go to bed with whom you like,' Maggie said.

Jaysus, Peggy thought, the bold woman; Sodom and Gomorrah aren't in it. 'Is that why you're not married? So that you can go to bed with whoever you like?'

'No,' said Maggie. 'If I met a man I truly loved, and really wanted to marry, I would marry him. But I haven't met that man yet.'

'If you did meet him and you did get married, would you still sleep with other men?' Peggy said.

'If I met my ideal, I would probably not want to sleep with other men,' Maggie said. 'But I would reserve the right to do so.'

'I think that's disgusting,' Peggy said. 'Marriage is a sacrament.'

'I don't know what that means,' Maggie said. 'It sounds like more Catholic mumbo-jumbo to me. But I do know that marriage can be a trap, a prison from which the woman can never escape. Look at how it works. The man is always supposed to propose to the woman. Why? Why can't a woman propose to a man?'

Peggy didn't have an answer to that one.

'And look at what can happen when a man and a woman do marry,' Maggie said. 'Supposing she finds she doesn't love him? Supposing she finds that he beats her? Supposing she finds he's a drunk? What can she do? It's only a few relatively rich middle-class women who can afford a divorce. Working-class women have had it; they're doomed. That's not for me.'

Peggy thought for a moment. 'Would you like to have children?'

'Yes. Yes, I would,' Maggie said. 'But only with the right man. I would want to be quite sure about that. Now. What about you? Would you like to be married?'

'Yes,' Peggy said.

'And have children?' Maggie said.

'Oh yes,' Peggy said. 'Of course.'

Maggie laughed. 'Well, I'll give you a bit of advice, Peggy. You're just about to start training as a teacher. You should wait until you've finished that training before you get married and have children. Then you will have a qualification and can always earn a living. And that means you are independent and can stay that way. If you want to. Does that make sense?'

'Yes, I think it does,' Peggy said. 'It would be a shame to start all that studying and have to give it up to look after a family.'

'It would indeed,' Maggie said.

The front door opened. 'Cooee!' Catherine called.

'We're in the sitting-room,' Maggie shouted.

Catherine came in and collapsed into an armchair with a gasp. 'That Gardner Street hill is a killer when you're carrying the messages,' she said. 'What have you two been up to? You look as thick as thieves.'

'Peggy was asking why we're not married,' Maggie said. 'So, we were discussing the position of men and women.'

'Men?' Catherine said. 'Don't get me started.'

Maggie laughed. 'Well, Peggy said she wanted to know.'

Catherine leaned forward and looked at Peggy. 'The reason why we're both socialists and suffragettes is because the position of women is systematically inferior to that of men. Women are always portrayed as subordinate, illogical, weak, indecisive and fit only for occupations as carers and servants. But who painted that portrait? Men. Men who claimed to be superior to women - but had not been elected to that position. Men and women aren't born unequal, Peggy, but men make women unequal. That's why we start by campaigning for votes for women. And although that campaign is decades old now, men still treat it with contempt. That's why our campaign became militant – we smash windows, set fire to pillar-boxes and so on. And go on hunger-strike if sent to prison. If you want to know about the differences between men and women, Peggy, you should be aware of what happens to the women who go on hunger-strike. They are force-fed. And if they resist, they are punished by having the feeding-tube stuck in their rectum. And …'

'Rectum?' Peggy said.

'Up their bum, Peggy,' Maggie said.

Peggy gasped. 'I don't believe it.'

'It's true,' Maggie said. 'You ask Mrs Crawfurd. She's collected the stories of women force-fed in Perth Prison.'

'It gets worse,' Catherine said. 'Some women have had

the tube inserted in their vagina.'

'Vagina?' Peggy said.

'Here,' Maggie said, placing her hand over her groin.

'Jesus, Mary and Joseph,' Peggy gasped. Down there?

'Jesus, Mary and Joseph were conspicuous by their absence, Peggy,' Catherine said. 'That kind of treatment has nothing to do with feeding. It's deliberate sexual torture to punish women and break their will. By doctors. By male doctors.'

Peggy looked from one sister to the other in horror. 'But who could do such an evil thing? All men can't possibly be like that. Archie, Archie isn't like that.'

'No, you're right, Archie isn't like that,' Catherine said. 'He is an exception to the rule, along with some other men. Archie isn't like that because he, like us, was brought up as a socialist. We socialists believe in a different morality, one based on love and caring rather than oppression and competition. So, we've substituted ten socialist commandments for the religious ten commandments.'

Catherine looked at Maggie. 'Look forward to the day?' Maggie nodded assent.

The two sisters chanted:

'Look forward to the day when men
And women will be free;
As brothers and as sisters live
In peace and unity.'

Peggy nodded.

'While I remember, Peggy,' Catherine said, 'Mrs Crawfurd asked if you could help her leaflet the women in the South Govan Housing Association tomorrow morning. You can take the morning off.'

'Of course,' Peggy said. Maggie smiled at her and said, 'How about a nice cup of tea?'

As Peggy watched the kettle boil, she thought she could understand why women should be equal to men. But the idea of women going to bed with anyone they wanted, even within marriage, was plainly a mortal, a very mortal, sin. Maggie and Catherine were going far too far; they were in danger of losing their immortal souls. But then … but then Maggie looked so happy after going to bed with whatshisname – Charlie. She was positively glowing. I wonder what it's like to produce such happiness? Can that be love? Can there be love outside marriage after all? What's the words of that ould song again?

I know my love by his way of walking
And I know my love by his way of talking
And I know my love dressed in a suit of blue
And if my love leaves me what will I do …

And still she cried, 'I love him the best
And a troubled mind sure can know no rest.'
And still she cried, 'Bonny boys are few
And if my love leaves me what will I do?'

Part 3.

Chapter 24:
Backlands.

Peggy met Helen Crawfurd at the Pearce Institute, and as they set off down Morrison Street, Helen handed Peggy a packet of leaflets.

'We'll do Harmony Row today,' Helen said. 'The ILP is holding a meeting about what happens to rent control after the end of the War, for you can be sure the factors will want to put the rents up again, and we're not having that. There have been no repairs or maintenance done since the start of the War, and a lot of the houses are in shocking condition. So, we've got to let the women know what's what. We'll do each close together on the left hand side right down to the bottom, then come up the other side.'

'Right you are,' Peggy said.

Harmony Row was a long street of tenements. Like Neptune Street, there were three houses on each landing in the close, a room-and-kitchen on each side and a single-end in the centre, with an outside toilet on each half-landing. Helen and Peggy overlapped, leafleting one landing each. Peggy noticed that there were two things common to each close; the number of weans, and the smell. Even although there was an absence of children of school-age, toddlers were everywhere, playing in the close, the street or the back-green, most of them in bare feet and much-patched hand-me-down clothes. And there was a pervasive, pungent odour in the closes, a mixture of dirt, urine, stale food, soot and coal-gas. Imagine living your whole life in a kip like this, Peggy thought, bringing up a family in a small, one-roomed house. But there were thousands upon thousands of people in Govan and all over Glasgow doing just that.

An hour or so later, they neared the bottom of the street. 'In here,' Helen said, turning into a narrow wynd. Peggy followed; there was only enough room to proceed in single file. They came out of the wynd to find another tenement, three storeys high, a few feet away. The whole area was gloomy and there was an overpowering smell of shit. Peggy gagged and looked round. In the right-angle at the corner of the external tenement was a midden overflowing with human shit.

Helen held a handkerchief to her nose. 'This is called a backland, Peggy,' she said. 'The demand for housing is so great that they've built another tenement in the back-green of the original tenement. There are no toilets at all inside the backland, so people just do it in chanties and empty them into the midden. Come on, let's get rid of the leaflets and we'll see if Mrs O'Hara can offer us a cup of tea.'

As they climbed the stairs, it was so dark that Peggy could hardly see the letterboxes to post the leaflets. She noticed that a steady trickle of water was seeping down the stair. Then she realised from the stench that it was piss. Peggy gagged again; what in the name of God was next? When they reached the top floor, Helen knocked at a door.

'Mrs O'Hara,' Helen said. 'It's Mrs Crawfurd.'

A voice called, 'Come in, Helen, come in. The door's open.'

Helen and Peggy stepped inside the single-end. Although it was the middle of the day, it was so dark the gas-mantle was lit. Peggy could see a young woman sitting beside the fire in the grate, nursing a baby.

'This is Peggy O'Donnell,' Helen said. 'Peggy, this is Mrs O'Hara. She's from Ireland, like you.'

The young woman turned her head, and Helen exclaimed,

'Oh my God!' She had a black eye, a split lip, and a deep open cut on her cheek leaked blood. Peggy gasped with horror. Oh my God, it was bad enough when the Da slapped me, but that man has taken his fists to his own wife, Mother o' Mercy.

'Who did that, Kathleen?' Helen said. 'Was it your husband?' Kathleen nodded.

'Where is he?' Helen said.

'At the pub,' Kathleen said.

'Why did he do that?' Helen said.

'Because I went on the sufferagette demonstration up town. Someone must have seen me and told him.'

'Have you any iodine or plasters in the house?' Helen said.

'No,' Kathleen said.

'Peggy,' Helen said, 'run up to the chemist's and get a bottle of iodine and some plasters. Have you got some money?'

'Aye.'

When Peggy came back, Helen had rolled up her sleeves and was dipping her hankie in a bowl of warm water and patting Kathleen's mouth and cheek. Peggy handed her the iodine and plasters. Helen opened the iodine bottle, and tipped a few drops on the edge of her hankie.

'This will sting a bit,' she said.

Helen patted Kathleen's cheek carefully; the young woman groaned. Peggy winced.

'That's the ticket,' Helen said as she carefully placed a plaster over the cut.

After they had a cup of tea, Peggy and Helen went back out onto the street.

'Shouldn't we go to the Police?' Peggy said.

'That's precisely where we're going,' Helen said. 'If you want to join the movement, you'd better learn what we're up against.'

They hurried down Harmony Row towards Govan Road.

As they entered the police station in Albert Street, Helen said, 'This used to be the Govan Burgh Hall until they built the new one.'

'Good morning, Mrs Crawfurd,' the Desk Sergeant said with a smile. 'Good to see you again. And what is it today? The state of the middens? Rent strikes? Votes for women? The socialist revolution?'

Peggy could see that although he was smiling, the Sergeant was uneasy.

'I've come to report a crime, Sergeant MacKay,' Helen said. 'A bad case of wife-battering. At 947 Harmony Row, backland, entry 1, three up, first right. The name is O'Hara.'

'Och aye,' the Sergeant said. 'Michael and Kathleen O'Hara. I know them. He's a drunken brute, and she's not up to much. Irish, of course.'

'"Judge not that thou be not judged." Matthew, seven, one,' Helen snapped. 'I'm not interested in your offensive opinion, Sergeant. I am interested in what you propose to do about this particular drunken brute.'

Peggy shifted her feet and coughed. She had never heard anyone speak to a policeman like this before. And she was furious at his smart remark about the Irish.

'Mrs O'Hara was badly hurt, Sergeant,' Peggy said.

'And who might you be, Miss?' the Sergeant said.

'I'm Peggy O'Donnell.'

'Would that be the O'Donnells of one-oh-one-one Neptune Street?'

'That's right,' Peggy said.

The Sergeant scribbled something. 'Aye. We know your family.'

'Well,' Helen said. 'What do you propose to do, Sergeant MacKay?'

The Sergeant spread his hands. 'What can we do, Mrs Crawfurd? You know what's it's like. We'll go down to the house and Mrs O'Hara will refuse to make a complaint. She …'

'She's terrified her husband will beat her again,' Helen said. 'You know what it's like, Sergeant. Until you treat violence against women as the crime it really is, it will continue and get worse.'

Peggy held her breath. She admired Helen's persistence in giving out to the Sergeant, but was apprehensive about her directness. The Sergeant sighed. 'Very good, Mrs Crawfurd. I'll have the incident looked into.'

'Thank you, Sergeant,' Helen said. 'Come on, Peggy. We have the socialist revolution to attend to.' As they left the police station, Peggy could see the Sergeant grinning and shaking his head.

'There you have it, Peggy,' Helen said. 'The Police don't take what they call "domestics" seriously, believe you me. They say what goes on between a man and his wife is their own business. And the Sergeant has a point. Unless the police are very careful in the way they caution O'Hara, he is likely to beat his wife even more seriously. I know him; he's a bully and a drunk. So, we're taking a risk reporting it. But I think it's a risk worth taking. We can't allow this wife-battering to continue.'

'So, what can we do?' Peggy said.

'We've got to force the police to treat domestic violence as a serious crime like any other forms of assault,' Helen said. 'Women like Kathleen who stand up for their rights have got to be protected, not battered.'

'It's a sin,' Peggy said.

'You're right. That's exactly what it is,' Helen said. 'It takes a great deal of courage for working-class women in this city to fight for their rights.'

Begod, you're right there, Peggy thought. Why is it that women have to fight so hard for their basic rights? It's a sin right enough, and God shouldn't be after letting it happen.

They crossed the road. 'Wait till you see this,' Helen said as she turned into another wynd. In the back-green area of the tenements were three or four whitewashed single-storey cottages grouped round a small drying-green with washing hanging from a line, propped up by a clothes-pole. Peggy gaped at the incongruous sight.

'They're weavers' cottages,' Helen said, 'more than a century old. They built the tenement rectangle right round them. The cottages are damp and insanitary, and should be knocked down immediately. But the housing situation is so bad that they've always got tenants.'

'That's a sin too,' Peggy said.

'Aye,' Helen said. 'That's why the ILP campaigns for municipal housing. There's no profit in small tenement houses anymore, so the developers won't build them.'

As she walked along Dumbarton Road, Peggy thought: it's time to make a decision. These women – Catherine and Maggie MacDonald, Helen Crawfurd, Mary Barbour - are right. They really care about the working-people, especially women, and try to do something about it. They're brave and principled, and prepared to face the consequences of their actions – setting pillar-boxes on fire, smashing windows and giving policemen a roasting. I admire them. So, I'm going to join them. She opened the door of the Partick ILP branch office in Anderson Street.

Later, as Peggy walked back along Dumbarton Road, she saw Father Gallagher coming towards her. He grabbed her by the arm.

'Peggy O'Donnell,' he hissed. 'You hussy. You've forgotten the Fifth Commandment. 'Honour thy father and they mother.' And if that weren't bad enough, you're a damned Judas, a traitor to the One, Holy, Catholic and Apostolic Church. You'll burn in Hell ...'

Peggy wrenched her arm out of the priest's grasp. 'Take your hands off me,' she hissed, glaring at the priest. '"If I speak with the tongues of men and of angels, and have not charity, I am become as a sounding brass or a tinkling cymbal." You should remember that, Father. *Slán agat.*'

As she strode off down the road, Peggy could hear the priest choking with rage, and grinned to herself. Maynooth mongrel.

Peggy went into the sitting-room where Catherine and Maggie were drinking coffee.

'Get yourself a cup and saucer,' Maggie said. 'The coffee's still hot. And there's a freshly-baked currant scone.'

'I will,' Peggy said. 'But first, I've something to show you.'

'What's that, then?' Catherine said.

Peggy showed them her brand-new red ILP membership card. Catherine and Maggie jumped to their feet and kissed Peggy on both cheeks.

'Welcome to the Party, comrade!' Maggie said.

'A comrade and a sister,' Catherine said.

The three women hugged each other, all smiles. Maggie hurried out of the room and returned with a framed picture.

'Here, Peggy,' Maggie said. 'A wee present. It's the ten precepts of the Socialist Sunday Schools, sort of like the socialist Ten Commandments.

Peggy read:

— *Love your schoolfellows, who will be your fellow-workmen in life.*

— *Love Learning, which is the food of the mind; be as grateful to your teacher as to your parents.*

— *Make every day holy by good and useful deeds and kindly actions.*

— *Honour the good, be courteous to all, bow down*

to none.

— *Do not hate or speak evil of anyone. Do not be revengeful, but stand up for your rights and resist oppression.*

— *Do not be cowardly. Be a friend to the weak, and love justice.*

— *Remember that the good things of the earth are produced by labour. Whoever enjoys them without working for them is stealing the bread of the workers.*

— *Observe and think to discover the truth. Do not believe what is contrary to reason, and never deceive yourself or others.*

— *Do not think that those who love their country must hate and despise other nations, or wish for war, which is a remnant of barbarism.*

— *Work for the day when all men and women will be free citizens of one fatherland, and live together in peace and righteousness.*

Peggy looked up and smiled. 'Now isn't that the grand thing,' she said. 'Thank you. Thank you very much. I'll treasure this.'

Chapter 25:
Model Lodging Houses.

Catherine came into the kitchen just as Peggy finished putting the dishes away.

'I'm writing a pamphlet for the ILP on 'The Housing Question," Peggy,' she said, 'so I'm going on a series of housing tours in the city centre with Mr Fyfe, the Chief Sanitary Inspector. Would you like to come? I think you'd find it interesting.'

'Yes, I would,' Peggy said. 'I couldn't believe some of the things I saw in Govan with Mrs Crawfurd. People shouldn't have to live like that.'

'No, they shouldn't,' Catherine said. 'So, it's up to us in the ILP to do something about it. The Moderate Party won't do anything because it's the Moderates who own the bloody slums and make a fortune out of them.'

Catherine introduced Peggy to Mr Fyfe. He was a tall, clean-shaven man with a pleasant, open face but a brisk manner, and he looked you right in the eye.

'There are basically two types of lodging-house,' he said to Peggy. 'First, there are unofficial lodging-houses run without any kind of license or supervision, what we call the 'low' type. You could say this is an example of private enterprise. Basically, these are rooms in single-ends or rooms-and-kitchen where the owner or tenant lets out a space in a bed or on the floor to all-comers. These lodging-houses cater to the unemployed, the homeless and the hopeless. But they also often double as brothels and shebeens. They're grossly over-crowded and insanitary, but it's practically impossible to control them, although we do try. The second type is Model Lodging Houses built and run by the Corporation of Glasgow in which we offer basic accommodation, cooking and washing facilities. We control these Models, so we make every effort to enforce a minimum of public health regulations. They cater to itinerant workers, and those who're making an effort to stay out of the low type of lodging house. We're going to visit both types today, starting with the low type. There are dozens of this kind of lodging-house in the Calton area.'

As they made their way into a dark close, the first thing Peggy noticed was the smell. It was like the smell in the Govan backland, only worse, the unmistakeable odour of decay. It was all she could do to keep from throwing up, as she climbed a narrow stair. Mr Fyfe rapped at a door.

'Corporation,' he said.

The door opened and he entered, followed by Catherine and Peggy. A fire blazed in the grate. Peggy saw a man and a woman asleep in the inset bed, while an elderly woman sat in a chair in front of the fire. A fully-clothed man lay asleep on a thin mattress beside the wall, snoring loudly, a near-empty whisky bottle clutched in his hand. A slatternly young woman sat beside him, her back against the wall, nursing a baby. A small pile of grubby thin mattresses was stacked in a corner. There was nothing else in the room; the floor was filthy, and the single window was so dirty that hardly any light penetrated the gloom. My God, Peggy thought, how could anyone sleep in such a kip, and would you listen to yer man snoring?

'How much do you charge for a bed space, Mrs Black?' Mr Fyfe said, opening a notebook.

'Fourpence a night, usually,' the old woman said.

'Daylight robbery,' Catherine whispered.

More like night-time robbery, Peggy thought. 'Where do

you sleep?' she asked the old woman.

'In the chair.'

'How many lodgers do you take?' Catherine said.

'As many as I can get,' Mrs Black said.

As they went down the stair, Peggy held her nose and kept her mouth shut tight against the stench.

'That's not the worst I've seen,' Mr Fyfe said. 'Not by a long shot.'

'I wouldn't want to see worse than that,' Peggy said.

'Quite,' Catherine said. 'I don't think I could cope with worse than that. How do you do it, Mr Fyfe?'

'It's my job. I have to do it,' he replied.

Later, Mr Fyfe stopped in front of a huge stone building. 'This is the Garscube Home Model Lodging House,' he said. Peggy craned her neck and looked up. She counted five storeys; it looked more like a warehouse than a place where people lodged.

'It used to be a mill,' Mr Fyfe said, 'but the Corporation acquired it in 1892 and turned it into a Model. The ground floor is used for communal facilities – a kitchen with hotplates, toilets, a laundry and a shop – and the upper floors for dormitories. And there's a laundry, drying room and barbers in the basement. The charge is threepence-ha'penny a night. We'll have a good look round so that you get the idea.'

They entered the building. As Mr Fyfe and Catherine greeted the manager, Peggy peeked into the kitchen. There was a large coal-fired hotplate which made the room very warm. Several men in threadbare clothes were frying bacon on the hotplates. Other men lounged about or sat in the heat reading newspapers. One man, with a nose so broken it was concave, and wearing a cloth cap at a rakish angle, was assembling a rosewood flute. Peggy caught a quick movement out of the corner of her eye. She turned to see one of the men frying bacon glance over his shoulder to see who the visitors were. As quick as a flash, another man grabbed the rashers, stuffed them in his pocket, and shot out of the door. When the bacon-fryer turned back, he stared at the space where his rashers had been. He roared, looked round angrily, then sprinted out of the door. Peggy couldn't resist a smile.

The man with the flute lifted it to his mouth and started playing. Peggy sat down and listened as Mr Fyfe and Catherine talked to the manager. The man had a lovely lilting Irish style. She recognised the tune he was playing as *The Sligo Maid*. He went on to a second tune she recognised as *The Woman of the House,* but she didn't know his third tune. Peggy stood up and went over to him.

'That was grand,' she said. 'I know *The Sligo Maid* and *The Woman of the House,* but I didn't know the last tune.'

'It's *The Sailor's Bonnet*, a Sligo tune,' the flute player said.

Peggy stuck out her hand. 'I'm Peggy O'Donnell from County Donegal,' she said.

The flute-player shook her hand. 'Cathal Sweeney from Tubbercurry in County Sligo.' He gestured, sit-down.

'So, what's a nice Donegal girl like you doing in a Model?' Cathal said.

'I'm just visiting,' Peggy said, 'to see what it's like in a Model.'

'Well, you see it all,' Cathal said. 'It's not for the likes of you, girleen.'

'Do you never think of going home?' Peggy said.

Cathal laughed. 'Not a bit of it, Peggy. What could I bring home? I'm broke, I've two smashed legs from when a trench collapsed on me, and me belly's not too good either. No, I stay here where I can make do. I go out with the bhoys in the squad, sharpen their tools, do their messages, make the tea and fry up their food, and they give me a few bob. I've no complaints.'

Peggy saw Catherine beckoning her at the entrance to the kitchen, so she went into her handbag, and opened her purse without taking it out. She slipped a half-a-crown into Cathal's hand. 'Get ye a pint, Cathal, and keep playing, so. *Slán leat.*'

'God bless you and keep you, Peggy O'Donnell,' Cathal said.

As Peggy left the kitchen and joined Catherine and Mr Fyfe, she heard Cathal playing *The Donegal Reel*, and smiled to herself.

They climbed up to the top floor. The rank smell of human sweat and unwashed bodies hung in air, along with a dash of disinfectant. It's the smell of poverty, Peggy thought; sure, you can't get away from it in Glasgow. Pausing to get her breath back, she saw a long, narrow, dark wooden corridor which ran the length of the building. On either side of it were dozens of small wooden doors. Mr Fyfe opened one to reveal a cubicle about seven feet by five, containing a wooden bunk, a stool, a shelf, and a small cupboard. The wooden floor was bare. A thin, soiled, straw mattress lay on the bunk along with a grubby Army blanket. The wooden walls stretched up about eight feet, and Peggy saw that the roof space was open but covered, with a mesh of chicken-wire. Looking at the bed, she resisted the temptation to scratch herself.

'The boudoir,' Catherine murmured.

'It's not up to much,' Mr Fyfe said, 'but it's better than the low type.'

Divil a lot of difference, Peggy thought. She shivered as she looked up at the high ceiling. 'It's freezing in here,' she said.

Mr Fyfe nodded. 'Yes, there's no heating. The men sleep in their coats. If they've got one.'

As they left the Model, Mr Fyfe said, 'You should also see the ticketed houses, Miss O'Donnell. The Sanitary Inspectors visit them in the middle of the night to make sure they are not over-crowded. Would you like to go round with one of my Sanny Men?'

'I've already been round,' Catherine said. 'But you should go, Peggy. It will complete your housing education.'

'Yes, I'd like to go,' Peggy said, without any idea of what a ticketed house was.

'Right you are,' Mr Fyfe said. 'I'll talk to my Inspectors and give you some dates.'

On the way back to the West End in the tram, Peggy and Catherine were silent for a while.

'If I hadn't seen it with me own eyes, I wouldn't have believed people could be living in such conditions in the twentieth century,' Peggy said.

'I know,' Catherine said. 'And we are talking about thousands upon thousands of people. Two-thirds of Glaswegians live in single-ends and rooms-and-kitchens with outside toilets. The only way to tackle such a gigantic problem is to build municipal housing with government subsidies. That's what the ILP is aiming at. John Wheatley has made a start by proposing to build cottages at an annual rental of £8 with the surplus profit from the tramways. We can only solve such a huge problem by thinking big.'

Peggy nodded her agreement. 'Very big.

Chapter 26:
Ticketed Houses.

Mr McCallum was a stocky man with a no-nonsense manner like his boss, Mr. Fyfe.

'I'm Mr McCallum, Miss O'Donnell, Sanitary Inspector for the Eastern Police District. Mr Fyfe told me you wanted to see round the ticketed houses.'

'That's right,' Peggy said.

'Do you know what the ticketed houses are?'

'I haven't a clue,' Peggy said.

The Sanitary Inspector explained that in order to tackle the immense problem of overcrowding in small houses, with serious public health consequences, the Corporation of Glasgow had passed a Police Act in 1862. All these houses were measured up, and then their capacity was computed. A round metal disk or 'ticket' stating its maximum legal limit was then screwed to the door; children under eight counted as half-a-person. So, you could have a ticket which displayed: 3½. Then, from midnight until about four in the morning, the Sanitary Inspectors would raid these houses, and would prosecute the tenant if the house contained more occupants than was permitted by the ticket.

'In the middle of the night?' Peggy said. 'That's fierce harsh.'

'I agree,' Mr McCallum said. 'But we've simply got to control overcrowding because it results in epidemic diseases like cholera and typhus.'

'Surely the answer is to build new and bigger houses,' Peggy said.

'That's one way of doing it right enough,' Mr McCallum

said. 'But who is going to build them? The wages in Glasgow are too low for workers to afford higher rents. So there's no profit in new housing for builders. In the meantime, I have to do my job, although I sometimes find it difficult. Do you know how many ticketed houses there are?'

Peggy shook her head.

'There are over twenty-three thousand containing over eighty-five thousand people. And many of them are illegal shebeens and brothels. Do you know how many prostitutes there are in Glasgow?'

'No,' Peggy said.

'There are said to be seventeen thousand,' Mr McCallum said. Peggy gasped.

'Let's go, and you can see for yourself how it works. But please, leave all the talking to me,' Mr McCallum said.

'Sure, and I will,' Peggy said.

It was half-past-midnight when they climbed a tenement stair and stopped outside a door displaying a metal ticket which said: 3. The noxious smell was familiar.

'This is a room-and-kitchen,' Mr McCallum said, 'a small room-and-kitchen.' He rapped at the door, holding his notebook and a lamp. A moment later, feet could be heard shuffling towards the door.

'Who's there?' called a woman's voice.

'The Sanitary,' Mr McCallum replied.

The door creaked open. Peggy saw an elderly woman wearing a nightgown. Mr McCallum went straight into the house motioning Peggy to follow. She could see that although the furnishing was spartan, the house was clean, and neat and tidy.

'How many people are in the house?' Mr McCallum said.

'Just the three of us,' the elderly woman said, gesturing towards the bed. 'He's asleep.'

Peggy could see the head of a man, snoring, in the bed.

'And in the room?' Mr McCallum said, consulting his

notebook.

'Just herself.'

Mr McCallum knocked at the door of the room and to Peggy's surprise, breenged straight in, holding up his lamp. Peggy could see a young woman in the bed. She woke up and shaded her eyes.

'For the love a God,' she said. 'What's going on?'

'Sanitary,' Mr McCallum said. 'Are you on your own?'

'Of course I am,' said the young woman. 'What do you think I am?'

Mr McCallum's eyes swept round the room. He caught Peggy's eye and gestured. A man's jacket and trousers were on a chair with a pair of boots underneath. Oh my God, Peggy thought. Without warning, McCallum reached down and yanked the blanket and sheet off the bed, to reveal the naked woman, and a man in his shirt-tails.

'You bastard,' the young woman shrieked as she covered herself with the sheet. The man stretched, grinned, and said, 'Good morning to the Sanny Man – and his bit of stuff.'

'Shut your mouth if you know what's good for you,' Mr McCallum said, scribbling in his notebook. Peggy wished the floor would open up and swallow her.

McCallum said to the elderly woman, 'You'll be hearing from us.' As they left, the woman winked at Peggy. The door slammed behind them.

'What are you going to do?' Peggy said.

'Between thee and me – nothing,' Mr McCallum said. 'It's my discretion whether or not to prosecute. The young woman is the older woman's daughter; she works as a prostitute. But there was only one extra person in the house, so I'm going to give it a miss. She works as a prostitute because she has to. Her mother and father are past it, but they're decent enough people.'

As they traipsed down the stairs, Peggy thought; well, he may be a Sanny Man, but he's got a spark of humanity about him.

They carried on down the street, entered another close, and climbed the stair to the top floor. Mr McCallum adjusted his lamp to give more light and knocked at a door with a ticket saying: 4. 'It's a single-end,' he said.

The door opened, a man appeared yawning and blinking, and Mr McCallum strode straight in. There were two men asleep in the bed. So where does the man who opened the door sleep? Peggy thought. She noticed a draught in the room, looked round and saw that the window was wide open. Mr McCallum reached down under the bed and pulled out the hurley bed. It contained two men. Then he noticed the open window. He leant out and lifted his lamp.

'Come in out of there, you idiots' he called, 'it's dangerous.'

Two men in their shirt-tails crawled back in through the window, embarrassed looks on their faces. McCallum consulted his notebook, and addressed the man who had opened the door.

'Mr Meikle. That's seven people in a house measured for four. You'll be hearing from us.'

As they went back down the stairs, Peggy said, 'Were they so scared they climbed out of the window onto the roof, in the middle of the night?'

'Aye,' Mr McCallum said. 'A man fell to his death from the roof during a raid last month.'

'That's a sin,' Peggy said. 'That shouldn't be allowed to happen. You're just persecuting poor people and disturbing their sleep.'

McCallum shrugged in a helpless manner. 'What else can we do, Miss O'Donnell? These raids go on night after night, all round Glasgow. They're necessary. There's no other solution.'

The ILP hall was packed. As they sat waiting for the meeting to start, Archie said, 'Well, Peggy, what have you learned from your housing visits?'

'I've learned that the housing situation in Glasgow is diabolical,' Peggy said. 'The houses are far too small for the big families living in them. And all this raiding in the middle of the night by the Sanitary Inspectors is just pecking at the surface. It's not the people's fault that they're forced to crowd into these wee houses. And the raiding is … is humiliating. It's just punishing the poor for their poverty and adding insult to injury.'

'Ten out of ten,' Archie said. 'You've hit the nail on the head, Peggy. We must … ah, there's John.'

Councillor John Wheatley appeared and slapped the table-top with his hand. 'Comrades,' he said. 'It's time the capitalist class, and their lackeys, the Factors, realised a simple truth in Glasgow. The housing problem can't be solved by private enterprise. The problem's too big for that. The only way that decent, sanitary housing for the working-class can be provided is by the state subsidising it. Such housing should be built by Direct Labour and tenanted and managed by local authorities. We must put an end to warehousing the poor and force the Government to provide decent houses for the working-class. That's the priority of the Independent Labour Party; that's the central plank of our election manifesto in Glasgow, and we hope you will support us.'

As the storm of applause died down, Peggy turned to Archie and said, 'More power to yer man. He's got the right ideas.'

'He has that,' Archie said.

But Peggy began to realise that supporting Wheatley's ideas was going to cause trouble because neither the government nor the Corporation of Glasgow showed any enthusiasm for building good, subsidised working-class housing.

Chapter 27:
Proceed with Caution.

Several months had passed, it was now the summer of 1917 and Peggy was due to start as a Junior Student in Hillhead School with the new session in September. The War was dragging on, the casualty lists were getting even longer, and conscription had been introduced. Peggy asked Conal to come up to the sisters' house to discuss this.

'There's no way the bloody British Army's getting me,' Conal said. 'That's the Army that executed sixteen Irishmen after the Easter Rising.'

He intoned:

'O but we talked at large before
The sixteen men were shot,
But who can talk of give and take,
What should be and what not
While those dead men are loitering there
To stir the boiling pot?'

'William Butler Yeats,' Conal said, 'and he's a fecking West Brit. But he got one thing right. The pot's boiling right enough. The Brits are rattled enough at what's going on in the Ould Sod to declare an amnesty for all the prisoners captured after the Easter Rising. Is it any surprise the bhoys that are left from the Irish Volunteers and the Irish Citizens' Army are starting a new army? And another thing. One dead son is enough in the O'Donnell family. If I'm called up, I'm off over the water, true as God.'

One thing Peggy was sure about was that Conal knew his own mind.

Peggy met her mother in the busy Rialto café in Govan, but they managed to find an empty table at the back away from the chattering crowds of housewives out shopping.

'What's the craic, Ma?' Peggy said.

'Things are grand, thanks be to God,' Brighid said. 'Your Da's working most days as there's a steady stream of boats from Ireland, so the money situation isn't bad at all. Conal's doing fine at the newspaper and gives me his digs money regular as clockwork – although I hardly see him he's so busy. If it's not *Forward,* it's Sinn Fein. And if it's not Sinn Fein, it's the Celtic.'

Peggy laughed. 'That's our Conal right enough.'

'But I'm worried about this conscription,' Brighid said. 'Conal could be called up any day. He …'

'Don't you worry about that, Ma,' Peggy said. 'Conal won't go. He'd go home beyond as quick as a flash.'

'God bless the mark,' Brighid said.

'And Tim?' Peggy said.

'It looks like Tim has a vocation for the priesthood,' Brighid said. 'He's been talking with Father Gallagher about the junior seminary. Sure, it would be an honour and all, but I still worry about it. It's a hard life being a priest in Glasgow. And never marrying. Anyway, it's all in the hands of God.'

Peggy nodded and kept her counsel; she didn't want to start an argument with her mother. Brighid took Peggy's hand.

'Would you never bring yourself to see your father, Peggy? I know he misses you, and he's sorry for what he's done. And you're his only daughter. And he's really proud of you going on to be a scholar and a teacher and all. Only …'

'Only what, Ma?' Peggy said.

'Only why couldn't you do it in a Catholic school? You'll lose your faith doing it in a Protestant school. Father Gallagher is always on at us about that.'

'Father Gallagher and his likes are the reason why I don't want to study in a Catholic school,' Peggy said. 'I want to learn to think for myself. And as for the Da, it's up to him to apologise to me. Sure, and I'm not going crawling to him. He hit me. I didn't hit him.'

Brighid smiled. 'You're your father's daughter right enough,' she said. 'The pair of ye are as stubborn as ould donkeys.'

Catherine and Maggie sat down facing Archie in her sitting-room.

'Look, Archie,' she said. 'You've got to face facts. It would be a big mistake to go courting Peggy while she's doing her Junior Student's Certificate. You're in the same school, for God's sake, and you're ten years older than her. Peggy's highly intelligent, make no mistake, but she's still a naïve country girl. She's not a sophisticated townie like you. She's learning fast, but she still needs to be protected. That's where we come in.'

'That's why we think she should continue to stay with us,' Maggie said. 'We can help her with her studies. And help her keep out of trouble.'

'Do you not think that's being a bit, em, patronising?' Archie said. 'You said yourselves she's intelligent. And she's twenty – twenty-one later this year. She's a grown woman.'

'Archie,' Catherine said. 'You've got political enemies. You've even got a couple in the school. Think of the scandal if it came out you were seeing a student teacher in your own school. You would be accused of exploiting the girl. Whichever way you played it, you would be in the wrong. The capitalist newspapers would just love it. 'Older teacher seduces innocent young student teacher in the same school.' It could ruin your career as well as hers. Your enemies would have a field-day.'

'That's right,' Maggie said. 'Besides which, you've got

to give Peggy the space to concentrate on her studies and finish her course successfully. And learn for herself what kind of woman she wants to be. She's got good instincts, and she should be allowed to develop them in a natural manner, at her own pace.'

'And what about Elspeth Mavor?' Catherine said. 'You know she's set on you. She wants to marry you, for heaven's sake.'

'Elspeth's a nice woman,' Archie said, 'but I don't want to marry her. I'm afraid I don't love her. And she spends an awful lot of time telling me what to wear. She wants me to be respectable. Fat chance of that.'

'Then you must tell her,' Maggie said. 'You must bite the bullet and tell her that you don't love her, that you don't have a future together. It's dishonest not to.'

'All right, all right,' Archie said. 'I will.'

'And you must promise to leave Peggy alone until she finishes her training,' Catherine said.

Archie scowled. 'I promise.'

'If it's going to happen, it will happen, Archie,' Maggie said. 'Give it time. Don't rush the girl.'

Peggy twirled in front of the long mirror in the hall. She was wearing a silk slip, a full skirt nearly to her ankles, and a long-sleeved cotton blouse that the sisters had given her. My goodness, she thought, quite the toff.

'Look, Peggy,' Catherine said. 'We've got some more clothes that we've grown out of, and we'd like you to have them. It seems a pity to waste good money buying new clothes for school when you could use these. We've a few blouses, skirts and dresses, a jacket or two and a coat.'

'Thank you,' Peggy said.

'That outfit really suits you,' Catherine said. 'Quite elegant, really.'

'Yes. You look great, Peggy,' Maggie said. 'A real

schoolmarm. But you must wear a hat.'

'I'm not used to hats at all at all,' Peggy said.

'Oh, ladies must wear hats in the street, 'Catherine said, 'especially lady school-teachers. Here, try this one.'

Peggy put on a broad-brimmed hat with a coloured ribbon trailing from it. She looked at herself in the mirror, tipped the hat slightly, and not having worn one since her interview, burst into a fit of the giggles. The doorbell rang.

'I'll get it,' Peggy said, as Catherine adjusted the hat to a less rakish angle.

There was an appreciative whistle. 'Well, well, well, would you look at that stoater,' Archie said. 'She's far too gorgeous for a mere school.'

'Ah, get away with you,' Peggy said. 'You're after codding me.' But she felt a thrill of excitement at Archie's compliment.

'You look very smart,' Archie said. 'You'll take Hillhead School by storm. That is, if you're not signed up for the pictures first!'

Peggy couldn't help laughing, but felt embarrassed as Maggie handed her a lipstick, and said, 'Just to finish off the image of the perfect young school-teacher.'

Later, as they all sat in the sitting-room drinking coffee, Catherine said, 'There's another thing, Peggy. You're going to have to rein in your political activity. First of all, you're not going to have much free time because you'll have homework – preparing lessons and the like – in the evenings. Second, as a trainee teacher, it's simply not advisable to be seen involved in radical socialist politics. You've no idea how much the Tories hate us. If they went out to get you, you could be withdrawn from training just like that.'

'That's right,' Maggie said. 'So, ca' canny, as the engineers say.'

'But … but Archie's heavily involved,' Peggy said.

'Yes, he is,' Catherine said, 'but he's a graduate of the university, and an experienced teacher. You're neither. And he's a man.'

'John McLean was a graduate of the university, an experienced teacher and a man,'

Peggy said. 'But they fired him.'

'They did,' Maggie said. 'But John is a die-hard, and a bit reckless. Archie is a die-hard, but he's not so reckless.'

'I don't like the idea of stopping working for the Party just because of a job,' Peggy said. 'And it's an important time with the Clyde Workers Committee calling for a 40-hour week.'

'Aye, it is an important time,' Archie said. 'You're right there. But you're not an engineer, Peggy. My suggestion would be that you continue with women's issues until you finish your training. These are just as important as the forty-hour week. Rent restriction and the housing problem are going to explode at the end of the War. And these are issues you know about. Agreed?'

Peggy shifted in her chair for a couple of moments. 'All right. Agreed.'

Chapter 28:
School.

Archie met Peggy at the double iron school-gates.

'Well, well, you do look the part, Peggy,' Archie said, taking in her smart coat, knitted cardigan, white silk blouse, grey skirt, heels and the hat with the coloured ribbon. The current fashion for women was an hour-glass figure achieved by tight corsets, but Catherine and Maggie had pooh-poohed that idea as unnatural and dangerous for women's bodies, so Peggy wasn't wearing one. But she felt ill-at-ease as she was totally unused to all this finery, on the one hand, and her loose clothes displayed her natural curves, on the other.

'A regular schoolmarm,' Archie said. 'Mr Maxwell will assign you to your class. And remember, just be yourself. Good luck.'

'Thank you,' Peggy said, quaking inside while still managing to carry herself erect.

'I'm assigning you to Mrs Morrison's class, S2,' Mr Maxwell said. 'Kirsty is not only an experienced teacher, but also she has mentored Junior Students in the past. So, she'll look after you, and you could learn a lot from her. I think you'll get on well.'

He knocked at the door of the Women Teachers' Staffroom. A middle-aged woman opened the door.

'Ah, Mrs Morrison,' Mr Maxwell said. 'This is your new Junior Student, Miss Peggy O'Donnell, who is from Ireland. Miss O'Donnell, Mrs Morrison.'

Peggy saw a smartly dressed woman, about fifty with a

buxom figure and an air of brisk efficiency. She smiled and extended her hand. 'I'm pleased to meet you, Peggy,' she said. 'Mr MacDonald has been singing your praises. Thank you, Mr Maxwell. Give me a moment to collect my papers, Peggy, before we go into the lions' den.'

As they walked along the corridor, Mrs Morrison explained what they were going to do. 'I'll introduce you to the class,' she said. 'Then you sit at the back, listen, and make any notes you wish. I may ask you the odd question, but for the first few days, it's best if you just observe how we do things. Alright?'

'Oh, yes,' Peggy said. 'That's grand.'

'It's a good class where most of the pupils actually want to learn,' Mrs Morrison said, 'so that's half the battle won.'

Mrs Morrison introduced Peggy to the pupils, and she went and sat at the back of the class followed by many curious eyes. She soon realised that Mrs Morrison was a gifted teacher. She imposed order on the class from the first moment, had a warm manner but brooked no nonsense, and noticed everything. She asked questions, encouraged the shy, and praised good answers. The class was geography, and the country in question was Ireland. Mrs Morrison went through the main towns and cities, rivers, mountain ranges, and came on to exports. The pupils chanted cattle, bacon, and dairy produce including eggs, cheese and butter.

'Have we missed any important exports, Miss O'Donnell?' Mrs Morrison said, taking Peggy by surprise.

She thought for a moment, and then said, 'People.'

The class laughed, but Mrs Morrison stopped it quickly, and said that from 1845 to the present day, Ireland's biggest export had in fact been people. She started writing with chalk on the blackboard:

Population of Ireland
1841- 8 million
1851 - 6.5 million
1911 - 4.4 million

'As a result of *An Gorta Mór*, the Great Potato Famine in Ireland, which lasted from 1845 to 1849, the population dropped by nearly 50 per cent in 70 years, as you can see,' Mrs Morrison said. 'A million people died and another million emigrated in the immediate aftermath of the Famine. Thousands upon thousands came to Glasgow, so that nowadays, it's reckoned that two-thirds of the population of the Greater Glasgow area are of Irish descent. So, Miss O'Donnell was quite correct in what she just said. Write these figures down in your jotters.'

As the pupils scribbled away, Mrs Morrison flashed a smile at Peggy.

At lunchtime, Peggy and Mrs Morrison headed towards the female staff room.

'Sure, and you know your stuff about *An Gorta Mór*, Mrs Morrison,' Peggy said.

'Call me Kirsty, Peggy,' Mrs Morrison said. 'I should hope I do know my stuff. My family were Protestants from County Donegal. Not all Irish are Catholics, you know. And the Famine killed Protestants as well as Catholics.' She stopped at the staff-room door, put her hand on Peggy's arm, and recited:

'Great distress was in the west,
Disraeli got a dreadful scare,
The land of Connaught, depend upon it,
It was near to be civil war;
Gladstone now will quell the row
And I hope next year there will be no need;
Believe me now, it's true you'll find
You'll see a row about the seed.'

'Good woman yourself,' Peggy exclaimed. 'That's a new one on me. Although I know the song *Skibbereen*, of course.'

'So do I, Peggy. So do I,' Mrs Morrison said.

As they ate their lunchtime sandwiches, Kirsty said,

'Now Peggy, I'd like you to prepare a forty-five-minute, one-period lesson on the nature and effects of the Famine in County Donegal. For next week. You'll find a lot of reference material and possibly even some photographs in the Mitchell Library. Do you think you can do that?'

'I'll give it a go,' Peggy said. 'How do you want me to present it?'

'That's entirely up to you,' Kirsty said. 'But the idea is to put some flesh on the bones of the statistics, to illustrate them with some real human stories. If you think I can help you, ask me. Agreed?'

'Agreed,' Peggy said. 'I can remember some of my grandmother's stories of the Famine in Donegal.'

'Good,' Kirsty said. 'That's exactly what we want to hear.'

Peggy was astonished at how many holdings of official reports and enquires about the Famine there were in the Mitchell library, not to mention travellers' accounts, each one more harrowing than the last. She took copious notes and, at home, wrote down everything she could remember from her grandmother's stories. When she assembled her lesson, she realised it was far too long and detailed. She was groaning out loud over her numerous sheets of paper on the kitchen table when Maggie came and asked what the matter was. Peggy explained.

Maggie sat down opposite Peggy and said, 'Now. Don't look at your notes, but tell me the story of the Famine in Donegal, emphasising what you think are the main points in the narrative.'

'When the potato crop failed in 1845, it meant that the peasantry had to go to the shops for food,' Peggy said. 'But, that meant prices rose sharply as the supply of foodstuffs dwindled. The people couldn't afford them, so they were forced to eat grass and seaweed. As there was no money to pay the rents, there were wholesale evictions. Typhus broke out, and thirteen thousand people died in the county between 1845 and 1850. Those who could emigrated on coffin-ships to Canada and the United States. On the island of Arranmore, the landlord evicted the whole population and told them to make their way to Donegal Town, where a ship was waiting to take them to America. It was mid-winter, freezing cold and there was deep snow on the ground. My grandmother remembered seeing these people freezing on the quay in waiting for the ship, with no cover at all. A few decent landlords and the Quakers set up soup-kitchens and tried to feed them from what became known as Famine Pots.'

'That's very good,' Maggie said. 'It's concise and clear. Now write that down on three or four pages, and you'll have your lesson. You'll find you will remember additional details to exemplify your points as you go along.' Maggie paused. 'I remember Catherine told me about the poem you recited to her about the money-lender. What was it called?'

'*The Gombeen Man*, by Joseph Campbell,' Peggy said.

'Right,' Maggie said. 'Can you think of an Irish poem about the Great Famine?'

Peggy thought for a moment. 'Yes. Yes, I can.'

'Excellent,' Maggie said. 'Recite that to the children at the end of your lesson, and it will provide a fitting conclusion.'

On the day of the lesson, Peggy did as Maggie suggested. Her pupils seemed mesmerised by her story.

'Here's what a traveller said about one cottage during the height of the Famine,' she said. She read out from a typed sheet:

> 'One dirty cabin, not more than twelve feet
> square contained 17 persons. Two or three of
> them were full grown men, gaunt and hunger
> stricken, willing and wishful to obtain work,
> but unable. The mothers, crouching over a few

> embers of turf, looked misery itself. Two or three half-naked children were lying in one corner of the room, partly covered by an old rug, while several other children were at the time stowed away in darkness and filth.'

You could have heard a pin drop in the class. The children stared at Peggy in disbelief.

'Now, boys and girls,' Peggy said. 'This isn't a story. This isn't a fairy-tale by Hans Christian Anderson. This actually happened. Some of my ancestors died in the Famine. My granny can remember seeing the people from Arranmore Island freezing on that quay when she was a girl. And it could've been prevented. The problem was … the problem was that the British government simply didn't care about the Irish people. And when eventually they realised the scale of the Famine, what they did was too little, too late. The catastrophe had already happened. Do you understand, children?'

'Yes, miss,' the pupils chorused.

'I'll finish the lesson with a poem about the Famine, so,' Peggy said. She took a deep breath, and recited:

'I saw fathers, boys and girls,
With rosy cheeks and silken curls,
All a-missing and starving
For a mouthful of food to eat.
When they died in Skibbereen
No shrouds or coffins were to be seen:
But patiently reconciling themselves
To their desperate, horrid fate.
They were thrown in graves by wholesale
Which caused many an Irish heart to wail.
And caused many an Irish boy and girl
To be most glad to emigrate.'

There was a dead silence as she finished. Peggy walked to the back of the class and sat down. Mrs Morrison stood up and said, ‘Thank you, Miss O’Donnell, for that moving account of the Great Famine in County Donegal in Ireland. Class – dismiss!’

The pupils filed out, quieter than usual. Peggy approached Kirsty, who took her hands in her own.

‘Peggy, my dear,’ Kirsty said, ‘you are a natural. You nearly had me in tears.’

Chapter 29:
Erin Go Bragh!

As Peggy pored over her English lesson plan in the kitchen, the telephone in the hall rang. Someone answered it, and Catherine shouted, 'It's Conal for you, Peggy.'

'Hello,' Peggy said.

'It's me,' Conal said. 'How's about ye, Peigeen?'

'I'm grand,' Peggy said.

'Can you meet me in half-an-hour in the University Café?' Conal said.

Peggy hesitated, thinking of her lesson preparations.

'It's important,' Conal said.

'All right, so,' Peggy said, and hung up.

Catherine passed and said, 'What's Conal up to now?'

'I don't know,' Peggy said, 'but he's up to something.'

Peggy could see that Conal was excited for he turned his cup of coffee round and round.

'It's like this, Peggy,' he said. 'Sinn Fein is gaining ground by leaps and bounds in the Ould Sod. Dillon and his Home Rulers are finished, even if they don't know it yet. The Irish people are finished with Britain. What with the executions and now conscription, we've had enough of the Crown.'

'What does the Da say to that?' Peggy said.

Conal grinned and put his hand over his mouth. 'I have to keep me trap shut in the house. The Da is still an old-fashioned Home Ruler even although he didn't approve of the executions. To tell ye the truth, I'd have rented a place of me own by now except that I don't want to leave the Ma on her own, especially now that Tim is going for a priest.'

'Is that for sure?' Peggy said.

'Yes, he's starting at Blairs College in a few weeks. So, I'm going over to Dublin for a couple of weeks,' Conal said. 'I'm going to cover things for *Forward*, and freelance articles for the *Herald* and other papers.'

'And work for Sinn Fein,' Peggy said.

Conal nodded. 'That's right. And work for Sinn Fein. That's where the future of Ireland is, Peggy. Not with the Brits.'

'You better be careful,' Peggy said. 'You'll have the Peelers here and in Dublin watching out for you.'

'I know,' Conal said. 'But I'll be watching out for them.'

'That would be wise,' Peggy said. 'The Brits are in big trouble. The Somme is nothing but a slaughterhouse, there's no sign of an end to the War, there's widespread opposition to conscription, the Clydeside workers are agitating, and the Government doesn't know what to do about Ireland. They'll be watching Sinn Fein like hawks.'

'Jaysus, I know that,' Conal said. 'But we're watching them closely. And at home, we have the advantage.'

'Just be careful. Write to me and let me know what's going on. And keep in touch with the Ma because she'll be worried for you. And don't do anything foolish.'

As 1918 grew to a close, Peggy saw that Conal's predictions proved uncannily accurate. The Man-Power Bill introduced conscription of all men over the age of eighteen and met with nationwide resistance. John McLean was everywhere, speaking against the War; he was arrested, tried, given five years penal servitude, and freed after seven months following public uproar. Helen Crawfurd and her colleague Agnes Dollan led the Women's Peace Crusade, holding kitchen and street meetings, and leafleting non-stop, a task in which Peggy helped. In Ireland, the General Election saw Sinn Fein gain seventy-three seats, but they refused to go to

Westminster and founded Dail Eireann, the Irish Parliament, where there was talk of declaring independence. What was happening in Ireland was the talk of the steamie. Brighid told Peggy that quite a few of the young Irishmen in the Irish Channel had vanished, apparently back to Ireland. She also brought the sad news that Donnie MacCaskill had been killed on the Somme. Oh God, Peggy thought, first Eamonn, now Donnie. All these fine young men are being slaughtered. Where was it all going to end?

The agitation in the Clydeside shipyards and engineering works continued apace, where shop-stewards' committees now seemed to be running production. The Clyde Workers' Committee accelerated its campaign for a 40-hour week. In January 1919, the Committee sent a delegation to the Lord Provost of Glasgow asking him to convey the demand for the 40-hour-week to the Prime Minister. He asked them to come back for a reply on Friday January 31st. A huge demonstration was planned in George Square on that day, with workers marching in from all districts of Glasgow. Peggy decided that this was an occasion she could not miss. So, she approached Mrs Morrison with some trepidation, asked for the day off and explained why.

'Of course you can have the day off,' Kirsty said. 'I wish I could go myself. My father was a shipyard engineer at Harland and Wolff's, and it's a crime that these men work the hours they do in the conditions they do. They deserve a forty-hour week and I hope they get it.'

'I agree with you completely,' Peggy said.

'So off you go,' Kirsty said. 'But we'll keep this between ourselves, and if anybody asks, I'll say I gave you the day off to catch up on your reading. How does that sound?'

'That sounds wonderful,' Peggy said. 'Thank you so much.'

Chapter 30:
Bloody Friday, January 31st, 1919.

Peggy was first off the subway at St. Enoch Square station. Running up the stairs, she dodged between the trams in Argyle Street and strode up Queen Street towards George Square. In her long skirt, shaped jacket, white silk blouse and broad-brimmed hat, she stood out amongst the streams of working people heading in the same direction. Her height – five feet seven inches – and her erect and graceful carriage caught people's attention; she marched rather than walked.

A clatter of hooves rang out behind her, and a dozen mounted police in two files trotted past; Jesus, Mary and Joseph, she thought, would you look at the size of them peelers! They've got the cheek to run down the Irish, but do they know that all their horses come from Ireland? Passing Royal Exchange Square, the sound of the rhythmic tramp of feet, the oomphah of a brass band and a surge of singing floated down to her. She reached the top of the street just in time to see a long column of workers led by the 40-Hours Strike Committee and Mrs Reid carrying a red flag as big as a blanket march into George Square, singing:

Then raise the scarlet standard high,
Within its shade we'll live and die,
Though cowards flinch and traitors sneer,
We'll keep the red flag flying here.

Peggy joined in singing the familiar anthem, and the Glaswegians were – what was it they said again? – fairly giein' it laldie, the song echoing and booming round the stone walls of the square.

In the square, Peggy looked round; it was nearly noon. Although it had rained earlier, a pale winter sun now gleamed, and the day was heaving with thousands upon thousands of people. The brass three-masted ship perched on a globe on top of the Merchants' House building glittered in the sun. The air was full of the pungent smell of unwashed bodies and damp clothes, while clouds of cigarette smoke billowed over Peggy's head. Two women wearing expensive fur coats chattered their way past in a miasma of perfume, ignoring the demonstration, probably heading for the Willow Tearooms in Sauchiehall Street.

The crowd was composed mainly of men from the shipyards and engineering shops wearing cloth caps. But there were plenty of women and children too, including a cheerful bunch of mill girls in headscarves, arms linked, singing *Tipperary* in tune with the brass band. A small boy jinked past Peggy, dribbling a ball between the legs of the bystanders.

'Gaun yersel, son,' a worker laughed, 'you'll get a gemme forra Celtic yet.'

Vendors were busy selling the *Forward*, and also *The Worker* and a wide range of other socialist pamphlets. Dozens of well-dressed onlookers stood at the windows of the North British Station Hotel, the office buildings at the west end of the Square, and on the flat roof of the Post Office. Willie Gallagher was haranguing the crowd from the plinth of Gladstone's statue, while every lamppost near the statue had two or three men clinging to it.

Peggy knew from the 40-Hour Strike Committee's Bulletin that the leaders had warned the Corporation to stop the trams running, so she was surprised to see one passing in front of the Post Office. There was an angry roar from the crowd. She reached the pavement as the tram turned into South Frederick Street. She was just in time to see a worker dart forward, pull the tram's trolley down from the overhead electric cable and cut the rope. A soldier in the uniform of the HLI slung a punch at the worker, who promptly belted him back, flooring him. That's torn it.

An order was barked. The line of Policemen in front of the City Chambers drew their batons and charged into the meeting, clubbing the strikers indiscriminately. As the crowd careered across the square, Peggy was lifted clean off her feet for a couple of seconds and spun round, arms pinned to her side, unable to move and scarcely able to breathe. The demonstrators rallied, and with a ragged yell, counter-charged the police.

Peggy tripped on something soft. Looking down, she saw an unconscious mill girl lying on her side in a sodden flowerbed, the clear imprint of a muddy boot stamped on her face. Peggy bent down to help the girl, but the crowd surged around her and she was dragged away. Then, right in front of Peggy, a moustachioed constable batoned a worker on the head. His cap flew off, and blood sprayed over Peggy's face. The injured man's wife screamed as she tried to support him. As the policeman, well over six feet tall, swung his baton again, Peggy grabbed his wrist.

'For God's sake,' she shouted, 'that's a harmless wummin.'

The policeman tried to break free, but Peggy held onto his wrist. He grabbed her arm with his other hand, but she walloped him with her handbag, and he staggered back, dropping his baton; Peggy kicked it into the melee. Another policeman threw a punch at her; she ducked the blow. The policeman's helmet fell off; Peggy grabbed it and launched it into the man's face before taking off into the crowd. As she did so, she heard someone shout her name and glimpsed her father battling his way towards her, but he was swirled away.

Peggy was now on the north side of the Square. Suddenly, she saw Conal and Harry McShane commandeer a lorry full of crates of lemonade which had been forced to a halt in front of the hotel. They climbed on board. Pumping the horn, Conal steered the lorry through the seething crowd. He turned left into North Frederick Street, scattering a line of policemen pursuing demonstrators. Her heart in her mouth, Peggy barged her way through the crowd and watched from the safety of a close-mouth.

In low gear, Conal drove the lorry to the pub near the top of the hill, slewed it broadside across the street, bonnet to the wall, stopped the engine, and yanked on the handbrake. Harry jumped out and yelled at a group of demonstrators fleeing up the hill. They stopped and quickly unloaded the crates, making a barricade across the street beside the lorry, piling the crates on their sides with the necks of the bottles to hand. Conal shouted at other strikers to bring crates of empty beer bottles out of the pub. Behind them, at the top of the hill, a gaggle of local women and children shrieked encouragement.

A large group of policemen charged up the hill at the barricade, batons drawn. The strikers threw a hail of bottles at them, and the police fled in an explosion of shattering glass. Behind Peggy, there was a roar of triumph; they must have driven the peelers all the way back to the City Chambers.

The police at the foot of North Frederick Street were reinforced by half-a-dozen mounted officers. Peggy watched them come trotting up the hill, their long truncheons resting on the shoulders like sabres, followed by the officers on foot. Bloody Cossacks; the bhoys have had it if they get in amongst them. But she saw Conal jump out in front of the demonstrators, waving his arms, an empty beer bottle in each hand.

'Wait!' he shouted, 'wait!' He sprinted back behind the barricade.

When the mounted police broke into an uphill trot, he yelled, 'Now!' A barrage of bottles arced through the air, and the police broke and cantered downhill to yells of derision from the strikers. Peggy slipped between them, and gathering her skirt in one hand, ran up the hill towards Conal, but he vanished into Cathedral Street.

Peggy glanced round the group of angry men. She could see from their campaign medals that many were ex-servicemen, spoiling for more action. When half-a-dozen policemen appeared at the top of John Street, there was a howl of rage from the demonstrators. The constables fled along Cathedral Street, and the chase was on. A couple of the policemen ducked into a tenement close, and the workers and Peggy swarmed after them. Her eyes lit up and a grin spread across her face as she realized the police were trapped like rats in a box. But in the back court, the policemen had vanished. A window on the second floor shot up, a housewife leaned out and bawled, 'The polis is behind the midden, boys.'

The men ran round the midden, beyond which was a high wall. Peggy saw the two terrified policemen jump up and try to scramble over into the adjoining back-court, but the demonstrators grabbed them by the legs, pulled them down, and showered punches and kicks on them, to the vocal encouragement of several women hanging out the tenement windows. Peggy realized with a sickening lurch of her stomach that the peelers were likely to be battered to death.

'Right,' she snapped, 'that's enough, lads.'

The workers stopped and stared at the young woman in astonishment. Take charge quickly, girleen, or there will be blue bloody murder.

'Right,' Peggy yelled. 'Off with their clothes.'

With a roar of glee, the demonstrators ripped the uniforms and underclothes off the policemen. A burly worker stepped back and swung his boot to kick one of the policemen in the balls, but Peggy grabbed his arm.

'No, that's enough,' she said again. 'Leave him be.'

The men propelled the naked policemen towards the close. As they passed underneath, a housewife emptied the contents of a chamber-pot over them, screeching, 'Take that, ya swine.'

The demonstrators threw the policemen out into the street, and fell about laughing as the naked, barefoot, bloodied men limped away towards the High Street, pursued by catcalls and showers of missiles. Peggy hadn't seen Conal since the fracas in North Frederick Street and was worried for his safety. But she knew he was covering the demonstration for the *Forward*, so she hurried off towards the office.

When Peggy burst into the *Forward* office, she saw Conal and the editor, Tom Johnston, a veteran socialist, having a heated argument. Suddenly, seeing her, Tom broke off what he was saying, and stared. Conal spun round, and gasped.

'My God, Peggy,' he said, 'your face is covered with blood. What on earth …?'

Peggy took her hand-mirror out her bag, scowled at her bloody reflection, and wiped her face with her handkerchief.

'The police attacked the strikers without any provocation,' she said. 'That's what happened. There was a hell of a fight.'

'All right, all right,' Tom said. He turned to Conal. 'Write up your story.'

As Peggy watched and added her contribution, Conal spent the early part of the evening typing up his story, even although they knew that Saturday's edition had already been printed and distributed. Conal pulled the last sheet of paper out of his typewriter, added it to the others, and handed them to the editor. Tom read the story and laughed out loud.

'"The *Glasgow Herald* as the mouthpiece of disordered capitalism cries steadily for the iron heel,"' Tom said. 'I like that.'

'The Strike Committee was disordered too,' Conal said. 'They didn't have any plan for action. They should've been talking to the soldiers in Maryhill Barracks right at the start of the strike. If they'd joined the strikers, they could've taken Glasgow over.'

Tom sighed. 'This is Glasgow, Conal, and it's nineteen-nineteen. It's not Dublin in nineteen-sixteen. And it's the City Chambers in George Square, not the Winter Palace. What the ex-servicemen want is work, and what the workers want is a forty-hour week, not a revolution. But after that riot, they're not going to get any reduction in their working hours.'

'We'll see about that,' Conal said. 'There must have been twenty or thirty thousand people in George Square. They didn't turn out on a January morning for nothing. And they were carrying a Red Flag, not a St. Andrew's cross.'

Tom stood up and walked over to the window. 'The trouble with you Irish is that you judge everything by what happened in the Dublin Post Office in nineteen-sixteen. I've told you before; it's not like that here. This is a different country. There's no tradition of violence amongst the working people in Scotland.'

'Jaysus, that's a pity,' Conal retorted. 'Because there's a tradition of violence *against* the working people of Scotland. That was a police riot today, Tom. The Peelers attacked a perfectly peaceful crowd; they went fecking mad, so they did.'

Tom returned to his desk and sat down again, shaking his head. 'Look. I agree. From what you say, the police did use excessive force. But …'

Peggy snorted and said, 'But nothing. Do you know what I think?'

'What?'

'I think the Government deliberately rejected the Forty Hour week demand to provoke the strikers. I think the police attack on the crowd was deliberate. I think they want to smash the movement now the war's over.'

'That's a conspiracy theory for which there's absolutely

no evidence,' Tom said. 'I will not print speculation, Peggy. The authorities would close the paper. This is a time to keep our heads.'

Peggy slammed the door as she stormed out of the office.

Chapter 31:
Bloody Friday: Aftermath.

Early the next morning, Peggy took the subway up to George Square to see the aftermath of the riot. Crunching through broken glass, the first thing she noticed was the large flagpole at the north end leaning at a crazy angle. Then she saw three cloth caps and an empty woman's shoe on the pavement; one of the caps was full of dark congealed blood. Turning, she froze. Young, helmeted soldiers were patrolling the square in pairs, with slung rifles and fixed bayonets. A barbed wire barricade stood in front of the doors of the City Chambers. Harry McShane appeared.

'I don't believe it,' Peggy said.

'You better believe it, comrade,' Harry said. 'Look up there.' Peggy's eyes followed the direction of Harry's pointing finger. She saw a sandbagged Vickers machine-gun at the edge of the flat roof of the Post Office. Harry turned and pointed again; there was another machine-gun on top of the North British Station Hotel.

'There are hundreds of troops,' said Harry. 'They've brought them up from England by train. They're just daft laddies who haven't been in action. I went up to Maryhill Barracks last night with some of the comrades to talk with the soldiers, but they're locked in. The officers are afraid they might join us.'

'Right,' Peggy said.

'Come on,' said Harry, 'let's try and talk sense to these squaddies.' He and Peggy approached a couple of young soldiers.

'Comrades,' said Harry, 'why …'

'I'm not your fucking comrade,' a soldier said. 'I know what I'd like to do wiv you, you Scotch bastard.'

'Fuck off,' his mate said, unslinging his rifle. 'This is better than bottles.'

An officer appeared and jammed his swagger-stick under Harry's chin.

'Stay away from my men, you Bolshevik scum,' he said. 'Or I'll let them loose on you.'

Peggy put her hand under Harry's elbow and towed him away as the officer loosened the flap of his revolver holster.

'You should be ashamed of yourselves,' Harry shouted, 'we're all workers together.'

'Jaysus, leave it, Harry,' Peggy said. 'These gobshites would shoot us as soon as look at us. Don't cast your revolution before swine.'

Back in the *Forward* office, Peggy and Conal discussed Saturday's local newspaper coverage of the riot with Tom Johnson. Peggy was still shaken by her encounter with the soldiers.

'It's clear that most of the reporters were appalled by the violence,' Tom said.

'They were,' Conal said. 'But listen to the language in the leaders. Here's today's *Glasgow Observer.*'

He read aloud:

> *'The main cause of the trouble is to be found in the fact that the workers have allowed the powerful machinery of their trade organizations to be seized by Extremists who have imbibed the Bolshevist dictum that force is right ... '*

'That's the Catholic paper,' Tom said. 'They're going to say that anyway.'

'Alright. But how about the *Herald* leader?' Conal replied, reading aloud again:

> *'It is impossible to repress indignant comment on*

the disgraceful proceedings of yesterday in George Square and other parts of the city. Those primarily responsible are of course the men who from the outset flouted law and decency, and deliberately set themselves to paralyse the orderly functioning of the community.'

Tom groaned. 'What do you expect? It's the local capitalist press.'

'I know,' Conal said. 'It's about time we got rid of those local bloody capitalists. Look. This was all planned. The government knew it was going to reject the Forty Hour demand. They took a week to reply so that they could plan how to transport the troops and the tanks up to Glasgow. And they didn't use the lads from the Royal Scots Fusiliers in Maryhill Barracks. They've all been in Flanders; they know what it's really like out there. No. The troops they sent are all raw recruits from England who will obey their officers. They'd mow the workers down just like that. That's the reality, boss. It was a conspiracy.'

'It's farcical. It's, it's nonsense,' Tom said. 'It's a complete over-reaction. Glasgow isn't St. Petersburg, for God's sake.'

Peggy slapped the desk with her hand. 'No, it's not,' she snapped. 'But it's the nearest bloody thing Britain has got to it.'

Chapter 32:
A Casualty of the Riot.

When Pat O'Donnell came to, it was to a blinding pain in his head. He looked around, but his vision was clouded by black spots. He tried to raise himself, but a wave of nausea made him fall back. His head felt heavy; he fingered it to find that it was covered with bandages. With difficulty, he rolled on his side and his vision began to clear. He was in a side room of a hospital ward. A nurse bustled in.

'Ah, there you are, Mr O'Donnell,' she said. 'Back in the land of the living.'

Pat tried to reply, but all that came out was a gurgle. Holy mother o' God, Pat thought, what's the matter with me? The nurse felt his forehead, tutted, and said, 'I'll just go and fetch the doctor.'

She returned with a tall, middle-aged man in a white coat, wearing pince-nez. He smiled at Pat, and said, 'Good morning, Mr O'Donnell. I'm Professor Walker. How do you feel?'

Pat tried to say that he had a fierce pain in his head and felt sick, but again, only a gurgle escaped his mouth. The Professor sat on the bed beside him.

'Now, Mr O'Donnell. Can you hear me? If you can, please nod your head. Good. Do you know where you are?'

Pat shook his head.

'You're in the Royal Infirmary,' the Professor said. 'You received a bad head injury in the riot in George Square two days ago, you've been unconscious, and you've had a stroke. Your skull was fractured. I've operated on that, but we suspect there may be internal injuries to your brain.

That's what's preventing you from speaking for the moment. I want you to rest and give yourself the best opportunity for a complete recovery. Nod if you understand.'

Pat nodded and tried to ask the numerous questions which crowded into his head. What day is it? Are Peggy and Conal safe? What happened in George Square? Where's Brighid? The last thing he remembered was fighting his way through the crowd to rescue Peggy from a policeman. He tried to say, where's my family? But again, no sound came, and he slumped back on his pillow, a tear trickling down his cheek. He felt utterly helpless. The doctor patted his shoulder, had a word with the nurse, and left the room.

The next day, Professor Walker ushered Brighid and Conal into his office.

'Sit down, please. Sit down,' he said.

He sat himself and addressed Brighid. 'Mrs O'Donnell, I'm afraid to say that your husband received a serious head injury in the George Square riot. This has caused a stroke, which in turn has affected his brain. He's lost the power of speech, although his eyesight and hearing appear to be functioning normally. And his sense of balance also seems to be affected. He can't walk, although I can find nothing organically wrong with his legs. I think it must be a complication of the stroke.'

Brighid could not control the sob which sprang from her mouth. 'Holy Mary, Mother o' God. Will he, will he be able to speak again, doctor?'

'I don't know, to be perfectly honest,' the Professor said. 'We don't know a lot about the brain. It may heal itself. Or it may not. I simply cannot tell.'

'And the walking?' Brighid said. 'Will he be able to walk again?'

The Professor spread his hands. 'Again, I can't tell. Only time will tell.'

'Will he be able to work again?' Conal said.

'I doubt it very much,' Professor Walker said. 'He's a docker, isn't he?'

'Aye,' Conal said.

'If he can't speak, and he can't walk, he can't work,' the Professor said. 'It's as simple as that.'

Brighid was weeping silently now. Conal clenched his fists and said, 'All that caused by a blow from a police baton. Could you testify to that?'

'No. No, I'm afraid I could not. The injuries are consistent with a severe blow to the head. But in all honesty, I couldn't swear that they were caused by a Police baton.'

'Oh for God's sake,' Conal said. 'What else could have caused them?'

The Professor shrugged, and said, 'He could have fallen in the crush and been kicked accidentally on the head. Or fallen and hit his head on the ground or the end of a bench. It's impossible to tell without witnesses. Do you have any witnesses?'

'No,' Conal said. 'Nobody saw what happened. He was found lying on the ground unconscious when it was all over. And brought here in an ambulance.'

'Then I very much regret that I couldn't testify as to what caused the injuries,' the Professor said. 'All I could really do is to describe their nature.'

Conal stood up. 'So, the Peelers are going to get away with it. Again.'

Professor Walker also stood up. 'Mr O'Donnell. I would really like to help you, but the fact of the matter is that we don't know for certain if your father's injuries were caused by the Police.' He turned to Brighid, who was wiping her eyes with a handkerchief.

'Mrs O'Donnell. I'm sorry,' he said. 'I'm truly sorry, believe me.'

Chapter 33:
Peggy's Decision Time.

In her mother's kitchen, Peggy poured Conal a cup of tea. Brighid had gone to the church to ask Father Gallagher to say a mass for Pat.

'So, there you have it, Peigeen,' Conal said. 'The Da's banjaxed; he'll never work again. The Ma's praying her heart out for his recovery, but let's face it, that would literally be a miracle.'

'I know,' Peggy said. 'It's a complete disaster. We're going to have to nurse Da at home when he's released from hospital. And that will be a full-time job.'

'Aye,' Conal said. 'And I'm off over the water. I'm needed at home, for the good of the cause.'

'For the good of the cause?' Peggy said. 'Home Rule for Ireland?'

'No,' Conal said. 'Independence for Ireland. I'm sorry to leave you in the lurch, Peggy, but it's something I've got to do. What are you going to do?'

'I don't know,' Peggy said. 'I'll have to think about that.'

'Right, so,' Conal said. 'I'll be leaving in the next couple of days, but I'll come and see you before I go. *Slán is beannacht.*'

'*Slán,*' Peggy said, returning Conal's kiss.

Well, that's torn it, Peggy thought; that's put the cat amongst the pigeons. If I come home to help Ma look after the Da, it's the end of the teaching. I'd be too busy to study and prepare lessons. And I don't see how I could continue with Catherine and Maggie. Then I'd be trapped in the ould routine of the Ma and Father Gallagher nipping me head about going to Mass and telling me what I can and can't do – like going out with Protestants. But I don't want to go back to that world; I want to continue studying to be a teacher and staying here with Peggy and Catherine. And Archie, if the God's honest truth be told. But I can't leave the Ma on her own with the Da; that wouldn't be fair. And we can't go back to Donegal; there's nowhere to go to. Oh God, what am I going to do?

Later, in the kitchen, Brighid said, 'You mustn't give up the teaching, girleen. You've come too far to leave it.' Peggy's jaw dropped.

'Yes,' her mother continued. 'Pat and I are proud that you've been taken on to train as a teacher. We always knew you were as sharp as a sickle. Sure, didn't Mister O'Neill come to the house when you were a Monitor back home to ask us to let you go on to teacher training college. He said you were more than capable of doing the course.'

'I never knew that,' Peggy said.

'You may be as sharp as a sickle, but you don't know everything, Miss,' Brighid said. 'Will you stay on working for the ladies above?'

'Yes, yes, I think so,' Peggy said. 'They want me to. And I'm happy there, and I learn a lot from them. They're good women. I'd like to stay on with them.'

'And why wouldn't ye?' Brighid said. 'Morag MacCaskill sings their praises. But there's one thing you've got to remember, Peggy O'Donnell.'

'What's that, Ma?'

'We're your family, not the MacDonald sisters. I'm your mother and Pat is yourfather. And Conal and Tim are your brothers. And Eamonn, God rest his soul, was also your brother. Never forget that.'

'As if I ever would, Ma,' Peggy said.

'Now, what about your father? Are you going to go in and see him? He needs you, now that he is bed-ridden,' Brighid said. 'You're his only daughter. And he loves you, you know.'

Peggy took a deep breath and looked right at her mother. 'I'll try and remember that next time he hits me. So no, I'm not going to go in and see him. That would be hypocritical. But I will come and see you every Saturday when I finish work. And if you need me, you can phone the house. Catherine and Maggie will always know where I am.'

'You've become a hard, hard woman, Peggy. May God forgive ye.' Brighid said. 'I'll pray for you.'

'You do that, Ma. You do that.'

Up in Partickhill, Maggie asked, 'So what have you decided to do, Peggy?'

Peggy exhaled heavily and stared at Maggie for a moment.

'I've decided to continue with the Junior Certificate course. And I'd like to stay here, if you'll still have me,' Peggy said. 'I don't want to go back home to Neptune Street If I did that, it would be the end of the teacher training.'

'You're as welcome here as the day is long,' Catherine said. 'We've already told you that. And we mean it. We will support your training every way we can.'

'Thank you,' Peggy said.

'You've made a very brave decision, Peggy,' Archie said. 'You've broken some important family ties. I hope you don't regret it.'

'So do I,' Peggy said. 'But it's my decision, and if I've made a mistake, sure it's me that's got to live with it. There's no going back now.'

Catherine, Maggie and Archie exchanged glances; that was the simple truth. Archie smiled and raised a clenched fist. 'So, it's – Forward!' he said. The three women laughed.

'What's happened about the Forty-Hour Strike?' Peggy said.

'The men have gone back to work,' Archie said. 'But they have gained a forty-seven-hour week. That's not forty hours, obviously, but it's ten hours a week less than they have been working to date. So, the men have two hours extra per day in bed. I can tell you they're pretty happy with that. And although the strikers didn't win their main demand, they've gained a great deal of experience of self-organisation through the shop-stewards' committees. That can't be bad.'

'While I remember, Peggy,' Catherine said, 'Helen Crawfurd would like you to join a small committee of women along with Mrs Barbour of Govan and Mrs Ferguson of Partick that is advising John Wheatley on the design of the kitchens in possible new municipal cottages. Would you be interested?'

'Sure, and I would,' Peggy said. 'What would men know about kitchens?'

Everyone laughed.

'We've got to keep a close eye on the housing and rents issues,' Archie said. 'Now that the Royal Commission has reported, and the Corporation wants to build municipal housing at Mosspark, you can be sure that the Moderates will try to sabotage that policy.'

'What do you think they'll do about rents?' Maggie said.

'Oh, they'll try and get the 1915 Rent and Mortgage Interest Restriction Act repealed and put the rents up. That's as sure as eggs is eggs,' Archie said. 'They'll argue there hasn't been any rent increase for five years.'

'But there have been no repairs and maintenance done for five years,' Peggy said.

'Precisely, comrade,' Archie said. 'That why we've got to watch them like hawks. Things are heating up. Now that the Representation of the People Act has given men over 21 the vote …'

'But not women,' Catherine said.

'But not all women. Not yet,' Archie said. 'Only women over the age of thirty with property qualifications have the vote, but universal suffrage will come soon. That's guaranteed. They can only delay it, they can't stop it. The contribution of women to the war effort was too great to ignore. So now we have the chance to elect more socialist MPs, and get more of our people – men and women – elected on to Glasgow Council. We have a real chance to change things, to make life better for the working-class.'

'Chance would be a fine thing,' Peggy said.

Chapter 34:
The Teacher Taught.

One of the things that Peggy found difficult to deal with in the school was the language of the pupils. Most of them spoke in the Glaswegian dialect, which was all but incomprehensible to Peggy. For example, as she went into the school one morning, she saw two boys pushing and jostling each other. One yelled, 'Gonnae no dae that!' What on earth does that mean? Peggy thought.

Later, she asked Mrs Morrison. Kirsty laughed, and said, 'The literal translation would be: 'Are you not going to not do that.' It's a double negative, Peggy, used for emphasis. In fact, it's incorrect English. But most of the children speak Glaswegian at home and to each other. However, we insist that they speak English in the classroom and write English in their compositions in the hope that it rubs off. They need to be able to speak and write Standard English for job applications and interviews.'

On another morning, Peggy met Kirsty on the way to the school. As they reached the entrance, a woman came up to them; Peggy recognised her as the mother of one of the pupils.

'Oh, Mrs Morrison,' she said. 'Ah just wanted tae tell you that Johnnie's no hissel just noo. His da done a wee murder and is in the jail.'

In the staffroom, when they had recovered from laughing, Peggy said, 'I wonder what a big murder would look like.'

'Precisely!' said Kirsty.

Peggy watched Mrs Morrison carefully. She noticed how deftly Kirsty controlled the class. She took charge from the moment she came into the classroom, instigated a learning atmosphere right away, and brooked no nonsense. She was not averse to giving pupils the belt, but did so infrequently, and then only for ill-discipline. Kirsty told her that most children actually preferred a teacher who wouldn't let them misbehave.

'Look, Peggy,' Kirsty explained, 'children need boundaries. It's your job to set these boundaries. You're not here to be liked. But you must be respected. You're a school-teacher; they are school-children. You must take charge. Do you see what I mean?'

'Yes, I do,' Peggy said. 'But I think it's easier said than done.'

'You've got the personality to do it,' Kirsty said. 'Trust me. Of course, it's difficult in the beginning. I found it difficult. But start by being firm, and the job will become easier, I promise you.'

As time went by, Peggy also noticed the salience of English in the curriculum. She asked Mrs Morrison about this.

'Oh yes' Kirsty said, 'English is central to the curriculum. Language is how we express ourselves and communicate. So, it's vital that the children have a thorough knowledge of the classics of English literature and read widely. This facilitates rational thinking, clear spoken and written communication, and a critical awareness of style. We want the pupils to be competent and confident in self-expression; that's what the Inspectors of Schools look for. And it's character-building. So, besides the classic novels and poems we read as part of the curriculum, I encourage the pupils to read at home, and use Glasgow's public libraries. The whole point is to encourage independent thinking. Another way of doing this is to read them stories. The children love stories, but the trick is to get them to react to the stories by asking them questions. In fact, I'm going to start soon with Robert Louis Stevenson's *Kidnapped.* What I would like you to do is to read it to them for the last twenty minutes of every Friday, but have two or three questions about the content prepared. You can practice at home by timing yourself and see how many pages you can read comfortably in ten minutes or so. Then you can use the last ten minutes for your questions. Do you see what I mean?'

'Yes,' Peggy said. 'But I'll have to read *Kidnapped* first. I've never heard of it, or Robert Louis Stevenson.'

'Fancy that,' Kirsty said. 'It's a terrific story; you're in for a treat. It's a very Scottish story. You'll get it in the public library. And when you've read it, I would like you to tell me what you think the central theme is. Agreed?'

'Agreed,' Peggy said. 'I'll read it this weekend, so.'

After school, Peggy walked down Great George Street with her friend Donna MacAulay. Donna was from the Isle of Harris and was also doing the Junior Certificate in the school. So, the two young women compared notes frequently.

'The thing that's worrying me is the crit lesson,' Donna said. 'I don't fancy standing up in front of yourself and the class teacher and the Master of Method, and trying to teach a lesson. I'm after being terrified already.'

'It is pretty scary,' Peggy said. 'But I think the way to face it is to be well-prepared. Lookit, when I know what my crit lesson is, I'll prepare it and try it out on ye, and ye can do the same to me.'

'Now that's a good idea,' Donna said. 'We'll do just that.'

After Peggy had done the shopping on Saturday morning, she sat down in the kitchen with *Kidnapped*, and began reading: 'I will begin the story of my adventures …' She was soon captivated by the story and could not put the book down until she had finished. It was soon evident to her what the theme of the novel was.

Some weeks later, Peggy had read her class the first four chapters of *Kidnapped*; they loved it.

'Now, boys and girls,' she said. 'I want you to think about David Balfour climbing up the stairs in the tower of the House of Shaws in the pitch-dark. He can't see where he is going, there's no banister, and the stairs are uneven. Close your eyes and imagine it.'

The children shut their eyes. Peggy tapped the floor with her heels as she spoke. 'Up he goes, up and up. Then suddenly – there's a peal of thunder and a flash of lightning.'

Peggy growled the sound of thunder, and banged the desk with a pointer; the children jumped.

'What did he see with the flash of lightning?' Peggy said. 'He saw that the steps ended in mid-air. David must have been petrified. What does petrified mean?'

'Scared stiff,' a boy shouted.

'Good,' Peggy. 'That's right. Sure, it means he was scared so stiff he couldn't move. Eventually, with his back to the wall, he began to edge down the stairs.' Peggy flattened herself against the classroom wall and mimed creeping down the stairs. She stood up straight.

'Now,' Peggy said. 'Ebenezer Balfour must have known the stairs in the tower ended in space. Yet he sent David up there to fetch a chest which wasn't there. It was a barefaced lie. So why did Ebenezer send David up the stairs?'

'To murder him,' one boy cried.

'Possibly,' Peggy said. 'It looks like it. But why would he want to murder David, a harmless boy of seventeen?'

'There was something in his father's letter that told Ebenezer David was a danger,' another boy said.

'I'd say so,' Peggy said. 'It sounds like there was something in that letter which must have made David a threat to Ebenezer and the House of Shaws. What do you think?'

'Yes, miss,' the class chorused.

'Right, so,' Peggy said. 'What do you think is going to happen next?'

'Please, Miss,' a boy said. 'Ebenezer will try to get rid of David some other way.'

'That's what I suspect too,' Peggy said. 'We'll find out next week when the story continues. But in the meantime, what do you think the theme of this book is?'

A boy stuck up his hand and said, 'Please, Miss, fairness. What's happening to David isn't fair.'

'That's right,' Peggy said. 'Good. What's another word for fairness?'

'Justice,' a girl called out.

'Correct, Mary,' Peggy said. 'The overall theme of *Kidnapped* is justice. Well done. Class: dismiss.'

After the pupils had left the classroom, chattering away about the story, Kirsty laughed. 'That was very good, Peggy. I liked the sound effects; they made me jump,' she said. 'And you've got the children thinking about the story. Well done.'

That evening, Archie called, and Peggy told him and Maggie and Catherine what she had been doing in the classroom with the story of *Kidnapped.*

'Kirsty told me you'd done a good job,' Archie said. 'And she's nobody's fool. It sounds like you're doing well. Good on you.'

Peggy felt herself blush and looked down. 'Like I told you,' Maggie said, 'it's a great story and I knew you'd like it.'

'Stevenson is a master story-teller,' Catherine said.

'He is,' Archie said. 'And he was a very interesting man, Peggy. It was as if there were two sides to him: the serious, very Scottish, Presbyterian side, on the one hand. And the imaginative romantic, on the other. *Dr Jekyll and Mr Hyde*, in short.'

‘That’s another of Stevenson’s novels, Peggy,’ Maggie said. ‘You should read that too.’

‘Do you have a copy?’ Peggy said.

‘Oh yes,’ Catherine said. ‘We’ve most of Stevenson’s books.’

Chapter 35:
1920-1921: More Rent Strikes.

The ILP branch meeting was in ferment, the hall was full, and there was a din of excited conversation. 'Order, order,' Archie yelled. The hubbub died down. Peggy listened intently.

'Here's the situation,' Archie said. 'The new Rent Act proposes an increase of ten per cent on standard rents, that is, the rent at the 1914 level, and twenty-five per cent *if* repairs have been carried out.'

Peggy jumped to her feet and cried, 'But there have been no repairs carried out since 1914.'

'Quite correct, comrade,' Archie said. 'But the Notices of Increase in Rent are already being served by the factors. The ILP's position is that these increases are unacceptable, and the Party proposes that rent control be continued *sine die*. One-fifth of our people live in single-ends, and almost half-a-million in rooms-and-kitchens, the vast majority with outside toilets. To propose a ten per cent rent increase in such inadequate housing is an outrage. So, we are calling a twenty-four-hour strike on August 23rd to protest against these increases, with a mass meeting on Glasgow Green.' The meeting roared its approval.

On Monday 23rd, Maggie, Catherine and Peggy entered Glasgow Green and made their way towards Nelson's Monument along with streams of other people. The tenants had been asked to bring their Notices of Increase in Rent if they had received them, and Peggy could see that a large number of people were carrying them. Soon, a huge crowd was listening to Andrew MacBride, John Wheatley and Mary Barbour attacking the provisions of the recent 1920 Rent Act and calling for the continuation of rent control by the government. Then it was Archie's turn. He too attacked the proposed increases in rent. But he had something extra to say.

'Comrades! Last year, Lloyd George promised homes fit for heroes for our returning servicemen. But where are they? Two months ago, the Corporation of Glasgow invited tenders for its new council housing scheme in Mosspark. We have no idea when these houses will become available for tenants. And who will be the tenants anyway? As they're to be large cottage-type houses, the rents will be far too high for the average worker. So, it looks like the heroes are going to have to remain in the small and overcrowded tenement houses of Glasgow. Comrades, is this situation acceptable?'

'No!' roared the crowd.

'Correct,' Archie said. 'Rent increases of any kind are unacceptable at a time of economic and industrial depression. So, the ILP calls for an immediate rent strike in protest against the proposed increases. On rent day, simply refuse to pay the increase on standard rent. And to make the point to the Government, here's what we're going to do.'

He held up a Notice of Increase in Rent. 'Put your Notices of Increase in a pile and burn them. Like this.' Archie lit a match and set fire to the Notice in his hand. Soon a large pile of Notices were burning at the foot of Nelson's monument. Sure, he knows how to fire people up, Peggy thought, but where will all this end? She was distracted by an unfamiliar buzzing sound overhead. She looked up and saw a biplane swoop low over the Green with two goggled men looking down. Although she had seen photographs of aircraft in the newspapers, it was the first time Peggy had actually seen one, and she watched with fascination as it banked, climbed in a circle, and dived over the crowd again. The very next day, she saw a photograph of the demonstration in the *Bulletin* newspaper taken from the aeroplane.

However, within a month it was plain that the Rent Strike was not taking off in Glasgow. The ILP branches reported that the majority of people were paying the increases in rent, or at least part of them, and this was also reported in the press.

'I don't understand,' Peggy said. 'If the tenants could hold out in 1915, why not now?'

'The war's over, Peggy,' Archie said. 'The main reason for the solidarity of the strike in 1915 was popular outrage that the Factors had the effrontery to put the rent up when the men were away fighting at the Front. But it's a different time now, and I suspect that tenants are a bit weary of all the drama and excitement of the 1915 Rent Strike, and then the 40-Hour Strike. It looks like there are hard times coming, and people want to be sure that they've a roof over their heads. So although they don't like paying the increases, by-and-large they are doing so.'

Yes, that makes sense, Peggy thought. People were tired after the drama of the 40-Hour Strike and the violent events of Bloody Friday, not to mention the end of the War.

'Now Peggy,' Helen Crawfurd said, 'the Clydebank tenants are proving very solid in their rent strike. Some of the women are even following the factors' clerks around and threatening them.'

'Why is it so solid in Clydebank, and not in Glasgow?' Peggy said.

'Clydebank is a quite distinct wee town,' Helen said. 'The vast majority of the workers are employed in Beardmore's, John Brown's, and Singer's. The shipyard workers tend to live all together in Dalmuir while the Singers' workers live up in what the Bankies call the 'Holy City,' in Radnor Park. Singers built a lot of flat-roofed tenements up there for their workers, and the story goes a returning seaman said it reminded him of Jerusalem. And another thing. Clydebank is a ninety-nine per cent working-class town. There are very few middle-class people there. So, there's great working-class solidarity in the town. Anyway, the local women's committee has asked if we could send someone down to advise them on tactics, someone who was involved in 1915 here in Glasgow. As both Mary and I are heavily involved in trying to organise Govan, we wondered if you would go down and talk to the Bankie women.'

'Sure, and I'd be happy to,' Peggy said. 'But I could only go down at the weekend as I'm busy at school and preparing my lessons during the week. But I could manage next Saturday afternoon.'

'That's fine,' Helen said. 'Your local contact is Mrs Jennie Hyslop, who is one of the leaders down there. I'll tell her you'll be down next Saturday afternoon. And the Housing Association will pay your tram fare.'

Peggy sat at the front of the single-decker tram on the long journey from Partick to Clydebank. From Partick, the tram passed Thornwood and Whiteinch, then Scotstoun, and on to Clydebank itself. Peggy had never been this far west before and looked around with interest. Clydebank wasn't so different from Govan or Partick, with a familiar townscape of tenements and numerous shipyard cranes towering above them. She found

Mrs Hyslop without any difficulty, and soon a group of women were sitting in her kitchen over a pot of tea discussing tactics.

'We used brass bells, like school-bells, to call the women out in Govan when we knew the Factors were coming,' Peggy said. 'You can hear them a long way away. Could you get some here?'

'No bother,' Mrs Hyslop said. 'There's a brass moulder's

down the road. I'll order a couple this very day.'

'Good woman yourself,' Peggy said. 'Now. You told me that the local Factors are in fact based in Glasgow.'

'That's right,' Mrs Hyslop said.

'So to get into the town, they'd come along the Glasgow Road?' Peggy said.

'Aye,' Mrs Hyslop said. 'The only other way is down through Drumry, but that's the long way round. They're more likely to come in on the Glasgow Road, either by tram or motor-car.'

'Well,' Peggy said, 'in that case I suggest you send out patrols of men on bicycles along the Glasgow Road, in shifts, twenty-four hours a day, to keep an eye out for the Factors. And if they spot them, they can sprint into the town and raise the alarm.'

'We can organise that,' Mrs Hyslop said. 'But what next? What do we do when they arrive?'

'The thing is to make it impossible to serve the Notice of Increase of Rent,' Peggy said. 'So, there are two things you can do. First, when you know which close the Factors want to enter, you can pack it with women, and I mean really pack it. And just push them out. And it helps if you throw some bags of peasemeal at them as well.' The women in the kitchen fell around laughing.

'The second thing is this,' Peggy said. 'In spite of everything you do, the Factors might get into the close, for example, with the help of the Police. But the Notice of Increase has to be served on the right person. So, you could change the nameplates on the door. For example, supposing the person on whom the Notice is to be served is Mrs Hyslop, two-two, 137 Kilbowie Road. You unscrew her nameplate and put another one in its place. And you can put another neighbour in the house, with the same name as on the new nameplate. So, if the Factor gets as far as the door, and knocks at it, the neighbour would come out. The

Factor would say, 'Mrs Hyslop?' And the neighbour would say, 'No. Mrs McDermott. Can't you read?' The Factor will get completely confused and with a bit of luck, will go away. Do you see what I mean?'

'Aye, I do,' Mrs Hyslop said. 'That's very clever, Peggy, thanks very much.'

Over the next few months, Peggy watched the progress of the Clydebank Rent Strike with great interest. The locals were tying the factors up in knots, and they were only able to serve a few Notices. And a local Labour lawyer had won an important case against the Factors in the Sheriff Court. But Peggy could ill-afford to do more than read the *Glasgow Herald*'s and *Forward*'s reports on the strike, for she was fully occupied trying to make sense of subordinate adjectival clauses of place on her Junior Student's course at school.

Chapter 36:
A Woman Scorned.

Peggy was puzzled. She'd been in the school for nearly a term now, and on a couple of occasions, she had suggested to Archie that they go for a cup of coffee after school. He had declined, pleading another meeting, and hurried away, but she could see that he was embarrassed. What the divil was going on here? He had encouraged her to do the Junior Certificate course, and to do it in this school. And now he's ignoring her. Is he too high and mighty for a mere trainee teacher? She decided to confront him.

One day, Peggy waited until Archie left the school and was walking along Great Western Road towards Byres Road. She caught up with him.

'Hello, Archie,' Peggy said. 'Going home?'

'Oh hello, Peggy,' Archie said. 'Yes, I am, in fact.'

'I'll walk down Byres Road with you, so,' Peggy said. 'And maybe you'll tell me why you're avoiding me.'

'Em, er, I'm not avoiding you,' Archie spluttered.

'You could have fooled me,' Peggy said. 'Sure, since I started at school, I've suggested three times we go for a coffee, and you've made an excuse every time. Am I too junior to be seen with a real teacher? Is that it?'

'No, no, Peggy,' Archie said. 'It's nothing like that.'

'Well, what is it like?' Peggy said. 'I would surely like to know.'

'Look, Peggy,' Archie said as they turned into Byres Road. 'It's, it's actually a question of protecting your good name.'

Peggy stopped dead. 'My good name? What on earth

are you talking about, Archie MacDonald? There's nothing wrong with my name.'

'No, of course there isn't,' Archie said. 'It's to do with the fact that I shouldn't be seen consorting with a trainee. People might get the wrong impression.'

'The wrong impression about what?' Peggy said. 'Stop talking in riddlemerees.'

Archie shuffled and looked round nervously. 'If people saw us together, they might think, they might think I was taking advantage of you, you know, I was abusing my more senior position.'

'To do what?' Peggy said. 'To seduce me?'

Archie went scarlet. 'Well, yes, for example. People would start talking about you. They would say …'

'I don't give a tinker's curse about what people say about me,' Peggy said. 'Having a cup of coffee together is a completely innocent matter. If people think ill of it, bad cess to them. It's them that have the bad minds, the cheapskates.'

'I agree, Peggy,' Archie said. 'But we're also both known socialists. We've got enemies, and there are some teachers in the school who would love to make life difficult for us. I'm just trying to protect you.'

'Protect me, me arse,' Peggy said. 'I can protect myself, thank you very much.' Peggy swept off down the road, leaving Archie gaping after her.

As she approached Tennent's Bar, Elspeth Mavor came round the corner from Highburgh Road.

'Hello, Elspeth,' Peggy said.

Elspeth glared at her. 'Go back to the bog where you belong, you Irish tart,' she hissed, and hurried off. Jaysus, Peggy thought, it's definitely not my day.

'I can see that you're upset, Peggy,' Maggie said. 'But Archie's right. You've got to be careful. He's protecting you, and you've got to protect him. There's always a lot of gossip in schools, and some of it is malicious, unfortunately. There are teachers in that school who would love to do Archie – and you – down. My advice is don't give them the slightest opportunity, because if you do, they will seize it. So you have to be circumspect, at least until you finish your certificate.'

'Circumspect?' Peggy said.

'Cautious. Wary,' Maggie said. 'Do you understand what I'm saying? There are a lot of people out there who hate us socialists. We can't afford to give them the chance to slander us and damage our cause.'

'There are a lot of people out there who are cheapskates,' Peggy said.

'That's true,' Maggie said. 'But they are dangerous cheapskates, and don't you ever forget it.'

'Is Elspeth Mavor a dangerous cheapskate, or a simple cheapskate?' Peggy said.

'Elspeth?' Maggie said. 'She's neither. Why do you ask?'

'Because I saw her on Byres Road, and she called me an Irish tart, and told me to get back to the bog where I belong.'

'Oh dear,' Maggie said. 'That's not like Elspeth. She's upset at the moment.'

'That's no excuse to give out to me like that,' Peggy said.

'I agree,' Maggie said.

'So why did she do it?'

'Elspeth's been keen on Archie for a long time,' Maggie said, 'and she got it into her head that she and Archie were going to be married – even although Archie never proposed to her, or even encouraged the idea. Archie told her recently that he's not in love with her, and doesn't want to marry her, so she's feeling very sorry for herself. She feels she's been jilted.'

'I would feel like that too if it were me,' Peggy said. 'So, it's a case of Hell hath no fury like a woman scorned.'

'Yes, exactly,' Maggie said.

Peggy hesitated. 'But did they, em … did they …'

'Go to bed together?' Maggie said. 'No, they didn't. But Elspeth feels that Archie has abandoned her for you. So, she's not well-disposed to you.'

'But Archie isn't courting me at all at all.'

'No, he isn't,' Maggie said. 'But he is attracted to you. And Elspeth knows that. Women are especially sensitive about these matters. Under normal circumstances, Elspeth isn't at all a malicious person. So do you understand now why she attacked you?'

'Yes. But it wasn't my fault,' Peggy said.

'Agreed,' Maggie said.

'So, Archie is attracted to me, is he?' Peggy said.

'Yes, he is. I think you must know that, Peggy. You're a beautiful woman, with a lovely nature. There would be something wrong with Archie if he wasn't attracted to you.'

Sure, he's got a quare way of showing it, Peggy thought. But it's good to know he is attracted to me.

'Now,' Maggie said. 'I've just finished reading a most interesting book, which I think you might like.' She handed Peggy a book. Peggy read the cover: *Married Love or Love in Marriage*, by Marie Carmichael Stopes, ScD, PhD. Peggy looked up at Maggie, confused.

'What, why …?'

'Just read it, and we'll have a chat about it afterwards,' Maggie said.

As Peggy walked down the corridor to her classroom, she saw Archie coming towards her.

'Good morning, Mr MacDonald,' she said. 'It's a lovely day.'

As Archie passed her, Peggy winked, and whispered, 'Don't worry, I'll protect your good name.' She giggled internally as she saw a grin flit across his face.

Chapter 37:
The Crit.

Peggy and Donna received the news about their final crit on the same day; it was to be in the last week of term, in the last year of the Junior Certificate course. The Master of Method who would review the classes was Mr Maxwell, the head teacher.

'What's your topic?' Peggy asked Donna.

'Over the Sea to Skye,' Donna said.

'Be the holy man, what does that mean?' Peggy said.

Donna told her the story of how Flora MacDonald, a young woman who was no Jacobite, had risked her life to help Bonnie Prince Charlie escape from Redcoat-occupied South Uist over the sea to the Isle of Skye after the disastrous Battle of Culloden.

'At least I know the bare bones of the story,' Donna said, 'so that's a start. And there's a famous song about it all, called *The Skye Boat Song*.'

'Can you sing it to me?' Peggy said. Donna obliged.

'Do you know what?' Peggy said. 'I think you should sing it to the class when you do your Crit. It adds atmosphere to the story and you've a lovely voice.'

'That's a great idea,' Donna said. 'What's your topic?'

'The Battle of Bannockburn,' Peggy said. 'And I've never even heard of it.'

'Och, it was a famous victory in 1314,' Donna said. 'The Scots gave the English a right hammering.'

'I'm pleased to hear it. It's off to the Mitchell Library for me,' Peggy said.

Donna was on first. Peggy sat at the back of the class with Mrs Morrison and Mr Maxwell. She could not stop her leg trembling or her heart racing. She was well-prepared; she had scoured the Mitchell Library for material and when she had explained to the librarians what she was doing, they could not have been more helpful. Catherine and Maggie had helped her prepare, and Maggie had done the three drawings and the map for her, while Catherine donated an appropriate hairbrush. She had pitched her lesson to them and to Donna, had incorporated their suggestions, and had learned the poem off by heart. But she was still terrified. She watched as Donna started her lesson and noticed how pale she was. She's just like me, Peggy thought, scared out of her wits. But Donna started well.

'Everyone in Scotland knows the *Skye Boat Song*,' Donna said. 'Here's how it goes.' Donna sang the song, and Peggy noticed that some of the pupils were humming along to it. Out of the corner of her eye, she also noticed Mr Maxwell scribbling away in a notebook. I hope he's writing something positive, Peggy thought. Donna finished the song, and said, 'Now, boys and girls, what's that famous song all about? Here's the story.'

Peggy listened intently. Donna produced several cards with prints of portraits of Flora MacDonald and one of a 'Wanted' poster for Bonnie Prince Charlie. Peggy thought Donna was doing very well, and the pupils were certainly listening intently. Forty minutes later, Donna came to the end of her lesson, and said, 'After the Prince safely escaped to France, Flora MacDonald never heard another word from him, not even a letter of thanks for all the risks she took on his behalf. She eventually returned to the Isle of Skye, married and had a family. Then, at the age of fifty-two, which was a good age in these days, Flora and her husband emigrated to America, to South Carolina. But that is another story.'

Later, over coffee, Donna told Peggy that Mr Maxwell

had said that it was good lesson. But it could be improved by two things. First, by asking the children questions about the content to ensure that they had understood the main points. And second, by summarising these main points at the end of the lesson. But, Mr Maxwell had said, Donna was to be congratulated on thinking of singing the song to start the lesson; that, he said, was original and effective.

The next day it was Peggy's turn. She described how Robert the Bruce mobilised his Army to fight the English, and then rolled up the cover of the blackboard to reveal a chalked map of the battleground with the English and Scottish armies in different colours.

'Now you might think of the Bannock Burn as a wee stream,' Peggy said. 'But in fact, it was a fast-flowing burn with steep muddy banks. Bruce knew what he was doing; he'd forced the English to fight on ground of his own choosing, ground that was boggy. This was fierce clever, for it meant that the cavalry were slowed down if they tried to charge, and had no room to manoeuvre. And Bruce also had his men dig pits in this ground that they disguised with brushwood and turf. Now, the next important point was that Bruce had organised his army in four schiltrons. Does anyone know what a schiltron was?'

None of the children knew. Peggy produced a detangling hairbrush with metal tines, and walked amongst the pupils so that they could see it.

'A schiltron was a body of men who carried pikes or spears. They could be formed into a hollow circle or a rectangular shape. So, if you can imagine each tine in this brush as a spear, a schiltron was like a human porcupine. If the first rank of soldiers knelt down and grounded the butts of their spears with the blade facing out, and the second rank stood with their spears facing out over the heads of their comrades-at-arms, it was all-but impossible for the cavalry to break through. It worked like this.'

Peggy produced a first drawing of the schiltron with their spears held vertical and showed it to the class. Then she produced a second, with the spears halfway down, at forty-five degrees. And the third showed the schiltron ready to receive a cavalry charge.

'Of course this took training and immense courage, but Bruce had drilled his men. And he had also had them practice moving from a defensive hollow into a tight offensive line.' She drew this on the blackboard.

'So, first of all, the English cavalry were slowed down by the boggy ground,' Peggy said. 'And second, when they did charge, many of the horses fell into the pits. And third, when they did reach the schiltrons, the horses couldn't break the circular formation. And many of them were stuck on the spears of the Scots.'

Peggy could see Mr Maxwell writing away. God o' Gods, I hope I haven't put me foot in it. A girl raised her hand.

'Yes, Patricia,' Peggy said.

'Please Miss, does that mean that the horses were wounded or killed?'

'Yes, it does,' Peggy said. 'War in the fourteenth century was a horrible, bloody affair. Neither animals nor human beings were spared.'

'That's cruel, Miss,' Patricia said. 'The poor horses.'

'Yes,' Peggy said. 'War is cruel. All wars are cruel.'

There was a moment's silence while the children digested this. Peggy continued by telling the class how Bruce made the schiltrons move forward to the attack, and drove the disorganised English into the burn.

'If the knights on horseback went down into the burn,' Peggy said, 'they were banjaxed. The horses couldn't get up the muddy banks, and if the knights fell off, their heavy armour weighed them down, and they drowned. But the last straw for the English was when what were called the 'Sma' Folk' joined the battle. They were the Scottish Army's camp-followers, the men and women who were the cooks, nurses, farriers, and waggon-drivers. Bruce had put them out of harm's way behind a hill, but when they saw how the battle was going, they charged down the hill to join in, and the English thought it was another schiltron coming to attack them. They turned and fled; it was a complete rout. So, the Battle of Bannockburn was a great victory for the Scots, and eventually led to Scottish independence. And it inspired Robert Burns to write a poem about it, based, as it were, on Robert Bruce's March to Bannockburn. It has become a great song, which I will now sing to you.'

Peggy drew herself up to her full height, took a deep breath, and prepared to sing

Scots, wha hae. But the words would not come; her mind had become a complete blank. As she frantically tried to remember the words, she saw Mrs Morrison silently mouth the first line from the back of the class. Peggy gulped, took a deep breath, and launched into the song. She came to the last verse, and really let fly:

'Lay the proud usurpers low!
Tyrants fall in every foe!
LIBERTY's in every blow!
Let us Do – OR DIE!!!'

There was a complete silence for a couple of seconds. Oh Jaysus, Mary and Joseph. Then the children burst into spontaneous applause. Peggy didn't know where to look. Mrs Morrison stood up, came to the front of the class and held up her hands for silence. 'Thank you very much, Miss O'Donnell,' she said. 'Class: dismiss.'

As the children trooped out, Donna gave her the thumbs-up from the back of the class. Mr Maxwell came to the front of the class and gestured to Peggy to sit down at one of the pupil's desks. Peggy sat down hurriedly; she felt drained.

'That was a very good lesson, Miss O'Donnell,' Mr Maxwell said. 'It was succinct and well-prepared, and putting a map on the blackboard was most helpful. The hairbrush and the drawings were also good ideas. And both you and Miss MacAulay are to be congratulated on thinking of a song to illustrate your lessons. However, I will make the same suggestions to you as I did to Miss MacAulay. It's one thing to win the children's attention. It's quite another to make sure that the points you wish to make sink in and are retained. So, think up several questions in advance to ensure that the children have actually grasped what it is that you wish them to learn. Do you see what I mean?'

'Yes, sir,' Peggy said.

'The other point is this,' Mr Maxwell said. 'It's really helpful to summarise the main points of your lesson at the end. In your case, you could say something like: the Scots won the Battle of Bannockburn for three reasons. First, Bruce chose the ground on which to fight carefully, to give him maximum advantage, and lured the English into it. Second, he had trained the schiltrons well in both defensive and offensive operations. And thirdly, the Scots soldiers were much better led than the English; Bruce was a skilled military commander. Is that clear?'

'Yes, sir,' Peggy said. 'Thank you.'

'Finally, that girl asked a good question,' Mr Maxwell continued. 'It is worth emphasising the point that in the olden days, war meant the wholesale slaughter of horses as well as men, sickening as it may seem today.'

He smiled, and said, 'I wish all my teachers had voices like yours. Well done, both of you. Keep up the good work.'

Peggy and Donna celebrated by treating themselves to an ice-cream in the University Café. Opposite them, two students were having an animated discussion in Gaelic. When they left, Donna, a native Gaelic speaker, told Peggy they were arguing about Thomas Carlyle's 'Great Man' theory, which they had been studying in their philosophy class at the University. But she burst out laughing when Peggy asked her if the students learned anything at the University about 'Great Women' theory.

Chapter 38:
Female Organisms.

Maggie handed Peggy a slice of home-made sponge cake in the kitchen.

'So, you see, Peggy,' Maggie said, 'most men neither understand nor care about how our bodies work, or what it is that we want from sex. Men don't understand that women can actually enjoy sex. So we have to tell them, and slow them down. We have to educate them. But first, we have to know our own bodies. Do you follow me?'

'Yes,' Peggy said. 'But it's all a bit strange. The Catholic Church doesn't tell you any of that stuff.'

'Of course it doesn't,' Maggie said. 'Neither does the Church of Scotland. These churches are run by men. They operate by keeping people in ignorance and promising them pie in the sky when they die.'

Peggy burst out laughing. 'Pie in the sky when they die? I love it.'

Maggie laughed too. 'Yes, it is good, isn't it? It comes from a song by Joe Hill of the Wobblies, our American comrades, in their Little Red Songbook.'

'It's so apt,' Peggy said. 'The Church encourages us to put up with poverty and misery and exploitation on earth with the promise of pie in Heaven when we die. Sure, it's an anti-socialist programme, that's what it is.'

'That's right,' Maggie said. 'It's an explicitly anti-socialist programme and is designed to be so. That's where the genius of John Wheatley became evident. He showed the Catholic Church that a socialist struggle for better housing and public health wasn't a revolutionary campaign but a matter of simple if radical social policy innovation.'

'But yer man is entirely opposed to birth control.'

'I'm afraid he is,' Maggie said. 'That's a step too far for his Catholicism. That's why it's necessary to continue to campaign for control over our own bodies and reproductive rights.'

'Yes, that's right,' Peggy said. 'I can't believe God meant women to have a dozen children, or more, one after the other.'

'Neither do I, Peggy,' Maggie said. 'Neither do I.'

Catherine and Maggie were out, and the house was warm and still. Peggy ran a hot bath and dissolved some of the sisters' bath salts in it. She stripped, slid into the bath, and relaxed. Remembering her experience in the public baths, she began caressing her breasts very gently with the tips of her fingers. After a moment or two, her nipples stood erect, and Peggy continued stroking them. A warm, tingling sensation spread through her breasts. She slid the fingers of her right hand down over her stomach and began caressing between her legs while her left hand played with her nipples. She felt herself become wet, slid her middle finger inside herself, and began stroking upwards gently. Stretching her legs open, she began to move her finger faster; it seemed to develop a rhythm of its own. She slid another finger in. Suddenly, she shuddered, gasped, and grabbed the sides of the bath in case she slid under the water. She started to twitch involuntarily, and then went into two or three rapid convulsions. Peggy let her hands fall back into the water as her whole body seemed to relax, glowing all over. Before she knew it, she was dozing.

Peggy came to with a start. The bathwater was now tepid. She stood up, wrapped a towel round her, drained the bath and cleaned it. She looked at her face in the mirror; it wore a happy, relaxed, quizzical smile. Jaysus, she thought, so that was a - what was that word Maggie used? –'organism', that was it. Well, she thought, I'll have a few more of them, thank you very much.

'Marie Stopes is giving a lecture to the women's branches of the ILP in the Albion Hall next Saturday,' Catherine said. 'Would you like to go?'

'Oh yes,' Peggy said. 'I'd like to learn more about them female organisms.'

Catherine and Maggie glanced at each other. '"Organisms"?' Maggie said.

'Yes,' Peggy said. 'You know, that you were telling me about.'

Peggy looked astounded as Catherine and Maggie burst into peals of laughter.

'What, what's so funny?'

'It's orgasm, Peggy,' Maggie gasped. 'Orgasm. "Organism" is the living material of a plant or an animal.'

'Oh,' Peggy said. 'I see. Orgasm it is, so. Anyway, yes, I would like to go to the meeting.'

'We're trying to keep the meeting secret,' Maggie said, 'so keep it to yourself.'

'Why?' Peggy said.

'The Catholic Church organises demonstrations wherever Marie Stopes or one of her colleagues is speaking,' Catherine said. 'And they can get quite rowdy.'

'I see,' Peggy said. 'Mum's the word.'

On the day of the lecture, Maggie, Catherine and Peggy arrived at the hall early only to find a noisy crowd of protestors already in place. Peggy noticed that the crowd contained several priests and nuns. As they passed through the demonstrators, they were subjected to a barrage of abuse and catcalls. Suddenly, Peggy saw Father Gallagher, his face contorted with rage. He spotted Peggy and made a lunge for her, only to be held back by a couple of the demonstrators.

'Peggy O'Donnell,' he screeched, his spittle reaching Peggy's face. 'A trollop and a dyke-jumper. You're a disgrace to a decent Catholic family, nothing more than a whore for the Protestant baby-killers.'

'Get away out of there,' Peggy said, as she swung her handbag at the priest with full force. It hit him on the side of the face and he reeled back into the crowd, losing his balance. I've had enough of that man to last me a lifetime, she thought as she strode into the hall.

'Good shot, Peggy,' Maggie murmured.

Peggy listened intently as Marie Stopes spoke. She demonstrated that endless childbearing not only had an extremely negative effect on women's physical and emotional health, and infant mortality rates, but was also correlated to poverty and over-crowding in small houses. She made a lucid case for women governing their own fertility by means of birth-control, and then discussed the use of sponges saturated with olive-oil, and cervical caps or diaphragms. She condemned abortion, particularly back-street abortion, as unnecessary and dangerous, and argued that the practice would be rendered obsolete if effective birth-control was legitimised. As she spoke, there was a continuous racket of chanting and hymn-singing from outside which Dr Stopes calmly ignored. She stressed the necessity for legislation permitting birth-control, and the lobbying of politicians and the clergy to back it. Peggy was impressed by the clarity of her argument, and completely convinced by its logic. Dr Stopes was given rapturous applause by the women in the audience when she finished her address.

'Who could possibly quarrel with that?' Catherine said, as they clapped their appreciation.

‘Them hyenas outside,’ Peggy replied.

As they made their way outside, they were still barracked by the demonstrators although now a line of police had pushed them back a good bit. Peggy saw Father Gallagher shouting and waving his fist – but took some satisfaction from the fact that he now had a good-sized bruise on his cheek.

That evening, Maggie, Catherine and Peggy discussed the lecture, and the birth-control devices advocated by Marie Stopes. Peggy asked how the diaphragm worked, and Maggie drew her a sketch of its anatomical location and explained its function.

‘So,’ Peggy said, ‘if you don’t mind me asking, do you have these caps?’

‘Yes, we do,’ Catherine said. ‘We get them from the Netherlands.’

Peggy thought for a moment. ‘Could you get me one?’

‘Yes, Peggy,’ Maggie said. ‘Yes, we could.

Chapter 39:
1920: The Irish War of Independence.

Peggy had finished her Junior Certificate satisfactorily, and received a glowing report, which filled her with a well-deserved sense of achievement. She was due to commence teacher training in Dowanhill in the autumn. In the meantime, the news from Ireland was the Irish Republican Army had now resorted to full-scale guerrilla warfare and was attacking both the Royal Irish Constabulary and the British Army. RIC barracks were raided for arms, while Eamon de Valera was in the USA fund-raising. In the summer, Sinn Fein won a series of local government elections all over the country, and established its own 'People's Courts,' tax-collection, and policing. Peggy had heard nothing from Conal for weeks except a postcard from Schull in County Cork which said he was 'enjoying the landscape.' She knew that meant with a flying column.

Late in the year, Peggy walked up Gardner Street with Archie after an ILP meeting in the Partick Burgh Halls. The meeting had been concerned with ensuring that all working-class people entitled to a vote in both the municipal and parliamentary elections were on the Glasgow Voters' Roll, which hitherto had been seriously incomplete.

'I've decided to go to Teacher Training College rather than university so that I can continue my political work,' Peggy told Archie as they climbed the steep hill. 'It's a critical time, with a General Election due.'

'It's a brave decision to give up the idea of going to university,' Archie said, 'and reflects great credit on you.'

'We've simply got to make some progress at the next

Election,' Peggy said, 'or we'll lose the people.'

'I agree,' Archie said.

They stopped at the top of the hill. 'Well, good night, Peggy,' Archie said.

Peggy placed her fingers behind the lapel of his coat, drew him close to her, and kissed him gently on the lips. 'Good night, Archie.'

As Archie went off down Partickhill Road to his house in Havelock Street, a figure materialised beside Peggy out of the dark.

'I saw that, Peggy,' Conal said, a big grin on his face.

'Jaysus, Conal,' Peggy said. 'You gave me a fright.'

Conal took her arm. 'We'll take a turn round the block, so.' As they made their way down North Gardner Street and turned into Hyndland Road, Conal told Peggy that he had been in the IRA since the previous year, was involved in the recent shooting of British intelligence officers in Dublin, and had been told to go home and lie low for a few weeks.

'We have them on the run, Peggy, we're running the country now, and they know it. There's going to be a settlement sooner rather than later, that's what the Big Fellah says.'

Peggy knew that 'the Big Fellah' was the nickname of Michael Collins. 'And I've got work to do here with the volunteers as well,' Conal said.

'Right ye be,' Peggy said, 'but be careful. Where are you staying?'

'You don't need to know that,' Conal said. 'But I'm safe. If you ever need to contact me, leave a message with John Carney in the Sinn Fein office in Govan. Good night now, Peggy. I'll be in touch.' And he vanished down Clarence Drive. I hope he will be safe, Peggy thought, for what he's doing is very dangerous.

As Peggy turned into her close, she saw a movement out of the corner of her eye. Someone was lurking in the last close of North Gardner Street. When she got into the flat, she crossed to the sitting-room bay windows without turning the lights on and peeked down from behind the curtains. She saw the glow of a cigarette in the last close-mouth across in North Gardner Street. It's the Special Branch, she thought; I've got to let Conal know.

Peggy hurried out of the subway at Govan Cross, and along Govan Road to the Sinn Fein office.

'Good morning,' Peggy said to the young man behind the desk. 'I'm Peggy, Conal O'Donnell's sister.'

'How are you, Peggy? I'm John Carney. What can I do for you?'

Peggy glanced about; there was no one else in the office. 'Conal told me to come here if I wanted to contact him. Can you get a message to him?'

'I can try,' John said. 'What's the message?'

'Tell him the Peelers are watching the flat where I live.'

'Where's that, Peggy?'

'39 Partickhill Road. The Peeler was standing in the last close in North Gardner Street before Partickhill Road last night.'

'Right, so. Well spotted, Peggy. Leave it to me. See if you can work out if it's permanent surveillance, or just at night-time – without taking any risks yourself. Understood?'

'Understood.'

Peggy left the office and walked over to Neptune Street to see her mother.

'Your Da's getting a bit better, thanks be to God,' Brighid said. 'He's trying to speak now. He can't say proper words, but he's trying, and I can just make out what's he's trying to say. Have you seen Conal recently?'

'Yes, he came to see me last night. Do you know he's in the IRA, Ma?'

Brighid nodded and said, 'Sure you don't have to be in the Peelers to work that out.'

'Have you seen any strangers in the street recently?' Peggy said.

'No,' Brighid said. 'Why do you ask?'

'The Peelers are watching my house,' Peggy said, 'but I've sent a message to Conal to warn him. They're probably watching this house as well. If you see anybody loitering about, let me know and I'll get a message to him.'

'Jesus, Mary and Joseph,' Brighid said, 'where is all this fighting and killing going to end?'

'I don't know, Ma, I don't know. How's Tim?'

'He's grand. I got a letter from him the other day. He's enjoying his studies at the seminary – and he says he's praying for you to abandon your Godless socialism.'

'Much good may it do him,' Peggy laughed.

'And Father Gallagher was raging at me, saying that you belted him with your handbag outside a meeting.'

'I did, so,' Peggy said. 'And he deserved it.'

'Ah well,' Brighid said, grinning, 'sure he does think he's the flower of the flock, the same fellah.'

As Peggy walked back towards Govan subway station, two tall men in suits fell in beside her, one on either side. One handed her a warrant card, which read: 'Detective Inspector Campbell.'

'Just follow us to the Police Station, please, Miss O'Donnell,' Campbell said.

As they made their way to the police station in Albert Street, Peggy quaked with fear. What were they going to do to her? In the station, she was ushered into an interviewing room.

'Sit down,' Campbell said.

Peggy did so, trying to remain calm, but in reality, paralysed with fear. Campbell sat opposite her and opened a folder, while the other policeman stood somewhere behind her out of her line of sight.

'Mairead O'Donnell,' Campbell said, 'born in 1896 in the townland of Carrickfin in The Rosses, County Donegal. Father, Patrick O'Donnell; mother, Brighid O'Donnell. You are currently a teacher training student in the Glasgow Provincial Training College. Address: 39 Partickhill Road, Glasgow. Is that correct?'

'Yes,' Peggy said.

'You are well known to us as a trouble-maker, O'Donnell. You were present at the suffragette riot in the Saint Andrew's Halls in …'

'No, it wasn't a suffragette riot,' Peggy said, 'it was a police riot. You made an unprovoked violent attack on a peaceful meeting of women.'

Campbell glared at her. 'You were also involved in illegal activity during the Rent Strike in Govan in 1915, and the riot in George Square in January 1919. And you have participated in numerous demonstrations and marches. Now. We believe you know the whereabouts of your brother, Conal O'Donnell, who is wanted by the Dublin Metropolitan Police on charges of murder. Where is he?'

'I don't know,' Peggy said, 'and even if I did, I wouldn't tell you.' A charge of murder? Oh my God. Conal could be hung for that.

Campbell leaned back in his chair, and looked at Peggy for what seemed like an eternity.

'O'Donnell,' he said. 'You are an Irish citizen. We could put you on the Dublin boat tonight and deport you as an undesirable. The Dublin police would be waiting for you at the North Wall. Now where is Conal O'Donnell?'

'I told you, I don't know,' Peggy said. She decided at that moment not to say another word. So, she pursed her lips and stared at the wall above Inspector Campbell's head while he repeated his questions. After what seemed like hours, the policeman said, 'Get out of my sight. But make no mistake, O'Donnell; we're watching you.'

Peggy thought hard as the subway roared under the Clyde. She decided not to tell Catherine and Maggie about Conal, the police, and her questioning by Campbell. Although they were in favour of Home Rule, the war in Ireland was not their concern, and the less they knew about support for it in Glasgow, the better. In war, people get killed – and sometimes, the innocent.

Chapter 40:
1921: A Long Hot Summer.

Peggy tapped the thermometer in the hall; even at eight o'clock in the morning, it was in the high 60s Fahrenheit and climbing. It had been a glorious summer so far, with day after day of hot sunshine. All day long there was the clunk of tennis balls from the tennis courts across the road from the sisters' house. Today was the August Bank Holiday, and Archie had promised to take Peggy on a picnic in the countryside on their bicycles.

Peggy had become a proficient cyclist. Catherine had taught her to ride on Maggie's cycle in the safety of the Dowanhill School playground, and when she could ride without wobbling up and down the length of Partickhill Road, sent her round the West End. Her big test came when Catherine told her to freewheel down the steep hill of Gardner Street, controlling her descent with her brakes. Peggy managed this, if not without trepidation. Shortly afterwards, Catherine took her for a longer ride up Maryhill Road to Canniesburn Toll, down the Switchback to Anniesland Cross, along Great Western Road, and home via Hyndland Road.

Peggy enjoyed the experience so much that she decided to buy a bicycle out of her savings. So she went to Rattray's bike shop in Murray Street in the East End, and bought a Rudge-Whitworth No. 2 Aero-Special Lady's Featherweight cycle for fifteen guineas. She also bought a two-thirds-length cycling skirt. Shortly afterwards, Archie had accompanied her along the towpath of the Forth and Clyde Canal as far as Bowling, and back along

Dumbarton Road past the shipyards.

'You're riding like you've been doing it all your life,' Archie said. 'We'll go for a picnic on Bank Holiday Monday, in the countryside where no one will see us. Would you like that?'

'Oh yes,' Peggy said, 'that would be grand. Where are we going?'

'Ah-ha, to a secret place,' Archie said with a mischievous smile.

'Right so,' Peggy said, 'I'll make some sandwiches.' But thinking of the secret place, and hoping it was really secret, she also soaked a sponge in olive oil. It's high time I learned more about them organisms, I mean orgasms.

Archie and Peggy whizzed down the hill into Strathblane, carried on past Blanefield, and continued north and west through open country towards Killearn.

'What's that white building?' Peggy said.

'It's the Glengoyne whisky distillery,' Archie said. 'Not far to go now.'

A little further along the road, Archie dismounted and opened a gate. 'Up here,' he said, 'but we'll have to push the bikes for a bit.' They pushed their bikes uphill for about ten minutes until they encountered a fence.

'We'll leave the bikes here,' Archie said, 'nobody comes up here, so they'll be safe. But bring your sandwiches and whatnot.'

He led the way steeply downhill through a wood; Peggy could hear the babbling of water, but the undergrowth was so thick she couldn't see the source. All of a sudden, they emerged beside a deep pool into which a waterfall dropped for about twenty feet; the water sparkled in the sunlight. There was a patch of grass beside the pool studded with poppies, harebell, St. John's wort, ladies' bedstraw and common orchids, and shaded by overhanging trees.

'Oh, would you look at that?' Peggy said. 'Isn't that grand? How did you find it, it's so sheltered?'

'I nearly fell into it coming off a walk in the Campsie Fells some years ago,' Archie said. 'I don't think anyone else knows about it. I've never seen anyone else here.'

Peggy laid out a rug and put her packet of egg-and-cress sandwiches, her apples and a bottle of barley-water on it. 'Give me the bottle,' Archie said, 'and I'll cool it in the pool.' He wedged it in the shallows of the pools with some rocks.

Peggy took off her socks, shoes and sunhat, and stretched out on the rug. 'This is the life,' she said.

Taking off his shirt, Archie lay down beside her. 'It is.'

Peggy closed her eyes, feeling her skin glow in the heat. The rhythmic gurgle of the waterfall was accompanied by intense birdsong and the soporific buzzing of bees. She felt herself dozing off. Archie stirred beside her. 'Phew!' he said. 'It's very hot. Let's go in for a dip and cool off.'

'Oh. You mean … you mean …?' Peggy said.

'Yes,' Archie said. 'Let's strip down to our underwear. There's nobody here to see us.' He stood up, slipped off his shirt and shorts, and wearing only his underpants, dived into the pool.

Well, well, well, Peggy thought. In for a penny, in for a pound. She stood up, stripped off her blouse and cycling skirt and waded into the pool. It was cool, and much deeper than she thought, as she slipped and floundered out of her depth. Archie towed her into shallower water so that she could stand with her feet on the bottom. 'Can't you swim?' he said, taking her hands.

'No,' Peggy said. 'This is the first time I've ever been in the water. But I like it.'

She put her arms round Archie's neck; her legs floated round his waist. He put his hands on her backside and drew her to him. Oh, I hope he does, Peggy thought. He did; he kissed her deeply. Peggy nearly fainted with desire. He then lifted her up out of the water, put her down on the rug on her back, and lay down beside her, his arm round her middle. 'I've got something to tell you, Peggy.'

'What's that?'

'I've been selected to stand as the ILP candidate for the South Side constituency in the parliamentary elections.'

Peggy sat up so fast she fell across Archie's chest. 'Really?'

Archie's hand on her naked back steadied her against him. 'Yes,' he said. 'Really and truly.'

'Oh Archie, that is the most wonderful news.'

Without thinking, Peggy kissed him. The next thing, Archie's arms were around her, and they kissed like there was no tomorrow. Peggy pressed herself against his body; it's so hard, she thought, while mine feels like it's going to melt. Archie rolled her onto her side, put his fingers on her cheek, and whispered, 'Oh Peggy.' She ran the tips of her own fingers round his mouth; Archie drew them in with his lips and sucked them.

'Mister Archie MacDonald, socialist Member of Parliament for the South Side constituency of Glasgow,' Peggy said. 'Jaysus, wouldn't that be the grand thing altogether?'

Archie laughed. 'I've still got to get elected.'

'You'll be after running away with it,' Peggy said. 'Sure, it's almost entirely a working-class constituency.'

'That's true,' Archie said. 'But there are a lot of Orangemen who vote Tory in it.'

'You'll win it for sure,' Peggy said.

Archie put his hand round Peggy's waist and without thinking, she moved closer to him, hoping he would kiss her again.

'I've been thinking,' Archie said, 'and I've also had a chat with Mary Barbour, Helen Crawfurd and John Wheatley. We all think you should stand as ILP candidate for the

Corporation for one of the Govan Wards.'

'Get away with you,' Peggy said, 'I amn't clever enough to be a Councillor. The teacher-training is hard enough.'

'I don't agree,' Archie said, 'and neither do Mary, Helen or John. Or Catherine or Maggie, for that matter. You've got brains. And more importantly, you've got a good political head. You already know a lot about the housing issue, you're a good speaker, and you're a Party activist. I really think you should stand.'

The warmth and proximity of Archie's body made Peggy feel faint. She ran her fingers down his naked chest and looked up at him. 'Well, I'll think about it. But only if you insist.'

'I insist,' Archie said. He gathered her to him and kissed her again. Bells went off in her head and as she closed her eyes and returned the kiss, it seemed like shooting-stars were going off behind her eyelids. Her whole body ached with an indefinable but hungry desire. She felt his fingers caressing her breasts like a feather through her bra; her nipples hardened. His fingers stroked her belly gently, then slid between her legs, and held her there. Peggy felt herself go wet immediately, and her body stiffened.

'Sorry,' Archie murmured, withdrawing his hand.

'No, no, it's alright, I …' Peggy put her hands on his head, pulled him to her, and kissed him with all her might.

'Oh, Peggy,' Archie said. 'Do you …?'

'Yes. Yes. I do,' Peggy gasped.

Archie's hands moved behind her, unbuttoned her bra, and removed it. His fingers traced her breasts. He bent down and licked her stiff nipples. Peggy felt a warm surge flooding her body. Sitting up quickly, she leant down and slid off her knickers as Archie pulled off his underpants. He kissed her breasts and began to suck her nipples. His hand caressed her belly, moved between her legs, and opened her like a flower. Peggy felt his thing hard against her thigh. Suddenly, Archie rolled away from her, gasping.

'What's the matter, my love?' Peggy said.

Archie groaned. 'Oh damn, oh damn.'

Peggy wasn't sure what he meant, but she noticed his shoulders were shaking and was shocked to realise that he was crying silently. Whatever had happened must have been very important to produce such distress. She reached out, pulled him gently back to her, and folded him in her arms.

'I'm so sorry,' Archie said.

'There, there, my love,' Peggy murmured. 'It doesn't matter.'

Archie sobbed once as he relaxed into her embrace. Peggy held him tightly, stroked his back and covered his face with kisses. They lay like that for several minutes. Archie's hand slid down over her hip and moved between her legs. He held her there, his fingers resting on the curve. All Peggy was aware of outside their two bodies was the heat of the sunlight filtering through the canopy of the trees, intense birdsong, the pounding of their hearts and the buzzing of bees nearby. I wish we could stay like this forever, she thought; it's heavenly.

A little later, Peggy sat up; Archie was dozing. Her thighs felt sticky. She stepped into the pool and washed herself. Archie joined her and showed her how to float on the surface; they drifted about, cooling down in amiable silence.

'Would you like to learn to swim?' Archie said.

'Sure, and I would,' Peggy said.

'All right. I'll teach you in the Western Baths,' Archie said.

'Just as long as you can protect your reputation,' Peggy said. She squealed as Archie ducked her playfully.

In the evening, they stopped outside Archie's house. 'Would you like to come in and stay with me tonight?' he said.

'There's nothing I would like better,' Peggy said. 'But I

won't. I've a class at nine in the morning in Dowanhill, and if I went to bed with you, I wouldn't want to get up ever again.' She leaned forward and kissed Archie with attitude.

'Thank you, Archie,' she said. 'Thank you for a lovely, lovely day.'

Archie took the palm of her hand and kissed it gently. 'Thank you, Peggy,' he said. 'You're a lovely, lovely woman.'

As Peggy drifted off to sleep, she thought she had never felt so happy in her entire life. She felt like a new woman. So, this is what it's like being in love? It's wonderful. What could be sinful about something so ecstatic? God must surely have had a purpose when he created it.

Chapter 41:
1921: Reconciliation.

Brighid sighed as she poured Peggy's tea. 'Pat's going downhill fast, and that's the fact of the matter. He's managing to speak a bit now, but with difficulty. But I can tell he's not himself. I think he's lost the will to live. To tell ye the God's honest truth, I think he's on the way out.'

'I see,' Peggy said.

'Would you ever go in and see him? You'll never live at peace with yourself if he dies without you forgiving him. Ye can't carry a grudge all your life, Peggy.'

It's true, Peggy thought; I've been carrying my anger for far too long. And I would never be able to forgive myself if the Da died on me without some kind of peace being made.

'Right, so,' Peggy said. 'I'll go in and see him next time I come down. I just want to gather me thoughts first. Lookit, Ma, Archie and I are seeing each other regularly now. We're courting steadily; we're serious about each other. Da's got to accept that.'

'Sure, and he will, girl,' Brighid said. 'I'll be after having a word with him.'

'Would you ever?' Peggy said.

'I would.'

'But supposing he doesn't want to accept my forgiveness? Supposing he still rares up at me for seeing a Protestant?'

'He'll accept your forgiveness and he'll accept the fact that yer fella is a Prod,'

Brighid said. 'He may not like it in his heart of hearts, but he'll accept it.'

'I hope you're right, Ma,' Peggy said.

'I know I'm right. I've been married to the man for twenty-six years. I can read him like a book.'

Peggy sat facing the sisters in their kitchen, explaining the situation. 'So, there you have it,' she said. 'I'm going to tell the Da I forgive him and ask him to meet Archie.'

Catherine and Maggie exchanged glances. 'Both of us are very pleased to hear it, Peggy,' Catherine said. 'You're not the sort of person to carry a grudge for the rest of your life.'

'That's right,' Maggie said. 'Carrying anger eats away at you and can turn you into a very bitter person. And that's not who you are. Even if your father rejects your forgiving him, you will have done the right thing.'

'I want the Da to meet Archie, and accept him, and bless our relationship,' Peggy said.

'That's his choice, Peggy, and you've no option but to accept that,' Catherine said.

'But it sounds like your mother is on your side,' Maggie said.

'I think she is,' Peggy said, 'even although she has never met Archie. But I'm sure she will like him.'

'Och, Archie could charm the birds out of the trees. He's naturally charming. Of course your mother will like him. And your father too, probably,' Maggie said.

Oh Lord, I hope you're right, Peggy thought.

'These are for you, Mrs O'Donnell,' Archie said, handing over a bunch of roses.

'Would you look at that?' Brighid exclaimed. 'Aren't they lovely? Thank you, Archie, thank you very much. I'll put them in water in a minute. Come on now, Peggy, come and speak to your father.'

Brighid opened the door to the room. 'Here's someone come to see ye, Pat,' she said, ushering a hesitant Peggy inside and shutting the door. Peggy winced when she saw her father. He was sitting up in bed, propped up by pillows, and wearing pyjamas. Pyjamas? Peggy thought. Be the holy man, he's never worn pyjamas in his life. Pat's face was gaunt, he had lost a lot of weight, and his hair was now completely white. Tears sprang to her eyes; she hurried over to the bed and hugged her father.

'Oh Da,' she said.

Her father hugged her to him in a fierce grip, kissing her cheek and stroking her hair.

'*A Pheigí, a thaisce*,' he croaked. 'Let me look at you.' He let her stand up and managed a smile. 'Sure, me daughter's become a beautiful woman.'

'Oh Da,' Peggy said again, sitting on the bed and taking her father's hand in hers. 'It's good to see you.'

Pat smiled. 'Sure, it's even better to see you.'

Peggy took a handkerchief out of her handbag and wiped the tears from her eyes.

'Peggy,' Pat said, with an effort.

'Yes, Da?' Peggy said.

Pat struggled to articulate what he wanted to say; Peggy handed him a glass of water and he took several sips and coughed.

'I'm so sorry I hit ye,' Pat said. 'Truly sorry, and I hope …'

Peggy put her finger to her father's lips.

'Sssh,' she said. 'I forgive you, and that's that. It's all in the past now.' She kissed her father's forehead. Pat held on to her hands so tightly as if he were afraid that she might fly away.

'Archie's next door,' Peggy said. 'Can I bring him in to see you?'

Pat nodded and smiled. Peggy noticed that he seemed unsurprised. She opened the door, and called, 'Archie.'

Archie came into the bedroom. 'Da,' Peggy said, 'this is

Archie MacDonald. Archie, this is me Da, Pat O'Donnell.'

Archie shook Pat's hand. 'I'm pleased to meet you, Mr O'Donnell.'

Pat held on to Archie's hand. 'Mr O'Donnell me bollocks,' he croaked. 'My name is Patrick, Pat to me friends.' They all laughed.

'I can tell you're a dacent fella, Archie,' Pat said.

'How can you tell that, Pat?' Archie said.

'Because my daughter wouldn't go out with a blaggard,' Pat said with a grin.

They all laughed again – if not without a hint of relief.

'I'll bring the tea in now,' Brighid said, smiling happily.

Later, in the kitchen, Brighid and Peggy looked at each other; the rumble of Archie's voice could be heard in the bedroom.

'What on earth can they be talking about for so long?' Peggy said.

'*Ciúnas*,' Brighid said. 'It's all to the good if they are talking, you mark my words.'

Archie appeared at the door, a big grin on his face. 'Your father has a very good sense of humour, Peggy,' he said. Peggy smiled her relief.

'You've to bring me back down again soon,' Archie said.

'You're as welcome here as the day is long, Archie,' Brighid. 'Don't be a stranger.'

As Peggy and Archie walked arm-in-arm up the road to Govan subway station, Archie said, 'Well, how do you think it went?'

'It couldn't have been better,' Peggy said. 'But what on earth were you talking about for so long to the Da?'

'Oh, he asked me about the Clearances in Skye, so I told him about the Battle of the Braes. And then Pat told me about the Clearances in Gweedore, and how his father had been involved in the fighting. And then I told him how the ILP campaigned on the Land Question, and he said we were all on the same side.'

Peggy stopped and put her arms round Archie. 'I'm so happy you got on well,'she said. 'He's a good man, the Da. And if he likes you, we're laughing, for the Ma likes you a lot. She said you're very well-mannered.'

'Oh dear,' Archie said, 'my radical reputation's ruined.'

Peggy laughed, kissed Archie warmly, and a small boy passing on his bicycle wolf-whistled loudly. They held hands happily all the way to the subway station.

Brighid sat beside Pat's bed holding his hand.

'I'd say Archie is a good man,' she said. 'I can see why Peggy likes him. He's a well-mannered, kind man, and good-looking with it.'

'You're right there,' Pat said. 'Do ye think they'll get married?'

'I'd say so.'

'But will it be a Catholic wedding, and will Archie convert?' Pat said.

'Lookit,' Brighid said. 'It's their choice what kind of a wedding they have, and if we oppose it, it will only lead to bitterness in the family. So let them be. What is important is that Peggy and Archie are happy.'

'You're right,' Pat said. 'But then, you always were.'

Brighid smiled as she kissed her husband.

Chapter 42:
1921: The Big Push.

Peggy watched as Paddy Dollan, the Labour Councillor for Govan Central Ward, addressed the packed ILP meeting in the main hall of the Pearce Institute.

'So you see, this is our big chance,' Paddy said. 'Since 1918, Glasgow City has been represented by fifteen Members of Parliament instead of seven. The Representation of the People Act has increased the number of registered voters six-fold to over five hundred thousand. And women over thirty have the vote for the first time – and most of them are our people. The Anglo-Irish treaty has meant the Irish Nationalist organisations are now irrelevant, and the Liberal Party's in tatters. We have to muster the Irish Catholic vote into the ILP, and Comrade John Wheatley has done a good job in that regard by demonstrating that our socialism isn't the revolutionary socialism of Rosa Luxemburg or Karl Liebknecht. We've got to sell that to working people so that our Party is their natural political home.'

Archie, Peggy, Catherine, Maggie, Mary Barbour, and the others exchanged glances; Paddy was right.

'But working-class women under thirty still don't have the vote in parliamentary elections,' Peggy said. 'What about them?'

'Good point, Peggy,' Paddy said. 'One of the first things we'll do when we're in power is give all women over twenty-one the parliamentary vote. That will be a priority. But ...'

'But in the meantime,' Peggy said, 'women *do* have the vote in local elections. So, I would argue that we must connect with these women by showing them that we stand for the issues which most concern them. And the key issue is housing. We must emphasise that the ILP stands for continued rent control, the abolition of warrant sales, evictions and long leases, the prosecution of slum landlords, and the rapid construction of good quality municipal housing at reasonable rents.'

'I couldn't agree more,' Paddy said. 'And remember that many of these women worked in wartime munitions factories and have experience of trade-union struggles. So, we must canvas every house in every close in every street and ensure that all those who are eligible to vote, men *and* women, are on the electoral register. We must distribute pamphlets written in simple English stressing our support for a municipal housing programme and rent control. Mary and Peggy, you must mobilise the women in the South Govan Housing Association to make their men go out and vote in the parliamentary elections – for us. And the same women must turn out and vote for us in the local elections. Does that make sense?'

There was a murmur of assent.

'And we must maintain our contacts with our comrades in the Socialist Labour Party and the British Socialist Party, with their important membership in the shipyards,'

Paddy said. 'Alright. Let's do it then, the Big Push for the 1922 elections.'

Peggy was never so busy as in the ensuing weeks. Whenever she had a free minute from her teacher training studies, she was pounding up and down tenement stairs checking tenants' registration against the voters' roll, handing out pamphlets and leaflets, and addressing meetings. But she and her comrades felt a new optimism in the air; there was a feeling that the so-called Moderates in Glasgow, in effect an anti-Labour Tory-Liberal coalition, could be beaten in the local elections. The militancy of the 1915 Rent Strike and the 1919 40-Hour Strike still reverberated in the working-class neighbourhoods of Glasgow. People remembered the police attack on the demonstrators in George Square on Bloody Friday; and they resented it. And they also remembered the impassioned speeches of John Maclean.

The ILP orchestrated a ceaseless propaganda campaign stressing the central planks of its social policy, and making sure that these, and the personalities of its candidates, received maximum publicity in the popular press, and not just in its own newspaper, *Forward.* Peggy found herself much in demand as a public speaker. Her striking looks, her Irish accent, her natural facility with language, and her ready wit when heckled ensured that she always had a good audience. She was now a kenspeckle figure in Glasgow's working-class movement, and Archie finally persuaded her to put herself forward as an ILP candidate for the municipal elections.

At a Saturday morning meeting at Govan Cross, Peggy addressed a small crowd of men and women.

'The ILP wants to see the demolition of all unsafe and insanitary back-court wash-houses and the establishment of Corporation steamies in every neighbourhood,' she cried.

'We want to see supervised play-centres where our children can play safely instead of out on the street. And we want to see birth-control clinics established where women can receive advice about how to avoid endless pregnancies, and how to plan …'

'Go home, you Irish bitch, and don't peddle your filthy smut here,' a man yelled.

'If ye had teeth in your arse, ye could call it a face, you ignorant gobshite, and it would be a poor-face at that,' Peggy retorted. The crowd erupted with laughter, and to Peggy's surprise, she saw her mother and Mrs MacCaskill listening, with broad smiles on their faces.

'We need to force the Government to subsidise the construction of decent council houses for working people, at affordable rents, and not for toffs like the houses in Mosspark,' Peggy continued. 'And we need these houses now.'

A voice with a distinct Irish accent shouted, 'Fair play to ye, girleen,' and there was a roar of approval from the crowd. A familiar voice then called, 'How do you propose to subsidise these council houses, comrade?' Peggy recognised Archie; clever question, she thought.

'Councillor John Wheatley has already supplied the answer to that question, comrade,' Peggy said. 'He's already shown that the Corporation of Glasgow could build cottages from the tramway surplus at an annual rental of £8. Any more questions? No? Ladies and gentlemen, thank you for your time, and remember that the Independent Labour Party is the party of the working people, both men and women. Thank you.'

That evening, Peggy, Archie, Catherine and Maggie sat at home discussing strategy for the forthcoming elections.

'I'm not sure it's a good idea to go on about the birth-control clinics, Peggy,' Archie said. 'We've got to win the Irish Catholic vote and any mention of birth-control, which the Catholic Church condemns outright, is going to alienate these voters. We can't afford to take the risk.'

'Divil a bit of it,' Peggy said. 'Women now have the vote in municipal elections, and if we want to win their vote, we have to show that the ILP is committed to women's issues. We have to show that support for women's birth-control and women's health and safety is a matter of political principle for socialists as much as universal women's suffrage. We need to show that we're not going to sweep women's issues under the carpet as usual and promise them pie in the sky after we have successfully won the elections. I believe that working-class women will respond to such a principled stand.'

'I agree with Peggy,' Maggie said. 'The history of the last century demonstrates that men will systematically ignore women's issues. It's time to take a stand.'

'But the priests will preach against the ILP if it supports birth-control,' Archie argued.

'To hell with the priests,' Peggy said. 'They can preach to their hearts' content, but they can't control how Catholics actually vote. The ballot is secret. I say we continue with our campaign on social issues like housing and women's issues like birth-control. Women know what happens to their bodies with endless childbearing. The priests don't know, and they don't care. All they can say is that it is God's will – and God was a man. I say women will vote for a party which demonstrates that it cares for issues that affect them.'

There was a moment's silence in the sitting-room. 'Peggy's right,' Catherine said. 'We need to show that we've moral and political principles that we won't abandon because the Holy Joes oppose them. It's as simple as that.'

'Fair enough,' Archie said. 'That makes sense. Now, I think we all deserve a drink.'

Chapter 43:
A Proposal.

It was such a hot day that Peggy and Archie were drenched with sweat as they reached the top of Conic Hill. They sat and gazed at the view as Archie produced a water bottle.

'Would you look at that?' Peggy said. 'Now that is spectacular.' They could see the whole of Loch Lomond stretching away to the north, the water glittering in the sunlight, and a panorama of hills under the cloudless sky.

'Conic Hill is right on the Highland Boundary Fault Line,' Archie said, 'and it's continued along these islands.' He pointed. Peggy looked at them, then turned to see a big peak in front of them, not far away.

'That's Ben Lomond,' Archie said. 'It's a Munro, the southernmost Munro in Scotland.'

'What's a Munro?' Peggy said.

'It's a hill over three thousand feet. There are over 250 in Scotland. Ben Lomond is three thousand, one-hundred and ninety-six feet high.'

'Have you been to the top?' Peggy said.

'Many times,' Archie said.

'Do you like hill-walking?' Peggy said.

'It's my hobby,' Archie said. 'It's what I do for relaxation.'

'What are these hills over there?' Peggy said, pointing to the north-west.

'They're the Arrochar Alps.' Archie said. 'From left to right: The Cobbler, Beinn Narnain, Creag Tharsuinn, A' Chrois.'

'And have you climbed them too?'

'Aye. I have.'

'Could I come next time you go?' Peggy said.

Archie turned to her. 'Of course. I would like that.' He kissed Peggy gently. 'Now, where are the sandwiches?'

A little later, they lay in companionable silence in the baking sun. Peggy slipped her hand inside Archie's shirt; his skin was warm.

'Archie,' she said.

'Yes?' Archie said.

Peggy traced the line of his lips with his forefinger. 'Archie, I wonder, that is, I …'

'What do you wonder, Peggy?'

'I wonder … em … I wonder if you would marry me,' Peggy said.

Archie sat bolt upright in astonishment. 'Peggy O'Donnell, are you asking me to marry you?'

'Yes, that's exactly what I said. Didn't you hear me?'

Archie stared at her for a couple of moments. 'Yes, Peggy,' he said, 'I will. I will marry you and love you for ever and ever.'

Peggy reached out her arms, pulled Archie to her, and kissed him passionately. Just then, a party of walkers reached the summit; they paused as they saw the young couple lying together in a tight embrace. Becoming aware of their presence, Peggy released Archie, turned towards them, and said, 'It's a lovely day, isn't it?' – as if butter wouldn't melt in her mouth.

When the walkers moved on, Peggy collapsed in giggles. 'I have a terrible confession to make,' she said.

Archie raised his eyebrows. 'Oh dear. What's that?'

'I have an overwhelming urge to consummate our marriage right here and now,' Peggy said.

Archie roared with laughter. 'That's a great idea, but this place is busier than Sauchiehall Street. Look.' He pointed down the hill. Peggy looked down and saw a file of walkers making their way up towards them on the path.

'Ah well,' Peggy said, 'I'll have to delay my gratification, and preserve your reputation.'

Archie laughed so much he nearly choked.

That evening, Peggy told her mother and father about her engagement, but didn't say it was her who made the proposal. She didn't think they could handle that.

'What are you going to do about the wedding?' Brighid said. 'Have you fixed a date yet?'

'No,' Peggy said. 'We haven't discussed that at all. I've still a year of my teacher training course to do, and it might be a good idea to finish that first. We'll see.'

'Peggy,' Pat croaked, 'do ye love Archie?'

Peggy looked at her father with surprise. 'Yes, Da,' she said, 'I do. I love him very much. He's a good man, and I would be honoured to be his wife.'

'Then you have my blessing,' Pat said.

Peggy hugged her father. 'Oh, thank you, Da, thank you. That means so much to me.'

'But there's one condition,' Pat said.

Oh my God. What on earth does the ould divil want? 'What's that, Da?' Peggy said.

'If you have children, they've got to be brought up as Catholics,' Pat said. 'Archie's got to agree to that.'

Peggy felt a sinking feeling in the pit of her stomach.

'I'll have to discuss that with him, Da,' she said. 'We've not got round to matters like that yet.'

'Sure, ye do that now, and let me know what yer man says,' Pat said.

Brighid took Peggy's hand. 'All we want is for you to be happy, Peggy. Are you sure you want to marry Archie?'

'I'm very sure, Ma.'

'Then you have my blessing too.'

Peggy watched Archie's face; she could almost hear his brain digesting Pat's demand.

'I can't agree to that, Peggy,' Archie said. 'To do so would be hypocritical. I'm an agnostic, probably an atheist, but definitely not a Christian. If I agreed to your father's demand, it would only be so that I could marry you. I would actually never entertain the idea of any children we may have being brought up in the Catholic faith – or any other faith, for that matter. So, to agree with Pat's demand would be a lie. Further, the implication of his demand is that we would have to be married in a Catholic church, and I am not having that. I believe the Catholic Church is a corrupt institution, literally and metaphorically, and I won't have anything to do with it. I wouldn't even get married in the kirk, which is my family tradition. Sorry, but that's my position.'

Peggy reflected for a few moments. 'I understand your position, my love, and I agree with it. There can only be one outcome, then.'

'What's that, Peggy?'

'We'll have what they call an irregular wedding in the Register Office and forgo my father's blessing – and possibly my mother's,' Peggy said.

'You would do that?' Archie said.

'Sure, and I would,' Peggy said. 'I'm marrying you, not my father. But he'll have to be told.'

'That will be difficult,' Archie said.

'It will. But there's no alternative. We have to do it.'

Chapter 44:
1921: A Death in the Family.

As Peggy cycled back to the house, she reflected on her father's ultimatum. There was no way he would change his mind about any children being brought up as Catholics, so it looked like she and Archie would have to have an irregular marriage. But would her parents attend? She put her bicycle in the press in the close and locked the door. It was only a short bike ride from the College in Dowanhill to her home in Partickhill Road. She climbed the stairs and the front door opened just as she reached it, to reveal an agitated Maggie.

Peggy was startled. 'What's the matter, Maggie?' she said.

'There you are, Peggy,' Maggie said. 'I've been waiting for you. Bad news, I'm afraid. Your brother Tim phoned earlier this afternoon. I'm sorry to say your father has had another stroke, and it looks like he doesn't have long to live.'

'Oh my God,' Peggy said. She flew down the Gardner Street hill and sprinted to Merkland Street subway station.

When she reached her parents' house in Neptune Street, she had to sit down for a minute to catch her breath.

'The doctor says he's on the way out,' Brighid said. 'He had another stroke and he can't speak. Father Gallagher has been and given him Extreme Unction. Tim's in with him just now.'

As she opened the door of the bedroom, Peggy was quaking. She had no experience of death, on the one hand, and there was the unresolved business with Archie, on the other. She saw Tim in his seminarian's cassock, sitting by the bedside murmuring a prayer from his breviary. Pat was lying in the bed with his eyes shut, his hands on the quilt holding his rosary beads, his breathing a shallow, irregular, ugly gasping; his face was chalk-white. Tim stood up and indicated the chair to Peggy. She sat down and took her father's hand as her young brother went into the kitchen. Pat's eyes opened. He saw Peggy and smiled, grasping her hands in his. He tried to say something, but only a croak and a stream of spittle came from his mouth. Peggy took a handkerchief from her handbag, wiped Pat's mouth gently, and said, 'Sssh, Da, don't strain yourself.'

Pat smiled again; he tried to say something again, but only a rattle came from his throat, and his head lolled to one side. Peggy shrieked. Brighid and Tim rushed into the room as Peggy burst into tears.

'He's gone,' Brighid said, and closed his eyelids.

'*Requiem aeternam dona ei, Domine, et lux perpetua luceat ei. Requiescat in pace*,' Tim said.

'Amen,' Peggy and Brighid said. Brighid opened the window to let Pat's soul rise up to Heaven.

Later, in the kitchen, a cup of tea in hand, Tim addressed Peggy. 'I pray for you, you know, you Godless communist, and …'

'Shut your gob, you eejit,' Peggy retorted. 'I'm a socialist, not a communist, and you're too stupid to know the difference.'

'Peggy, Peggy,' Brighid murmured.

Peggy stood up and slammed her teacup on the table. 'I'm not about to listen to abuse from this ignoramus. Get away with you and get a decent job, you parasite. I'll see ye later, Ma.'

Peggy stormed out of the house and went straight to the Sinn Féin office in Govan.

She saw John Carney, and said, 'Me Da's just died, John.

I need you to get word to Conal and tell him to come home immediately for the funeral.'

'I'm sorry for your loss, Peggy,' John said. 'I'll do what I can, right away.'

There was a traditional wake for Pat. Brighid and Morag MacCaskill washed his body and dressed him in his Sunday suit. He was laid out in the front room, with candles at the head and foot of the coffin, and his hands clasped over his rosary beads. The clocks were stopped at the time Pat died, the mirrors were turned to the wall, and all the curtains drawn except those in the room, where the window was left open to permit his soul to go up to heaven. Peggy, Brighid and Morag worked like a production line in the kitchen preparing piles of ham sandwiches. In the early evening, numerous women neighbours came round to pay their respects, and the rosary was said. Peggy rattled backwards and forwards between the kitchen and the room, ferrying pots of tea and plates of sandwiches. The women told funny stories about Pat and the atmosphere grew lighter.

A song was called for, and Brighid was persuaded to sing '*Down by the Salley Gardens.*' When she finished, she burst into tears but was consoled by her neighbours.

Peggy was then also persuaded to sing, and she sang *The Curragh of Kildare,* but was unable to stifle a sob when she came to:

And straight I will repair
To the Curragh of Kildare
For it's there I'll find tidings of my dear.

About eight o'clock in the evening, the women left, and the men arrived – Michael, Pat's cousin, fellow workers from the squad of dockers, and friends from the Govan Irish Club, bearing bottles of stout and whiskey. A fiddle player and a flute player gave a rendering of *Limerick's Lamentation,* as suitable for the occasion, but a little later, when more whiskey had been drunk, played the altogether more cheerful *The Bucks of Oranmore.* They sat up all night, permitting Brighid and Peggy to snatch a few hours' sleep, telling stories about Pat, remembering the epic fight with Sammy McKee, singing the odd song and playing the odd tune. As the men prepared to leave at dawn, Michael summed up the common feeling: 'We'll never see his likes again.'

As Pat's coffin was carried out of St Anthony's Church, with the family following down the aisle, the uillean piper from The Irish Club played the haunting tune, *Caoineadh Cu Chulainn.* Ah Jaysus, Peggy thought, tears streaming down her cheeks, that's the right lament sure enough, it has nothing but death in it. And Eamonn played that tune. Conal took her arm and supported her. She had agreed to attend the requiem mass on the clear understanding that both Father Gallagher and Tim said nothing hostile to her. Brighid had agreed immediately to have a word in their ears. 'Sure, it's no time to be fighting over religion,' she said. 'We've enough sorrows of our own.' As the cortège left the church, Peggy saw Archie, Catherine and Maggie standing in a pew at the back, and nodded recognition.

Women did not attend the interment in Dalbeth cemetery, as was the Irish custom. So, Peggy helped her mother lay out the refreshments in the Irish Centre. As the mourners streamed in, she took a plate of sandwiches over to Archie and his sisters.

'Thank you for coming,' Peggy said. 'That was thoughtful of you.'

'We're here for you and your mother,' Catherine said.

'My goodness, it's like an Irish Republic in here,' Archie said, listening to the din of Irish accents.

'Let's hope there will be a real Irish Republic soon,' Peggy replied.

'Amen to that,' Maggie said.

That evening, Peggy sat with her mother, Conal and Tim in the kitchen.

'Pat was a good man, Ma,' Conal said.

'He was that, son,' Brighid said. 'All he ever wanted was to look after his family.

And find a steady job that would give him enough money to do that. Which he did eventually. He was a good husband, a good father, and a good worker, a good man entirely.'

'And a good Catholic,' Tim said. Peggy ignored his glare.

'He also wanted Home Rule for Ireland,' Conal said.

'He did that,' Brighid said. 'Sure, we all wanted that.'

'Well,' Conal said, 'I think Sinn Fein will be delivering an Irish Republic sooner rather than later.'

'God save the mark,' Brighid said. 'When are you going back to Ireland?'

'On the Broomielaw boat tomorrow evening, Ma,' Conal said. 'But I'll bring you out to lunch tomorrow, Peggy. Supposing I come round for you at half-past-twelve?'

Peggy sensed he had something important to communicate. 'That would be grand,' she said.

'And what are your plans, Tim?' Brighid said.

'I'm on the nine-thirty train to Aberdeen in the morning.'

Peggy stood up. 'Right, so' she said. 'I'm off to the subway. I'll come and see you tomorrow after I've had lunch with Conal, Ma. *Slán*, Tim. Safe journey.'

'Good night, Peggy,' Tim said. 'And God bless.'

'I'm working for The Big Fellah in Dublin now,' Conal said.

'I thought as much,' Peggy said. She knew that her brother meant he was in the IRA, for The Big Fellah was Michael Collins.

'We've got the Brits on the run, Peggy. We'll have the Republic before Christmas.

Collins and Griffith are going to London to negotiate a treaty.'

'If you think Lloyd George will permit the creation of an independent Republic, you need your head looked,' Peggy said. 'No British government can afford to do that. If it's Ireland today, it's South Africa and India tomorrow.'

'I don't agree,' Conal said. 'For all its Army, Royal Irish Constabulary, Black-and-Tans, Auxiliaries and Intelligence Officers, the Brits can't beat the IRA. They have no option but to grant us our Republic.'

'Well, we'll see soon enough,' Peggy said. 'But in the meantime, you be careful. This could all wind up in an ugly, bloody mess.'

'We'll try and avoid that,' Conal said. 'My job is to make sure that our people in Dublin city are prepared for any crisis.'

Peggy realised with dread that he meant the possibility of an outbreak of fighting within the Republican movement, which was far from unified.

'I wish you luck, Conal,' Peggy said. 'For ye may need it.'

'Thank you, Peggy. If you need to contact me, go through John Carney. Now tell me: are you going to marry the Archie fellah right enough?'

'I am indeed,' Peggy said. 'We haven't set a date yet, but probably in the spring of next year.'

'He seems like a sound man, to be sure. The Ma has a high opinion of him.'

'He is a very sound man, Conal,' Peggy said. 'Otherwise, I wouldn't be marrying him.'

'I'll dance at your wedding, so,' Conal said. Brother and sister both laughed.

Brighid handed Peggy a letter. 'This came for ye from the Sinn Féin office,' she said.

'Sure, it looks as if it has been in the wars.'

Peggy took the letter from her mother; it was simply

addressed: *Peggy O'Donnell.* She recognised Conal's handwriting, and saw that the envelope was creased and grimy, as if it had been through many hands. She sat at the kitchen table and read her brother's letter, watched by her mother.

'Ah Jaysus,' Peggy said, putting the letter down.

'What does Conal say?' Brighid said.

'He says Sinn Féin and the IRA are split over the Treaty, and there will be fighting between the two factions. He's in command of a unit in Dublin city. And he says not to worry if we don't hear from him for a while for he feels sure the fighting will break out sooner rather than later.'

'Jesus, Mary and Joseph,' Brighid said. 'Has there not been enough fighting and killing at home already?'

'I fear the worse has yet to come, Ma.' Peggy said. 'It'll be old comrades-in-arms against each other, and I think it'll be savage.'

'I'll pray for Conal, so,' Brighid said.

If a civil war breaks out, and that looks likely, Peggy thought, then he'll need your prayers.

Chapter 45:
Wedding Bells.

Peggy and Archie decided to get married in the spring of 1922. The civil wedding ceremony would be in the Register Office and the reception in the ILP hall in Anderson Street in Partick. Peggy knew that one of the women in the South Govan Housing Association was a confectioner and asked her to bake the wedding cake.

Peggy and Maggie discussed the design of the wedding-dress, and eventually plumped for a simple, straight, calf-length, lace model that Maggie sketched for the bride-to-be. 'The white lace will contrast beautifully with your dark hair,' Maggie said, 'and I'll also design a simple head-dress with a veil.'

While Peggy would have liked Conal to give her away, she knew that he was so involved in the tense stand-off in Ireland that he was hardly likely to come to Glasgow for a mere wedding. So, she asked her mother to do it.

'Oh no, no,' Brighid said, 'women don't give the bride away. I couldn't do that.'

'Look, Ma' Peggy said, 'me da isn't alive to do the honours, and Conal's too busy with the political situation in Dublin. And Tim's sent me a letter saying that a socialist wedding was a Godless ceremony, an occasion of sin which his conscience could not allow him to attend. So, it's only natural that you should do it as the oldest member of the family. Please, Ma. I would really like you to do it. To hell with tradition.'

'All right, Peggy,' Brighid said. 'I'll do it for you.'

A friend of Archie's lent the young couple his family's holiday home in Lochranza on the romantic Isle of Arran for their honeymoon. Archie was all for going there for a weekend beforehand so that Peggy could see the beautiful island, but she felt reluctant to make love with him before the wedding.

'I know it sounds daft,' Peggy said, 'and I know we've lain together with no clothes on, and we might well have made love then. But … but that's the way I feel. It just doesn't feel right. We'll have the rest of our lives to sleep together.'

'If it doesn't feel right, we won't do it before the wedding,' Archie said. 'But can we do it as often as possible after we're married?'

Peggy laughed out loud, and kissed Archie. 'Oh yes please.'

It was bright and sunny on the day of the wedding. Archie fingered his tie nervously as he sat in the Register Office with his best man, his cousin Kenny MacDonald. He heard the sound of horse's hooves approaching outside. They stopped. Archie glanced over his shoulder to see Peggy approach on Brighid's arm, looking radiant in her white dress. When the Sheriff pronounced them man and wife, they kissed enthusiastically.

The reception was friendly and informal. Kenny made a stirring speech in which he said that the young married couple constituted an exemplar of all that was progressive about socialist man and woman: dedicated, hard-working, principled, loving, and dedicated to a better future for the working men and women of Glasgow.

But what brought the house down was a long telegram from Conal in Dublin.

Kenny read it out:

'*The Black-haired Girl – Pretty Peggy – Bashful Lover – Before I was Married – Rolling in the Rye Grass – Haste to the Wedding – Kiss the Bride – Drink and be Merry – Joy of my Life – Scolding Wife.*'

Kenny looked round in bewilderment, but Peggy was killing herself laughing.

'They're tunes,' she gasped. 'They're the names of Irish tunes.' When this was explained, the guests fell about laughing too.

Later, by popular request, Peggy was persuaded to sing a song. 'Right, so,' she said. 'I'll sing *Farewell to Loughswilly.*'

There was a hush in the hall as Peggy sang:

Farewell to stately mountains
Of dear old Donegal
And twice farewell to Errigal hill
As it towers o'er ash tree and rowan
As I passed through the glen by Dunlewey Lake
With waters so peaceful and calm
With an ache in my heart I was forced to depart

From Gleantáin Ghlas' Ghaoth Dobhair
'Twas never my plan to travel afar
From my own beloved land
But the intrigue and the guile
Of the tyrant's hand forced me to leave my home
'Twas the wish of my heart to return again
If I could get money in store
And my days there to end among the relations and friends

Around the Gleantáin Ghlas' Ghaoth Dobhair
Farewell, farewell to Donegal
That county sweet and fairness
And to her brave men when the enemy came

Never cowered or bowed to the Gall
I hold in esteem all these women and men
And all children big and small
That dwell there in peace without worry or grief
In Gleantáin Ghlas' Ghaoth Dobhair.

That night, Peggy came out of the bathroom in Archie's flat into the bedroom, wearing a sheer silk white nightgown. She stood facing Archie, raised her hands, slipped the nightgown slowly off her shoulders, let it fall to the floor and stepped out of it.

'As often as possible?' she said.

Archie's eyes moved up and down over her naked body. 'Oh yes, Peggy,' he gasped. 'Oh yes. You're so beautiful.'

He lifted her up off the floor in his arms, carried her over to the bed, and laid her down on it. He lay beside her and Peggy turned to face him. As Archie caressed her breasts, she put her hand between his legs and held him, feeling him hardening. He stroked between her legs and Peggy felt herself going wet as he slid his fingers inside her. As he stroked her gently, Peggy thought she would die of desire, and pulled him close.

She opened her legs wide as Archie climbed on top of her. He braced himself up on his hands and smiled down at her. Peggy felt a sudden sharp pain, gasped, *oh*, and then he was inside her. She immediately felt a rushing sweet spasm, *yes*, wrapped her legs round Archie's buttocks, *yes*, and pushed her body up as if she wished to envelop him. Wave after wave of what seemed like warm light surged through her, and her body went into a series of uncontrollable convulsions as she clung onto him for dear life and screamed out loud as he pounded away. Archie collapsed on top of her, his whole body contracting in spasms. So that's what it's all about, Peggy thought, that's what a real orgasm with a man feels like. Oh my. It's gorgeous.

Chapter 46:
The 1922 Elections.

Election Day, November 15th, 1922, dawned cold, dank, and foggy and remained like that for the rest of the day. Peggy, Catherine, and Maggie decided to go to the election rally in the Metropole Theatre in Stockwell Street in the afternoon. Paddy Dollan was in the chair, and Archie was one of the speakers.

'We better go early,' Peggy said. 'I think it'll be mobbed.'

She was right. There was a crowd outside waiting for the doors to be opened, and when they were, she, Maggie and Catherine were swept inside by the rush. Peggy looked around, fascinated. The theatre was packed, and overflow meetings had to be arranged outside. When Paddy stepped forward to address the audience, there was thunderous applause.

Paddy looked round slowly, and said, 'Comrades, what do we stand for? What does Labour stand for? Labour stands for the People against the Peers, against the Profiteers, against the Slum Landlords, against the Stealers of Food from our babies, against the Warmongers, against all the Agents of the Rich Robbers of the workers. Labour is your only hope.'

The applause was so deafening that what he said next could not be heard. Peggy exchanged an excited smile with Catherine and Maggie; Paddy knew how to work an audience. Then it was Archie's turn. Paddy Dollan introduced him as 'the Labour candidate for the South Side – and the next Member of Parliament for that constituency.'

This brought more enthusiastic applause. Archie made all the usual points about a 40-hour working-week, an attack on poverty, the continuation of rent control, the acceleration of a council housing programme built by Direct Labour, and the emancipation of women. And then he said, 'Comrades, let me conclude by saying this. When Labour sweeps into Parliament led by the Clydesiders, we will not be asking for all these radical social reforms in our legislation. We will be demanding them!' There was a storm of applause, and Peggy contributed a piercing whistle. The rally ended with the William Morris Choir singing the 124th Psalm, the old covenanting anthem. Peggy did not know the words but listened as Maggie and Catherine sang them:

Restore our fortunes, LORD,
like streams in the Negev.
Those who sow with tears
will reap with songs of joy.

Those who go out weeping,
carrying seed to sow,
will return with songs of joy,
carrying sheaves with them.

Peggy met Archie outside after the rally. 'Let's go over to Bridgeton quickly,' he said. 'There's something I want to see.'

In Green Street, Peggy and Archie saw an effigy of McCallum Scott, the Liberal MPfor the Bridgeton constituency and candidate in the present election, slung from a rope stretched across the street. It was wearing Wellington boots and a bright red Tammy, and locals were pelting it with mud and stones. Peggy couldn't restrain a giggle. Just then James Maxton, the ILP candidate and a friend of Archie's, appeared.

'I'd nothing to do with it,' Maxton said. 'Honest.'

'I believe you. But it's still good fun,' Archie muttered, grinning. 'Good luck, Jim.'

Peggy and Archie made their way towards St Enoch

Square along with thousands of excited spectators banging drums, clanging bells, and whirling rattles. Processions came from every working-class district in the city. Peggy also saw charabancs displaying Clydebank and Kirkintilloch ILP banners. St Enoch Square, Buchanan Street and St Vincent Street were completely packed. A large screen had been erected in Buchanan Street onto which the election results were projected, and Peggy and Archie managed to find a space in a doorway. Peggy noticed that a large number of young working-class mothers were present, with their babies wrapped in their shawls, while a brass band played cheerful tunes. That's very promising, Peggy thought, so many women turning out.

'What a crowd,' she said. 'How many people do you think are here?'

'More than twenty thousand,' Archie said. 'There are at least as many people here as were in George Square on Bloody Friday.'

'Let's hope it doesn't turn out like Bloody Friday,' Peggy said.

Every time a Labour gain was projected on to the screen, a huge roar went up from the crowd. In a lull, a melodeon player started *The Red Flag*, and the crowd took it up.

'My God,' Archie said, 'They'll be able to hear this in Edinburgh.'

Another result flashed up on the screen; Archie had won his seat with a comfortable 3,000 majority! Peggy kissed him in the street while well-wishers thumped him on the back and shook his hand. The overall results for the City of Glasgow were flashed up on the screen:

Labour: 32% of the poll.
Conservatives:23%
National Liberals:11.49%
Independent Liberals:7.91%
10 Labour M.P.s elected, 4 Conservative, and 1 National

Liberal.

There are now 140 Labour M.P.s in Parliament.

In Scotland, Labour had won a landslide victory. The ILP had won fifteen seats nationally, with ten of them in the City of Glasgow alone. Peggy and Archie decided to go home in the middle of the night, they were beside themselves with excitement.

The next afternoon, Archie, Peggy, Catherine and Maggie sat in the sitting-room reading the newspapers.

'Listen to this,' Maggie said. 'It's from the *Glasgow Herald.* 'We cannot view without profound dissatisfaction the significant gains made by Labour in industrial Scotland and most conspicuously in the Glasgow constituencies. They have proved, however, that the policy of organising and arraying all the forces of moderation against the advocates of socialist, communist, and other fads, which we have consistently preached – and which has not been without its measure of success and encouragement – was the right one, and indeed the only one for those enamoured of stable institutions and sanely progressive government to pursue'.'

'Pompous bloody hypocrites,' Archie said.

'Let them stew in their own capitalist juice,' Peggy said.

'*Forward*'s got it right,' Archie said. 'We won the election in Glasgow on the housing and rents issues, and because we got the working-class women to turn out for us. And …'

Just then, the doorbell clanged. 'I'll get it,' Peggy said, getting up and discarding the *Herald*. She opened the door to find an excited Mary Barbour.

'Come in, come in,' Peggy said, ushering Mary into the sitting-room. Mary sat down, beside herself with excitement.

'They've finished counting the votes in the municipal elections,' Mary said. 'And I've been re-elected with an increased majority.'

The sitting-room echoed with congratulations – but Mary

held up her hand. 'And Peggy has been elected Councillor for the Linthouse Ward with a majority of over a thousand!'

Partickhill echoed with the whoops of triumph. Peggy was overcome, and didn't know where to look.

'A socialist MP and a socialist Councillor,' Catherine said. 'What a couple!'

On the evening of the Glasgow Labour MPs' departure for Westminster, Peggy accompanied Archie to the railway station. She laughed out loud as she saw the round tin lapel badge he was wearing. It read: 'High explosive. Handle carefully.'

Thousands upon thousands of Clydesiders packed into St Enoch Station and surrounding streets to see the fifteen new Scottish ILP MPs off. An extra carriage had been added to the quarter-to-eleven train to London for them. A brass band played *The Red Flag* as the MPs battled their way up the concourse towards the train, with thousands of well-wishers roaring out the socialist anthem, causing it to echo all round the city centre. Peggy clung onto Archie's arm as they sang:

Then raise the scarlet standard high,
Beneath its folds we'll live and die.
Though cowards flinch and traitors sneer,
We'll keep the red flag flying here.

At the end of the song, there was a silence as the MPs boarded the train. Archie leaned out of the window and said, 'Comrades, it's been more difficult getting into this station than into Parliament. Thank you all for turning out.' The laughter reverberated all round the station. Peggy kissed Archie for a last time as the train's horn blasted, and it began to move slowly forward. Forward, Peggy thought, we must always go forward.

Chapter 47:
Rest in Peace.

Several months later, Peggy was leaving a Committee Room in the City Chambers when a janitor accosted her.

'There's a note for you, Councillor MacDonald,' he said. 'An elderly woman brought it in. My, she was in a fair state of excitement.' He handed over the note. It was from Morag MacCaskill, and read: 'Come quickly, Peggy. Your Mother has had a heart-attack.' Peggy tore into her office for her coat, rushed outside, hailed a taxi in George Square and said, 'Neptune Street, Govan. As fast as you can.'

As the taxi-driver sped towards Govan, Peggy's heart was in her mouth, thinking please, please God don't let her die before I get there.

As Peggy arrived at the house, she met the family GP, Dr O'Neill, leaving. He took her into the kitchen and sat her down. 'Peggy,' he said, 'your mother's had a serious heart attack. I'm not moving her to hospital for to tell you the honest truth, she's not got long left. She's conscious, but I'm sorry, there's nothing more I can do for her. Father Gallagher has already given her Extreme Unction.'

'Thank you, doctor,' Peggy said. Taking a deep breath and trying to control her overwhelming fear, she went into the bedroom to find Morag sitting by the bed. Brighid was pale, and her face seemed to have shrunk, but she smiled weakly when she saw her daughter. Morag got up, gestured to the chair, and left the room. Peggy sat down and took her mother's hands. 'Oh Ma,' she said, stifling a sob.

'I'm fine, girl, don't you be worrying about me,' Brighid

said. 'How are ye?'

'I'm grand, Ma,' Peggy said. 'Busy in the Corporation, but as fit as a fiddle.'

'Good,' Brighid said. 'And how's Archie?'

'He's grand too, Ma. He and the other lads are giving them Hell in Parliament. They're calling them the 'Red Clydesiders'.'

'I know,' Brighid said. 'I read it in the newspaper. Good on them.'

Peggy lent forward. 'I'll let you into a secret,' she whispered.

'What's that?' Brighid said, her eyes widening in alarm.

Peggy smiled. 'Ma, I'm pregnant.'

Brighid grasped Peggy's hand. 'Oh Peggy, that's wonderful news,' she said. 'Thanks be to God.'

'I only learned yesterday,' Peggy said, 'and Archie doesn't know yet. He's due home at the weekend. And I want to tell him in person rather than send a telegram.'

'Quite right,' Brighid said. She took a deep breath and seemed to gather her resources. 'Will ye do something for me?'

'What's that, Ma?'

'If it's a boy, would you ever call him Patrick? After your father.'

'Sure, and I will,' Peggy said. 'And if it's a girl she will be called Brighid.'

'God bless you,' Brighid said. 'You're a grand daughter. I'm so proud of ye.'

Brighid smiled, sighed deeply, and closed her eyes.

After the funeral, when the mourners had all left, Peggy, Conal and Tim sat round the kitchen table. Peggy poured cups of tea.

'Well,' Conal said, 'we're what remains of the O'Donnells of the County Glasgow.'

'Don't forget there's another one on the way,' Peggy said. 'And who knows, there may be more after that. And what about yourself in the Ould Sod?'

'Sure, I've met a grand Dublin girl, right enough,' Conal said. 'She's a comrade-in-arms. But we're going to have to wait until the fighting's over, one way or the other, before we can even think about marriage.'

'Which I hope to God will be soon,' Tim said. 'This business of Irishmen killing Irishmen is a sin.'

'It is,' Conal said. There was a silence round the table. They all drank their tea.

Peggy looked up. 'Well,' she said, 'in the meantime, there's only one way to go.'

'What's that?' Tim said.

Peggy grinned and raised a clenched fist. 'Forward!'

Chapter 48: The Naming Ceremony.

Ten months later, Peggy and Archie stood in the Partick Socialist Sunday School Hall again. Peggy held their new-born son in her arms covered with a white shawl, while Catherine chaired the ceremony, and the children's choir stood ready. The audience included Maggie, Morag MacCaskill, Helen Crawfurd, Mary Barbour, Donna MacAulay and Harry McShane.

'Comrades,' Catherine said. 'We are gathered here today for the naming ceremony of Peggy O'Donnell's and Archie MacDonald's baby son. We hope and pray that this baby boy will grow up to be a caring, gentle and kind person, a good comrade, and a committed socialist like his parents. We hope that he will help to create the good city, with justice for its foundation and love as its law. The past cannot be changed, but the future is in our hands.' Catherine nodded to the choir and they burst into song.

Look forward to the day when men
And women will be free;
As brothers and as sisters live
In peace and unity.

When the children finished, Catherine said, 'Peggy, would you like to name your son?'

'I would,' Peggy said, and stepped forward, holding her baby proudly up in her arms. 'I name this boy Patrick Eamonn O'Donnell in memory of his late grandfather, and his late uncle, killed in the Great War.'

The children from the choir heaped white roses on

Patrick's shawl, while another added a single red rose. Catherine pinned a red ribbon to the shawl with the boy's name and date-of-birth. She then gave Peggy a gift-wrapped book.

'This is a present from the branch to Patrick Eamonn,' she said. 'It is a copy of William Morris's *News from Nowhere*, which he can read when he is older. We hope that it will inspire him as it has inspired thousands of our comrades.'

The pianist then played a chord, and everyone stood up and sang *The Red Flag*; its words seemed to thunder throughout Glasgow:

Then raise the scarlet standard high
Beneath its folds we'll live and die.
Though cowards flinch and traitors sneer
We'll keep the red flag flying here.

Archie nudged Peggy, grinning, and gestured towards their baby. With his eyes firmly shut, Patrick yawned mightily, and raised his right arm with a clenched fist.

'Sure, he's inspired already,' Peggy said, laughing.

The End.

Acknowledgements.

For assistance with the general historical background to this novel, including contemporary newspapers and memoirs, I am indebted yet again to the staff of Special Collections and the City Archives in the Mitchell Library, Glasgow.

Niamh Brennan, Archivist at Donegal County Council, assisted me with aspects of the history of the county.

For advice on the historical Scottish school curriculum, I am grateful to Professor Lindsay Paterson of the University of Edinburgh, while Dr Anne Cameron of Strathclyde University Archives kept me advised on the Junior Teachers Certificate.

Several friends also assisted me greatly. George and Mary Hunter helped with the issue of classroom discipline. Doireann Ni Bhriain of Dublin was both patient and helpful with numerous enquiries about Irish Gaelic and culture.

My neighbour Joan McGinlay from Derry, whose parents are from Co. Donegal, where she spent childhood holidays, kindly read the whole manuscript and commented on its authenticity.

Dr. Frank Herron, who was brought up in the 'Irish Channel' in Govan, briefed me on the minutiae of life in Neptune Street. Iain Fraser was good enough to give me his opinion on certain sensitive matters.

Govan Timologist Sean McDonagh kept me informed on cultural, geographical, historical and political aspects of the lives of the Catholic Irish in the area. Dr Anni Donaldson briefed me on irregular marriages in early twentieth century Glasgow, such as happened within her own family.

Meg McGuinness made several excellent suggestions about relevant songs and Deirdre Campbell managed to rescue the whole manuscript, which suddenly disappeared into the Great Cyberspace in the Sky when I was word-processing the last chapter!

Finally, I would like to thank Fija Callaghan, my Chief Editor at Ringwood, and her two Assistant Editors, Neil McDonald and Natasha Cunningham, for their numerous invaluable comments and suggestions during the process of getting this novel ready for publication.

About the Author

Now retired, Dr. Seán Damer was an academic sociologist for over 30 years, latterly a Senior Research Fellow in the University of Glasgow.

He is passionately interested in the urban history of Glasgow and has authored numerous scholarly articles and books such as *Glasgow: Going for a Song* and *Scheming: A History of Glasgow Council Housing 1919-1956.*

His interest in the Irish Connection stems from his own extensive research into the social history of the city, and the rich oral history of his own family.

Other Titles from Ringwood

All titles are available from the Ringwood website in both print and ebook format, as well as from usual outlets.

www.ringwoodpublishing.com

mail@ringwoodpublishing.com

The Volunteer

Charles P Sharkey

The Volunteer is a powerful and thought-provoking examination of the Troubles that plagued Northern Ireland for almost three decades. It follows the struggles of two Belfast families from opposite sides of the sectarian divide.

This revealing novel will lead the reader to a greater understanding of the events that led from the Civil Rights marches in the late Sixties, through the years of unbridled violence that followed, until the Good Friday Agreement of the late Nineties.

ISBN: 9781901514360 £9.99

Torn Edges

Brian McHugh

When a gold coin very similar to a family heirloom is found at the scene of a Glasgow murder, a search is begun that takes the McKenna family, assisted by their Librarian friend Liam, through their own family history right back to the tumultuous days of the Irish Civil War.

Parallel to this unravelling of the family involvement of this period, Torn Edges author Brian McHugh has interwoven the remarkable story of the actual participation of two of the McKenna family, Charlie and Pat, across both sides of the conflict in the desperate days of 1922 Ireland.

Torn Edges is both entertaining and well-written, and will be of considerable interest to all in both Scottish and Irish communities.

ISBN: 978-1-901514-05-6 £9.99

Where The Bridge Lies

Frank Woods

1941. The Clydebank Blitz robs Nessa Glover of her husband and five children. Struggling with her new reality she becomes a shipyard welder, and finds herself drawn into trade union activism. One day she visits Harmony, a commune built on notions of equality and unity, led by the charismatic Fergus Abercrombie. But not everything is quite as it seems at Harmony.

1980. Keir Connor is a traumatised war correspondent. When his father dies, he is left with a letter –a letter that takes him to Clydebank in search of answers. His journey leads him on to Harmony, now a residential school for disadvantaged children, as he tries to unlock the past. One thing is sure: Harmony is key.

ISBN: 978-1-901514-66-7 £9.99

Between Two Bridges

Brian McHugh

Between Two Bridges is a sequel to *Torn Edges*. New York, 1933: Prohibition is coming to an end. A few astute businessmen realise that by importing liquor before the Volstead Act is repealed, they can net themselves a small fortune. Charlie McKenna, an Irishman, is sent to complete the deal.

Glasgow, present day: Three old friends are lead back into their investigation of Julie's grandfather, Charlie McKenna, by the resurfacing of a battered diary.

ISBN: 978-1-901514-35-3 £9.99

Cuddies Strip

Rob McInroy

Cuddies Strip is based on a true crime and faithfully follows the investigation and subsequent trial but it also examines the mores of the times and the insensitive treatment of women in a male-dominated society.

It is a highly absorbing period piece from 1930s Scotland, with strong contemporary resonances: both about the nature and responsiveness of police services and the ingrained misogyny of the whole criminal justice system.

ISBN: 978-1-901514-88-9
£9.99

What You Call Free

Flora Johnston

Scotland, 1687. Pregnant and betrayed, eighteen-year-old Jonet escapes her public humiliations, and takes refuge among an outlawed group of religious dissidents. Here, Widow Helen offers friendship and understanding, but her beliefs have seen her imprisoned before.

This extraordinary tale of love and loss, struggle and sacrifice, autonomy and entrapment, urges us to consider what it means to be free and who can be free – if freedom exists at all.

ISBN: 978-1-901514-96-4
£9.99